ICARUS
DOWN

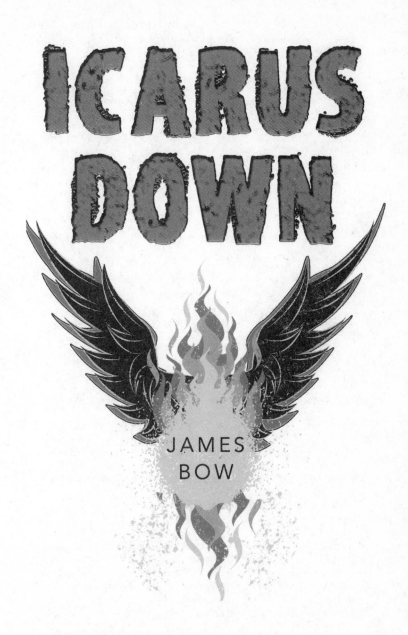

ICARUS DOWN

JAMES BOW

Scholastic Canada Ltd.
Toronto New York London Auckland Sydney
Mexico City New Delhi Hong Kong Buenos Aires

Scholastic Canada Ltd.
604 King Street West, Toronto, Ontario M5V 1E1, Canada

Scholastic Inc.
557 Broadway, New York, NY 10012, USA

Scholastic Australia Pty Limited
PO Box 579, Gosford, NSW 2250, Australia

Scholastic New Zealand Limited
Private Bag 94407, Botany, Manukau 2163, New Zealand

Scholastic Children's Books
Euston House, 24 Eversholt Street, London NW1 1DB, UK

www.scholastic.ca

The author is grateful for the assistance of the Ontario Arts Council
and its Works in Progress grant.

ONTARIO ARTS COUNCIL
CONSEIL DES ARTS DE L'ONTARIO
an Ontario government agency
un organisme du gouvernement de l'Ontario

Library and Archives Canada Cataloguing in Publication
Bow, James, 1972-, author
Icarus down / James Bow.
Issued in print and electronic formats.
ISBN 978-1-4431-3913-7 (paperback).--ISBN 978-1-4431-3914-4 (html)
I. Title.
PS8603.O973I33 2016   jC813'.6   C2016-900401-5

Cover image © Retrostar/Dreamstime

6 5 4 3 2 1   Printed in Canada 139   16 17 18 19 20

To Erin, destroyer of worlds . . .

THE FALL OF SIMON DAUD

CHAPTER ONE
BETWEEN FOG AND FIRE

SIMON:

My name is Simon Daud, and I was never the special one.

My brother Isaac, now, he was a golden boy. Everything came to him easily. He walked into a room and people smiled. He turned in his perfect schoolwork and his teachers smiled. He turned his bright eyes toward a girl, and *she* smiled. He went to the flight academy a year early, became the youngest fullfledged pilot in our colony's history, and the mayor himself smiled, and gave him a medal. In short, the universe smiled on Isaac. Right up to the day he died.

• • •

For a long time, I thought it was my fault. If you've read deep enough into the history books to bother with this annotation, you know that it wasn't. That puts you ahead of me, because when I remember it, it still *feels* like my fault.

Isaac shouldn't have been there, of course. The Creator only knows what strings he pulled. The senior pilot who accompanies the junior on his maiden flight is chosen at random, but obviously older, golden-boy brothers shouldn't be called on to supervise younger, unremarkable ones. But Isaac could always bend the rules.

"What are you doing here?" I shouted at him when he turned up that morning on the gantries outside Daedalon's flight bay. The hot wind rushing across the underside of the city was loud, and the cables that tethered the city to the anchors in the cliffs hummed like cello strings. They could put up all the vibration dampers they wanted, and maybe inside the cities you wouldn't notice, but any pilot or gantry spider would tell you: our cities *sang*. Daedalon, our largest city, had a bass thrum you could feel in your bones. The ornithopters around me hung like dragonflies in a spider web, their folded fabric wings surging and snapping.

"Seven senior pilots on shift and I drew *you*?" I said. "Honestly, Isaac, it isn't fair!"

He took the canister of batteries from me and raised his voice above the furnace wind. "Fair won't keep your flight level, cadet! Fair's got nothing to do with it."

There was no point in arguing with Isaac. He was

brilliant in his white uniform, the ridged fabric of his sleeve denoting his senior pilot rank with shadow. More ridging over his heart outlined the arrowhead of Iapyx, our home city. On his shoulder, above the rank insignia, was a man rising to the stars on wings of flame, in memory of our colony ship the *Icarus*, the emblem of Icarus Down.

Holding on to one of the plastic-sheathed cables, I inched to the two-man ornithopter. Beneath my feet — a kilometre down — clouds rolled over the floor of the chasm. Behind me was the stem of the city, added after we pulled our cities halfway up the cliffs. Its wall curved behind me and swept downward, narrowing like a funnel before vanishing into a black point in all that white cloud. Before me and behind, the cliff faces bathed us in shadow. At the top of those cliffs, I could see sunlight blazing off fused silica, too bright to look at directly. Up on those diamond lands, an ornithopter's wings would catch fire in minutes. A person would burn to death even quicker.

I climbed into my ornithopter. Isaac was all business as he pulled himself into the rear seat and did up his harness. "Personnel in," he reported. "Cadet, what's our weight?"

Between the pilot's seat and the rear seat, the ornithopter engineers had squeezed a small bank of gauges. I checked them, tucking my head down to avoid my brother's eyes. They were bright that morning, like he was planning something. "Two hundred kilos, even." I paused just long enough before adding, "Sir."

"Good. Battery levels?"

I had just put the batteries in myself. I did — I know I did — look at the gauge anyway. "Full power."

"Wings?"

"Lateral control reads true," I said. "Vertical control reads true. Rudder true. Green board." It wasn't green, of course, or a board; it was a series of wooden switches. But two generations beforehand, we'd been a star-faring civilization. Old words die hard.

"Tailhook reads true," Isaac said. I'd missed that one, but he didn't comment. He looked at me with his sunshine eyes and grinned dangerously. "Crank over."

I turned the winch, cranking my chair around to face the windshield. My back left the seat. My chest pressed against the harness. Now there was nothing in front of me but the hand and foot levers of the flight mechanisms and, beyond that, a kilometre-long drop. Now I was in charge. Isaac was just the navigator. Well, just the navigator who could wash me out of flight school with one report. He tapped the Morse lever. "Requesting permission to drop, pilot," he said.

I waited. Flight clearance had to come from Daedalon, the capital, and from Iapyx, which meant message by semaphore, which was slow, even if it was technically by the speed of light. Each city's semaphore tower could be seen on approach, and

I imagined Daedalon's now, standing atop the vast dome of the city like a wind turbine from Old Mother Earth, two arms twisting and aligning, sending our flight plan letter by letter. Poking into sunlight, the semaphore was a beacon that could be seen kilometres away by watchers huddled in their roof bunker on Iapyx. Watching through filtered mirrors, the semaphore operators would write each letter down, send the slip by canister to Iapyx's flight bay, which would reply, and then . . .

Hanging from its tailhook, our ornithopter swayed like a pendulum. Finally, the Morse lever clicked to life. "Iapyx is expecting us, pilot," Isaac said. "We are clear to drop."

I took a deep breath; I couldn't help it. "Drop," I said. And we did.

We fell. We needed to be clear of the cabling before deploying wings, but you could lose track of time when falling and it was always tempting to unfold too early. My mind said the name of my city — *one eye-a-pix, two eye-a-pix* — and when I got to ten, I heaved back on both hand levers. They fought. Even with powerful gears, it's no small thing to push wings out against that kind of speed. The wood handles shuddered; my arms shook. Then the levers jerked as the wind caught the wings and snapped them back and into their locks. The ornithopter swung around to level as if it had hit a tightly curved rail. It wanted to keep swinging, and head up, but I fought it. "Wings set," I reported. "Navigator, start engine."

Isaac hit the electric button — the only one on board — and the engine came up with a hum. The ornithopter's dragonfly wings started to buzz. We were away, flying level, pretty as a picture. I'd done it perfectly. Isaac didn't say a word.

As we came out from under the cable umbrella of Daedalon, I ran over the advice of our instructors. I pictured our ornithopter in the centre of the canyon, a moth flying the routes of a maze: left cliff face half a kilometre to port, right cliff face half a kilometre to starboard. Five kilometres ahead, the right cliff face angled in front of us. Iapyx was an hour away. I gripped the rudder controls and counted down to the next turn. Finally, the black rock on my port side fell away. I turned the rudder, felt the ornithopter bank, and held on until the chasm opened up in our front windscreen. This length was angled more to the south, meaning the sun cut lower on the cliffs, and I dropped us a hundred metres to compensate. On my left, the cliff face blocked Daedalon from sight.

"Very good," said Isaac.

I blinked.

"Let me be the first to congratulate you, Pilot Daud."

"You're supposed to file a report," I protested. "It has to be evaluated."

"Formality. You were never going to wash out, Si. You're the best cadet the flight school's had since . . . well, me. Didn't you know?"

"Uh . . . no?" My brother always provoked me to brilliant conversation.

"Trust me. Your wings are waiting for you at Iapyx. I ordered them myself."

"Oh," I said.

"In the meantime, here we are in the middle of nowhere, sky to ourselves, an hour's easy flying from any prying ears."

"Prying ears?"

"You'd be surprised," he said. "We need to talk, Si. It's important. It's — it's about Mom."

• • •

Mom. Is she even a footnote, now? Funny how things turn out, that you're reading about me. Simon Daud, age (at the time) sixteen. Older brother: Isaac, just turned nineteen. Father: Abram, a gantry spider by profession — one of the men who tended to the webs of cables that tethered our cities to the anchors embedded in the cliffs. Fell to his death in the colony's fifty-first year, age thirty. I was five. Mother: Hagar, map-maker, an aide to the mayor of Iapyx's planning committee. Died in the colony's fifty-fifth year. A suicide.

I was nine. That's old enough to be shocked, old enough to be angry. Young enough — maybe — to forget, or pretend you've forgotten. Isaac and I, far from the only orphans in that dangerous place, were raised in vocational school, without parents but with cheerful and competent teachers and hall mothers. We did well enough. We hadn't spoken about Mom in years.

• • •

We spoke about Mom, now, by ourselves in an or-nithopter, in a canyon that nobody had bothered to name. Isaac didn't ease into it, either. "I don't think she jumped, Simon."

"Well, I don't think she flew." The bitterness in my voice surprised me; I thought I was past that. "They found . . . parts of her, Isaac. There was an ID." Though, as I said it, it sounded vague. Found what? ID'd how? I hadn't been asked to make an ID. Had Isaac? What if he'd been wrong? My heart lurched like an ornithopter levelling out.

"I don't mean she's not dead, Si," he said. "I mean she didn't kill herself. Maybe." All of a sudden, he sounded preoccupied. He tapped a dial. How could he lose focus in the middle of telling me *this*? He went on. "I've been . . . working with some people. I think . . . maybe she was . . ."

"Spit it out, Isaac!" I said. The ornithopter had nosed up while I was distracted. I pushed the tail flap pedal to compensate. "You think what?"

"I think she was murdered," he said. Then, before I could even take that in, he snapped, "Did we check these batteries?"

"*What?*" And the batteries were fresh. I *know* they were. "What in sunlight are you talking about?"

"We've got half a bank, and sinking," he said. "Twelve amps. Eleven point nine."

"Is this a test?" I barked at him. "Emergency sim?

9

Pilots under emotional stress?"

"No," he said. "It's dropping. Look—"

I tried to crane my head around, but I couldn't see the indicators.

"What does this have to do with what you said about Mom?"

"Nothing," he said. "I think, but . . . Eleven point eight. Point seven five."

I gaped at him over my shoulder. "We can't make it to Iapyx on less than twelve amps."

"I know."

The wings buzzed. They hadn't changed pitch. We weren't slowing down. Not yet.

"We'll ditch," I said. "Put up flares. They'll come looking for us when we're over-time."

Isaac pulled the chart down from the roll above his head. A long pause. I tried not to ask him. Pilots didn't ask navigators, and navigators spoke out as soon as they had a fix. Simon Daud, playing by the rules.

"We're too far out." Isaac gave his clipboard a final tap with his pencil. "The rescue flight will be two or three hours, at least. The ticktocks will get us by then." We both looked down as he said it. Beneath the veil of white appeared dark shapes, the limbs of trees. The fog forest. The bottom of the world.

"Take us down," said Isaac. "Get us as low as you can."

I was pushing on the elevator pedals with both feet before it occurred to me that I was obeying without question, and I had no idea what the plan was. If we weren't going to ditch, why were we going down?

"Eleven point five," said Isaac.

Those battery readings were dropping fast. "A leak," I said. "An intermittent short somewhere."

"Maybe." There was a racket as he winched his chair around, pulled up the access hatch and poked around. "The bank's properly seated."

Funny how good news can be bad news. The connection between the battery bank and the cable that led out to the engine mounted at the front of the tail stem was the only thing that we could check on without landing. And there was no place to land.

"I'm going out," said Isaac. He reached for a set of smoked goggles.

"Out *where*?"

"On the roof. To check the engine connections."

Check the engine connections. In flight. It was a wild idea but, knowing Isaac, it might work. The engine was from interstellar days; nothing short of a supernova could make it go wrong. There were four cables connected to it, two for each wing pair. If there was a short, it was going to be there. It was probably just a matter of wiping some gunk off a plug.

"Keep going down," he said, his voice muffled as he wrapped a white scarf over the lower part of his face. "We'll need the room."

I saw what he meant, now. With him on the roof, the ornithopter would be tail-heavy, and would nose up, no matter what I did to keep her level. Up, toward sunlight. I heard the *click* as Isaac undid his harness, then the *chuff* of the door seal, and a deafening rush of wind.

"Take your parachute!" I shouted.

"Like I'd leave you!" he shouted back. But out of the corner of my eye, I saw the chute pack pull free from the rack. "Right back, Si!" And he went out.

I didn't have time to worry. It was all I could do to control the flight. The ornithopter lurched to port as Isaac swung out. I stomped on the portside elevator pedal and trimmed back the starboard wing pair. The next minutes were a wild, swinging ride as Isaac climbed over the fabric roof. I moved hands and feet fast, trying not to drop my brother into the clouds below.

"Hang on, hang on," I muttered. Ornithopters were maintained while hanging from their tailhooks in the sky. There were handholds everywhere. They were *designed* for climbing on. I thought all that, but I kept saying "Hang on, hang on," as if it were a prayer to the Creator.

Finally, the lurching stopped and the ornithopter nosed up hard. Isaac must be on the tail. I floored the pedals, but we kept climbing. I could hear Isaac shifting on the roof. I kept our glide true, right down the centre of the canyon, but going up. There was nothing I could do about that. If I cut speed any more, we'd stall and crash in the fog forest, never to be found.

It might come to that anyway. My heart thudded as I looked ahead. We were running out of shadow. The air glittered as the sun shone through the cap of fused silica above us.

"Isaac!" I yelled, jamming hard on the elevator pedals. "Isaac!"

There was no way he could hear me above the wind. I banged on the roof. "Isaac! We're going into sunlight!"

Suddenly every wire and strut could be seen through the fabric of the ornithopter. Isaac's dark bulk shifted as he moved toward the door hatch, thank the Creator.

The plane lurched again. I squinted, watching the cliff face through my eyelashes, unable to let go of the controls long enough to grab the smoked goggles that swung near my ear. Isaac's shadow fell across me. But at that moment, the cabin glowed brilliant. The temperature spiked. And worst of all, the controls went dead in my hands. We'd run out of time. Something vital had burned, and broken.

I wrenched around. Isaac was in the doorway. His clothes were smoking. Behind him, the wing was smoking. "Isaac, get back in!" I grabbed at the winch, trying to turn around, to reach him, to help him. Or just to hold on to him as we both died. *"Isaac!"*

He gripped the edge of the cab door. The skin of his hands was blackening. I remember the smell of cooking meat. I will always remember the smell of cooking meat. I remember the way he turned his hand over, peering at it as if curious. He didn't look like he was in pain.

The canvas by the doorframe caught fire.

Then the wing.

The whole plane was on fire.

I had the seat around; I fumbled with the buckles of my harness, trying to reach my brother.

The wing fell apart, and the wind ripped Isaac away.

I grabbed my chute and leapt, pulling it on as I fell. The ornithopter fell apart around me. Isaac's parachute ballooned out below me. I pulled the cord on mine; it deployed and jerked me upward viciously. The harness, half-on, cut into my armpits. I grabbed the chest strap, buckling it over my breastbone. The backs of my hands were already blistering.

Then, below me, Isaac's chute caught fire. It ripped open from the centre like petals falling off a flower. And then Isaac fell, his body alight. He hit shadow like a shooting star.

The air was so hot my lungs refused it, making me choke and gasp. I could smell my hair singeing away. Below, the veil of shadow was closer, but I wasn't falling quickly enough. I had forgotten to count. I had pulled the chute too soon. And now I was going to roast to death.

Of my brother, there was no sign.

Isaac. He had always led the way. I curled up, burning under the smouldering chute, and hoped I would follow him soon.

• • •

"Simon?"

A voice pulled on me like a cord. I woke from dreams of pain into soft white. The fog, I thought. I'd fallen into the fog. No. I was looking at a mottled white ceiling. It drifted above me.

"He has his eyes open. Simon, are you with us?

Monitors. Hospital smell. Out the window, the triangles and diamonds of the cables. Iapyx. My city. Workers were adding mylar and polishing the mirrors. My addled mind saw this and recognized the early preparations for Solar Maximum. That added to my confusion. How long had I been out?

I tried to turn to the voice, but when I did, my skin crackled with pain. It felt stiff. Plastic. My hands were curled into claws.

"Take it easy, Simon," said the voice. "The skin grafts will make it hard to move."

Skin grafts?

"Rachel?" There was a raspy sound that I could hardly believe was my voice.

"Simon!" Her face swung over me. The constellation of her features swam: the blond hair coiled in its snood, the freckles, the beauty mark star at the corner of her jawbone. The just-slightly crooked nose. Those eyes . . . In the hollow of her throat, the betrothal charm that had once been my mother's hung like a star. "I'm right here, Simon."

15

"Rachel . . . what . . . Isaac?"

There was a pause, and in that pause, I had hope. I had made it out. Had Isaac?

"I'm sorry." She looked away. "He's gone, Simon."

Isaac. I closed my eyes. There was a long moment's silence.

"How . . . How did they find me?" I said at last.

She forced a smile. "When you didn't arrive at your prearranged time, the pilots scrambled to look for you. They found your parachute snagged against the cliff wall."

"How . . ." I coughed and my chest cracked into a spiderweb of pain. "How long . . . ?"

There was a pause that was almost worse than the news. "You've been in a medically induced coma for three months."

Three *months*. I tried to get my eyes to focus. Rachel, her hair like the gentle sun of Old Mother Earth, leaned over me. There was a slash in her whiteness: a black armband on her sleeve.

Rachel, my brother's widow.

CHAPTER TWO
REHABILITATION

Third-degree burns don't heal. They leave behind scar tissue, raised and red, tight ropes of pain that pull every joint closed. My body curled in on itself: hands into claws, arms into a mummy cross, chin tucked, knees hooked up. If I didn't work at it, I found myself lying fetal.

Michael Dere was assigned as my rehabilitation officer. He was as thin as a reed and looked young to be a doctor, but the embossed rod-and-snakes on the arm of his uniform — circled to show his specialist rank — clearly identified him.

"Hello, Simon," he said as he introduced himself. He had a soft voice, but spoke quickly, like he had a lot to do. "Nurse Caan and I will work with you to get your body back to, well, about as normal as we can expect. Out of the bed, certainly. And out of the infirmary."

My face must have registered disbelief, because he nodded at me. "I know this doesn't seem possible from where you're lying, but there's a lot we can do to get you back to a more normal life. I won't lie: it will be hard work. You'll be getting to know me well over the next few weeks," he said.

I tried to hold up my hand. "I have to go to the bathroom," I whispered.

He nodded. "Yes. Getting to know each other *very* well." He fetched a bedpan.

Rehab is long and boring and painful. Michael would pull my arms open until I shouted with pain. He put rolls under my neck and made me throw my head back. He fitted me with compression garments to shape my new skin, and massaged lotion into my scars, twice daily, until he announced that my scars were "mature." I'll spare you further details, unless you want to hear about the triumphant time I held a fork in the numb pincers my hands had become. Eventually, I could get into a wheelchair by myself, if I had time and someone was there to catch me if I missed the grab bar.

Meanwhile, Rachel was in charge of getting me off the morphium. I gave her no trouble. It's addictive, knocks you out and gives you strange dreams. For me, those dreams were of fire and falling. Most days, I'd rather have the pain than the dreams.

And I liked having Rachel there. I liked having

her haul me up to drink the water to down the pill. I liked the way she brushed back my hair after she caught me from collapsing, and eased me back onto the pillow.

But as I lay in recovery, Rachel and I didn't talk. Oh, we had things to talk about: how the treatment was going, and how much less morphium I was going to take. But Rachel didn't ask me what happened on the ornithopter and, unasked, I couldn't find the courage to tell her. Our clinical conversation fell to awkward silences, and she had other patients to see. She drifted out. Like a ghost. Like a widow.

Is *widow* the right term? Isaac and Rachel had been betrothed, not married. It was almost the same thing, but they'd never taken the vows at Nocturne. What term do you use when someone's betrothed dies? Maybe widow serves.

I'd first met Rachel when we were kids. We were in second grade — or was it third? — and I just noticed her one day. She was walking from the art table to the hydroponic rack with scissors in her hand. I don't know what caught my eye. The way she moved, maybe, with such purpose. I watched her, holding a dripping paintbrush.

Well, we can be friends, I thought. And so we were.

But then, at Nocturne . . . it got complicated.

I remember a toy ornithopter my father had given me once. His face was a kind blur but I could remember his hands, the bar of calluses across his palms. The weight of the little toy, the crackling of the wings he'd made from bits of cable shielding, the smooth-sanded wood of the needle-body. "I'm a pilot!" I shouted to him. To this day I swear it was my dream first — flying — and not Isaac's. But he was older. He always led the way. Even with Rachel.

And now with Isaac gone . . . things were more complicated still.

• • •

At first, Michael and Rachel and an assortment of nurses and doctors were the only people I saw. That disappointed me. I had no family, and my friends from vocational school had moved on to jobs or apprenticeships, but the flight academy? I'd made time to socialize. I'd made friends. Or so I thought.

I suspect Rachel noticed my loneliness. She may have gone down to the flight academy and lit into them like the sun. Whatever she did, the next day I got a visit from much of my class.

They came in one group, bearing gifts.

"Hey!" Leah led the way into the room. She was the hotshot in our class. Liked speed. Had to be warned against doing barrel rolls in the chasms. "How's our downed bird?"

The room filled with people. I was delighted, but also embarrassed. I was wearing nothing but a hospital robe. I pulled the sheets higher. "Hey!" I reached for the crank to raise the bed, but I was nowhere near ready to lever myself up. I pointed at it. "Could you . . ."

"How you doing, lazybones?" Calvert came forward to crank me into a sitting position. He was a steady flyer, but preferred the mechanical side of things. He moved to slap my shoulder, but stopped short just in time. He patted my arm instead.

"You'd best get better soon," said Falk, "or I'll tell the flight master you're goofing off."

We all laughed at that. Well, them more than me. They laid their gifts on the bedside table. They had books from the library and flowers from the arboretum. They'd all signed a card. They talked in cheerful tones, but from the looks on their faces I knew I wasn't up to facing a mirror yet. It wasn't long before an awkward silence stretched.

"So," said Falk, his tone joking, "you got many calls from the press?"

The others glared at him. Leah slapped the back of his head.

"Sorry?" I said. "What?"

"Don't worry about that," said Leah, looking serious. "We're just glad you're alive."

"Yeah, we all are," said Calvert.

I kept waiting for somebody to make a joke, break all this seriousness, but nothing came.

A nurse rescued us, telling us visiting times were over. They said their goodbyes and left. I noticed that they hurried out of the room a lot faster than they hurried in.

I shouldn't have been surprised. We were pilots. We were young. We thought — they thought — they were immortal. I was a ghost they didn't want to face.

The light above my bed kept flickering, and twice it went out. Battery boys came to change the battery, and then the bulb, but it didn't help. It felt like something dark was coming.

I thought of Isaac. I thought of Mom. *I don't think she jumped, Simon.*

I even ordered up the coroner's report on her, but it had been routine, and long since recycled. I wasn't surprised. When your only source of fibre for paper is a forest inhabited by monsters, you don't keep records around for the heck of it.

Still, somewhere, someone made note of my request for the coroner's report, and decided it was time to turn Simon Daud, pilot, into something else.

• • •

It was just bad luck, I think, that the news came the day Rachel and I finally got around to really talking to each other.

She came in with my pills in a little cup. "A quarter grain." She sounded pleased about it. "Your last step-down, Simon. We'll have you off morphium entirely next week."

"Oh," I said. "Good." It *was* good, but it's hard to get excited about withdrawal tremors and rebound pain.

"I'm sorry. But it really is better." Rachel sat down on the edge of the bed. "You're being very brave."

I wasn't being brave, really. What I was doing, what I was good at, was following the rules, trusting that the people in charge knew what they were doing. Still, I wasn't about to contradict her. I liked her sitting there. The light through the mylar sheeting over the window was metallic, tarnished. Her white nurse's uniform looked silver. Her honey hair looked like polished wood.

Her — *wait.* "You took off your armband," I said.

Rachel glanced away. One loose curl of hair had poked through the netting of her snood and curved over the top of her ear. "Six months today."

"Is it?" Time had shortened and stretched for me in the hospital. The accident felt like last week. It felt like a million years ago. "Six months. Wow."

"Six months. And I still don't—" She cut herself off, stood up and put the pills on my tray. "I don't know what happened, Simon. No one has told me."

That would be because someone was a rat-fink coward. She'd loved Isaac. We could have shared that. But we hadn't.

She looked at me, waiting, and then her face folded up and she turned to leave.

"Rachel," I called after her. "Wait."

She turned. She waited.

"He died—" my voice cracked. "There was a faulty battery. He climbed onto the tail to check the connections. The weight made us go up . . ." I stopped, realizing I was holding out my hand, like an ornithopter, tipping the fingers upward. Beseeching. "We — ran out of room."

"A faulty *battery*?" she echoed. She glanced up at my troublesome light.

"I—" I didn't know what to tell her; it was such a stupid reason to die. "He was trying to save us, Rachel. He died trying to save me. I'm so sorry."

"Simon . . ." She turned back to me. Then the voicepipe connecting my room to the infirmary's central desk squeaked. She glared at it. "Oh, for heavens'—" She stalked over and pulled the end of the tube to her mouth. "Nurse Caan speaking." She put it to her ear.

As she listened, her frown deepened. "Are you sure?" she said into the tube. "He's just had medication . . ." She put the tube to her ear. "Well, why wasn't I informed?" I couldn't hear a thing, but Rachel's frown deepened. "I don't care if they sent a message, it isn't here now, is it?" Rachel's voice was getting more clipped by the second. "Well, yes, he is getting better, but—" Her lips tightened. "All right. I'll ask him." She hung up the receiver and turned to me. "You have visitors."

I sat up in my bed, wincing as my joints protested. "Really? Who?"

On the wall, the pneumatic tube clicked as a message container thumped into place. Rachel frowned, then went over and pulled the canister from the receptacle. She looked perplexed, and worried.

What visitors had to be heralded by message tube?

"Rachel." She looked at me. She was pale: I could see her freckles. "Who's here?"

Before she could answer, the door burst open. My hands went to my side and I sat at attention as Mayor Matthew Tal swept in, his robes of office billowing behind him. His entourage followed, carrying clipboards and pads of paper. One held a camera. All wore white, with the arrowhead insignia of Iapyx surrounded by an embossed circle, denoting the mayor's office.

"Mr. Daud," the mayor exclaimed. He glanced at his notes. "Simon! You're looking much better. In fact, you're looking great!"

"Um." I'd seen the expressions of my fellow pilots. I was fairly sure I didn't look great. "Uh, thank you, sir."

The mayor sat on the chair beside my bed. The room lights reflected off his bald spot and his chain of office. "Something like this deserves something more than just a lowly official, doesn't it?"

What was going on?

"Don't mind the photographer," the mayor went on. "For the newsletter, you understand. Iapyxians will want to know how the fallen pilot that his brave comrades rescued is faring."

The photographer raised his camera before I could react. The flash blinded me; I flinched, reminded of sunlight.

Another of the mayor's entourage leaned in, clipboard and pen at the ready. "So, Simon Daud, could you tell the citizens of Iapyx how your recovery is going?"

"Uh . . . Fine! They've been taking good care of me. I'm working hard." *I can even hold a fork.*

"Very good." The mayor slapped me on the back. I winced, but did not cry out. Rachel coloured red.

"Thank you!" I said, before she could jeopardize her career. "Thank you, sir; it's an honour."

The photographer spoke low near the mayor's ear. "Excuse me, sir, but we'll need to do the ceremony somewhere else. The lighting in here is totally inadequate."

"Hmm . . ." The mayor nodded. "The infirmary reception area, perhaps?"

"That will do nicely."

"Excuse me," I cut in. "What ceremony?"

The mayor beamed at me. "The ceremony where we award you your medal, son. Didn't you receive the papers?"

Rachel and I looked at the pneumatic canister that had arrived too late.

The mayor turned to the photographer. "Set everything up. Nurse, see to a wheelchair for Simon here." He turned his smile on me, like a semaphore shifting. "We wouldn't want you to miss your own medal pinning!"

There was organized chaos as the mayor and his entourage left the room. Rachel blinked, bewildered, but she went to a corner and pulled out the folded wheelchair.

A dark-sleeved arm gripped the armrest. Rachel looked up. Her eyes widened.

The man must have been standing by the wall the whole time. We hadn't noticed him.

"Nurse," he said. "Please go help the mayor. I'll see to Mr. Daud. Thank you."

It wasn't a request. Rachel looked from the man to me, flustered. Then she lifted her chin and marched out the door.

Once the door clicked shut, the man turned to me. My throat tightened.

Nathaniel Tal, the mayor's older brother, had been Iapyx's chief of security for as long as I could remember. He was tall and, like the security officers he commanded, wore the only colour to be found on clothes and uniforms on Iapyx. That colour was grey. His black hair was streaked with white. He was like a column of smoke standing behind the mayor's left shoulder. I had no reason to be afraid of him.

I was afraid of him.

Nathaniel rolled the wheelchair to the bed and unfolded it. He held out a hand for me. "Mr. Daud."

I took it, clumsy, and used the support to heave my legs to the side of the bed and over. He guided me into the chair. Once I was there, he put his hands on the armrests and looked me in the eye. "I want to talk to you about your last flight."

My stomach lurched, as it had when my ornithopter dropped off the gantry at Daedalon. The way he asked the question made me feel instantly guilty.

"Okay." I fought the urge to look away. "What do you want to know?"

He leaned back. "You departed Daedalon soon after you sent a message by semaphore to Iapyx. You had a normal flight through the first turn, but then you dropped three quarters of a kilometre before rising again into sunlight."

I nodded. "The batteries developed a fault. Isaac — the navigator — wanted to go out onto the tail to check the connections. He told me to fly down so we'd have room to rise. There wasn't enough room." My brow furrowed. "How did you know what we did?"

"Your white box told us," Nathaniel replied.

The white box. They'd found it.

"Then you know what happened." I felt a sudden rush of courage. "It's been six months. Wasn't there an inquiry? The white box should have told you — everything." Including what had caused the batteries to fail.

Nathaniel ran his tongue over his teeth. "Your white box developed a fault when you passed the first turn on your trip home," he replied. "It lost sound. So we don't know all of what happened in the cabin." His gaze bored into me. "What conversations you had, for instance."

I kept my mouth closed. What had happened after the first turn? Nothing that showed on my instruments. But Isaac had said, *Here we are in the middle of nowhere, sky to ourselves, an hour's easy flying from any prying ears.*

When I'd first heard that, I'd thought Isaac was being facetious. Afterwards, I'd been too busy being in a coma to remember that the white box would have recorded our conversation. Except that apparently ours hadn't. Which meant . . .

But *tampering* with the white box? Isaac often bent the rules, but he didn't break them!

"I also note that the selection of navigator was unusual for your flight," Nathaniel went on. "Your maiden flight, isn't that correct? Your older brother giving you your final grade? Surely that's a little . . . irregular?"

Feelings of guilt washed over me again. Nathaniel was trying to spook me. And doing a good job of it.

But as I thought about it, a resolve crept up in me to say as little as possible. My last words with Isaac belonged to him and me alone. "I wouldn't know, sir. I just followed orders."

His frown deepened. "So, what did you talk about?"

We talked about Mom. Or, we started to. "Stuff," I said. "Flying, mostly."

"Can you be more specific?"

I'm not used to lying. "He . . . he told me how good it was to be a pilot. And . . . the scenery."

He didn't look impressed. "The scenery."

"Yes, sir. You know, the cliffs, the fog and stuff."

"He didn't talk to you about the Grounders, did he?"

I stared at him. Why would Nathaniel ask about some flaky movement obsessed with moving our cities onto the foggy ground below, a place teeming with monsters? Why —

But Isaac's words echoed in my head. *"I've been working with some people . . ."* *"I think she was murdered . . ."*

"No," I said firmly. "Nothing about the Grounders. We didn't get much of a chance to talk about anything before the batteries developed a fault and we had to try to repair the ornithopter in flight." I leaned forward in my seat. "What is this? An interrogation? For what? My ornithopter developed a fault. We tried to fix it, but we couldn't do it in time. Isn't that what the white box said? What more could you find out from me?"

I glared at Nathaniel. He looked back at me. Silence stretched.

My resolve faltered. A question demanded to be asked. "What caused the fault in my ornithopter? Does the white box say?"

Nathaniel's face betrayed nothing. "The evidence was inconclusive."

There was a knock on the door. One of the mayor's assistants poked her head in. "Officer Tal? The mayor's ready."

Nathaniel nodded. He wheeled me out and into the corridor, toward the reception area.

"I have never had the chance to say I am sorry about your mother," he said.

I jerked, and tried to look up at him, but I couldn't crane my neck that far. "It's okay," I lied. "It was years ago."

"I worked with her," Nathaniel went on. "An

excellent assistant to the mayor. Her death was a great loss to the colony."

"Um . . . thanks. I appreciate that."

"I wish you well on your recovery." He turned a corner. "You'll be a great asset to the CommController."

I looked up at him so sharply, it made my neck ache. "What are you talking about?"

"Didn't you know?" He kept his eyes on the corridor ahead. "You've been deemed medically unfit to fly. I'm told that the flight master did what she could and pulled some strings, but there are plenty of flight instructors at the academy, I'm afraid, all with full use of their hands. Fortunately, the Communications Hub can always use additional personnel."

It was like the accident again. I could feel the ornithopter flying apart around me. "No," I said, all the strength gone from my voice. Not the Communications Hub. "I want to fly."

Nathaniel shrugged. "It could be worse. You could be a battery boy. Here we are."

He rolled me into the reception area, where the mayor and his entourage stood waiting, along with a crowd of onlookers. Leah and Calvert and Falk were there, along with the rest of my class. The press were there. Rachel stood at the edge of the crowd.

Nathaniel rolled me up beside the mayor and stepped back.

"Simon Daud," the mayor recited, raising a disk on a coloured ribbon and draping it around my neck. Flashbulbs burst, reflecting off the shiny surface, dazzling me. My eyes watered. "In recognition of your bravery in the face of danger, it gives me pleasure to honour you with this award of service on behalf of the citizens of Iapyx, in the name of the Creator of the Stars and the Captains of the *Icarus*."

Then he shook me by my ruined hand. "And congratulations on your reassignment to the Communications Hub."

CHAPTER THREE
LIFE GOES ON

I should have known my flying days were done. I could hardly hold a fork; how could I pull back on the wing levers? If I'd been honest with myself, the only career I had left to look forward to was with the battery boys.

A nurse-intern wheeled me to my room. I sat by the window, brooding.

The canister that had arrived ahead of the mayor sat beside the pneumatic receptacle. I pulled it onto my lap and fumbled with the latch. My clumsy fingers ripped the envelope, and papers scattered over my lap and onto the floor. Across my knee was a picture — a parachute snagged on a cliff face. From the parachute dangled a broken boy, his dark head bowed.

An artist's sketch of me.

It was the Iapyx newsletter, sent with the papers

announcing my medal and my transfer to the Communications Hub. Everyone in the colony would have seen the picture.

I started reading. It was about a brave fallen pilot, and his brave friends who had bravely rescued him. There was an update about his brave fight for life. I was still trying to find someone I knew in this story when Rachel knocked. Her breath caught when she saw the spill of papers.

I held up the newsletter. "Why didn't you tell me?"

"I didn't know they'd give you a medal today," she said. "I didn't know they'd do it in the infirmary."

"Not the medal," I shook the newsletter. "This. Does everybody think I'm a hero?"

Rachel opened her mouth, but I cut her off. "I didn't do anything! I just tried to hold the ornithopter steady while Isaac checked the connections! I just tried to keep her out of sunlight. I followed the rules and, you know what? I *failed*! How does *that* make me a hero?"

Rachel didn't say anything.

"I'd like to go to bed now."

She helped haul me out of the wheelchair and onto the bed, then pulled the covers over me. I thought she'd leave, but she stood there looking down.

"You're a hero because you lived," she said. "The pilots rescued you. People like to hear news like that."

"They had to pretty it up, though, didn't they? Wait till next week's photo, when they can see what the sun left behind! Do you suppose they'll like that?"

Rachel reddened, but I turned away. I listened to her footsteps recede.

The next few days, I picked at my food. Michael came and made me stretch. Rachel tried to cut my morphium; I snapped at her. There followed more exciting days of lying in bed. More pointless stretching. Pointless pain is harder. Rachel banned me from lying down during daytime hours. So I sat in my wheelchair.

One morning, Rachel came in with a cane under her arm. "Good morning, Simon," she said crisply.

I barely looked up. "Morning."

"It's time to start your walking exercises."

I sighed. "Do we have to do this now?"

"Yes. Your muscles have atrophied. Every day you don't get on your feet, you'll get weaker. Eventually you won't be able to walk. After that you'll get pneumonia and probably die."

My angel of mercy was in fine form this morning. I studied the wall.

Rachel gripped the handles of my wheelchair. "You're no use to the CommController if you can't walk from a pneumatic tube to a table. You need to get started. You've been in bed for seven months."

"It's not like it's my fault!"

Abruptly, Rachel tipped the wheelchair up, sending me sprawling to the floor.

"Get up!" She thumped the cane down next to my ear, then held it out for me. When I rolled over and grabbed at it, she pulled it away.

"Rachel, what are you doing?" My joints were sparking.

"The question is, what are *you* doing, Simon?" She pulled the cane away again. "Are you just going to lie there, or are you going to get up?"

"You threw me to the floor!"

"You're an idiot, you know that?" She thumped the cane near my ear again. "You're alive. You're not the one who *died*, Simon!" She stopped then.

"Rachel?" I looked up. She turned away. "Rachel, are you okay?"

"I'm fine." Her voice was muffled. She'd covered her face with her hands.

I struggled. Without the grab bars, it was hard to sit up, but I managed. "Rachel," I whispered. I crawled closer. I touched her knee, wishing it could be her shoulder.

She turned to me and knelt, and I hugged her. She buried her face against my chest, and I buried my nose in her hair. It smelled of flowers. We stayed there a long moment. My cheeks were wet.

When the silence wore out its welcome, I whispered, "I'm sorry."

"So am I," she whispered back. "Live, Simon. For him. Promise me?"

My voice caught, but I forced it out. "I promise."

"Well," she said, her voice muffled by my shoulder, "you're sitting up. That's something. Can you stand?"

"No way!"

She straightened up, kneeling tall, and put her

hands under my armpits. She heaved, and I tried to help, and before I knew it I was on my feet, holding on to Rachel for dear life while my feet screamed with pain and the room faded and spun around me.

She held me. Her face was close. Very close. Her eyes looked into mine, and I felt a tug like a pull of the parachute.

• • •

Weeks passed, and I began to walk again.

The stim technology Old Mother Earth had developed to keep early astronauts from withering away in cryosleep had not been lost, and it helped, but still, it took me a long time to rebuild my muscles. But I did it, for Rachel, for Isaac, and I tried not to think how I was walking toward a future I did not particularly want.

Meanwhile, the fall of Iapyx was beginning.

It started slow, and I missed the early warning signs. Isaac would have put it together, but he would have known what to look for. There was the flickering light above my bed. There was a cancer survivor in my rehab group who'd hurt her back when an interior stairway suddenly fell dark. Then there was a rush of people to the burn ward, from a rash of steam-pipe bursts. There were the message canisters that showed up for no reason — I missed them all. Even the last one, which was delivered right to my room. But, then, I had something else on my mind.

It was the day they issued me my Communications Hub uniform. I stared at the icon of a winged envelope on the sleeve — my sleeve — before I shrugged it on. I'd become flexible enough to get my own clothes on, but buttons were tricky. I was struggling to do up the collar, and working myself up into a good mope about the fact that it wasn't a pilot's jacket and never would be, when the message tube whistled and clunked.

I frowned at it in irritation. It had been the third one that week, and that was just canisters to my room. If *I* was getting that many misdeliveries, how many were being sent astray elsewhere?

I'd previously let the interns handle it, but this time I limped over. Wasn't this supposed to be my job in a few days' time? Maybe I should take care of it.

I peered at the label through the hatch window, and got a shock. It was from the semaphore office. To the *flight bay*. A flight plan. Somewhere out there, an ornithopter was hanging by its tail, waiting for clearance. Which wasn't coming. Because clearance authorization had been sent to *me*.

I stared at this ghost from my pulped past, then reached to open the hatch, and looked at my mottled hand. Stretching my fingers open, I took the canister in both hands and pulled it out. The weight surprised me and I almost dropped it. I steadied it against the wall while I gathered my strength. *I can do this*, I told myself. Then, with arms shaking, I inserted the canister into the intake tube, closed the hatch, and pressed the button to send it on its way.

As the hiss of delivery faded, I stared at my shaking hands. Was I really ready? For this? For everything?

I closed my eyes, closed my fists, and lowered them to my sides.

Rachel came in, then, like a ship at sail, striding as she had the moment I'd first noticed her. She beamed at me. "Simon! Your uniform!" She did up my top button, which I still hadn't fastened. Then, still close, she put her hand on my shoulder and said softly, "I know it's not the uniform you wanted."

"It's all right," I said. And it sort of was. Communications workers were useful, in a modest sort of way.

"It's good to see you in anything besides a patient's smock," she said. "Are you ready to face the world?"

I drew back. It was one thing rebuilding my body behind the closed doors of the infirmary. Heading outside made this more real. Out there, I would either succeed or fail. I wasn't ready to face the possibility that I might fail.

Rachel patted my shoulder. "You can do it, Simon."

I let her lead me through the corridors. Walking with my cane, I stepped outside the protective double doors of the infirmary and looked out onto the rest of Iapyx for the first time in nine months. People walked back and forth, heading to and from work, the library or the galley. Some looked at me, and some looked very quickly away, but nobody stopped to stare. Everybody was busy needing to be somewhere else.

I spotted a bench across the corridor and made for it, my cane clicking on the floor. Suddenly I felt a hand on my arm. Rachel was smiling at me, sympathetic, even as she shook her head. And before I could say anything, she turned and walked away quickly through the crowd. If I didn't want to lose her, I had to follow.

I struggled forward, dodging between moving people — or, rather, having them dodge around me. My body wasn't ready for quick movements yet. I followed Rachel until I got to the last corner, turned it, and stepped into the Great Hall.

At first I was startled by the expanse, though I was as familiar with it as anybody else on Iapyx. The mounded hills of grass, the trees rising up to the lights in the rounded ceiling, were still a shock after the grey corridors around it.

And I couldn't see Rachel anywhere. I looked out among the people walking around, individually or in pairs, a young family enjoying a picnic, and my heart twisted.

Then I felt her hand take mine, and my heart lifted.

"Another rehabilitation exercise?" I asked.

She smiled. "Michael's orders. He said you needed more than walking across a corridor to a bench. I just . . . interpreted his request a little creatively."

"Thanks," I said. I gave her hand a clumsy squeeze. She kept her hand in mine.

I suddenly felt awkward. I could feel the blush rising in my neck, where it broke against the scar tissue of my cheeks. I hadn't been to Iapyx's Great Hall since two Nocturnes ago. And that Nocturne had been with . . . I suddenly couldn't meet Rachel's gaze.

Nearby, someone shouted "Ticktock!"

I jerked up, then winced as my joints protested.

In a nearby copse of trees, a young boy was wandering around with eyes closed and arms outstretched. As he neared one of the trees, a young girl jumped out. "Ticktock!" she shouted. The boy jumped away before she could pounce at him. He staggered toward another tree, where another boy jumped out. "Ticktick!"

I chuckled. Just kids playing ticktock monsters. Two generations, that's what it takes to turn a nightmare into a children's game.

I looked out at the people sitting on the grass, or walking between the trees. "It's strange," I said again. "Everybody going about their business. I'd forgotten that people still did that."

I was turning to say something more to Rachel, something brilliant, doubtless, but when I turned she was looking at me, her eyes brimming. Her face was very close. Before I could do anything, she leaned up on tiptoe and kissed me.

On Old Mother Earth, there had been an ancient tradition about marrying your brother's widow. We had made a small revival of it on Icarus Down, and why not? We were also pilgrims, also refugees. I actually thought some of that, while my skin softened like butter under Rachel's lips, and my whole heart melted away. Simon Daud: looking for a rule to play by.

Rachel leaned back. She was flushed, and she was no longer crying. "See?" she said. "Life goes on."

CHAPTER FOUR
NOCTURNE

I should explain Nocturne. It may not mean anything to us now, but in our bleached-out colony under a too-bright sun, it was everything.

The life of Icarus Down swung around two points, as the planet spun on its slow fourteen-month-long day: Solar Maximum, when the sun peeked over the rim of our nearly polar canyon and for a few days (that's the twenty-four-hour-long Old Mother Earth variety) blazed at our city, and Nocturne, the few days when it set.

It was my last Nocturne that I'd last seen Isaac, before he'd met me on the gantries of Daedalon's flight bay. And it was during that same Nocturne that I lost Rachel to him.

I'd stood in the Great Hall of Iapyx, shoulder to shoulder with my fellow citizens, staring at the sun.

"It's just a projection, you know," said my friend Aaron. "A fake."

The setting sun was projected on a gigantic screen. It showed the fused silica cap atop the cliffs, the diamond lands stretching as far as the eye could see. The setting sun was a curved sliver of brilliance on the horizon.

"It's not a fake: it's a film of last Nocturne's sunset," I said.

"I'm just saying, Simon: it's not live. They've had that film for fourteen months. They could edit anything into it. It could be the view from Daedalon, or — anywhere."

This was pure Aaron, a guy who wanted to be an astronomer on a planet where the stars never shone, and who was forever questioning the status quo.

I was about to chide Aaron for his conspiracy theories, but just then the lights dimmed. The battery boys were on ladders, unscrewing the bulbs in the Great Hall to show the projection better. A roar went up from the crowd. Night was almost here. Nocturne, the end of white, the end of restraint. Nocturne: darkness and colour. There would be dancing. I had passed my exams and would be flying away to join the flight academy on Daedalon. But first, there was a ceremony to go through.

Mayor Matthew Tal strode onto the stage, and the crowd cheered. He gripped the podium and beamed at us. Then his face grew solemn. I clasped my hands. As one, we lowered our heads.

"We give thanks to Old Mother Earth," he called.

We answered in a unified chant. "The blue marble in space. Our birthplace. The cradle of our civilization."

The mayor continued. "We are sorry for what we have done."

"For the wars," we replied. "The pollution. The mistakes that drove us away."

"We give thanks to the ship," the mayor intoned.

"The *Icarus*," we replied. "Bearing thirteen cities to our second chance. Leaving the mistakes of our ancestors behind."

"We give thanks to those who went before us," called the mayor.

"Who prepared the way for us to land."

"We remember the accident," said the mayor.

As one, we lowered our heads. "We appeared too close to the sun."

"We remember the monsters," the mayor called out.

"Who ticked in the fog. Who made us raise our cities halfway up the cliffs."

"And so we live," the mayor prompted.

"Between fog and fire. Between darkness and light. In our webs, tethered to our cliffs. For tomorrow."

The mayor raised his arms in benediction. "Let us say the oath!"

Our chants echoed across the hall. "We pledge ourselves to the future of Icarus Down. Together we shall build the future, for ourselves and for the generations that follow. We shall leave the mistakes of Old Mother Earth behind."

Mayor Tal bowed his head. "In the name of the Creator of the Stars and the Captains of the *Icarus* . . ."

"We say it is so," we intoned.

The mayor turned to the projection, his arms outstretched.

The sun was almost gone. The sliver of brilliance shrank to a dot and vanished. The blazing sky turned dark blue. A roar rose up from the Great Hall and from all Iapyx. It swayed the lights. It buzzed in the soles of my shoes. Everybody was cheering.

At the podium in front of the screen, Mayor Tal brought his arms down and turned to us. "Let Nocturne begin!"

There was a crash of drums. There was the blare of pipes and fiddles. I was laughing. I followed the crowd. I tried to steer Aaron to the party, but I lost him. I didn't really care. It was here! Nocturne! Nobody would be sleeping tonight!

The Great Hall rumbled with practically the entire population of Iapyx. People filled all available space among the trees and the plant beds, and more and more streamed in from every door. Stages had been set up for the musicians. The rafters had been strung with flakes of mylar, winking as they reflected the lights below, giving us stars even if we couldn't see the real ones. There were tables laden with fruits and rare meats from the forest floor. Most people milled about. Others played impromptu games of kickball. Many danced.

All wore the boldest colours they could find:

scarves of red, blue and yellow, capes of black. The sun couldn't find us now, and turn that colour into flame. People ran through the crowds shaking hand-powered flashlights, turning them on and training them on their faces. The coloured cellophane over the bulbs gave brilliant red, blue and green tones to their laughing, joyous expressions.

"Simon! Isn't it fantastic?"

Suddenly, I had a purple scarf draped over my neck and someone pulling on both ends. I and the someone stumbled, and I instinctively grabbed on for support. When we caught our balance, I found myself staring at Rachel, her cheeks rosy and her eyes alive with laughter.

She'd changed out of her vocational school uniform and was wearing trousers and a loose-fitting, long-sleeved blouse. She had on a blue scarf and had also tied colourful ribbons — some fabric, some cellophane — around her waist.

"Do you like it?" She twirled. Her ribbons billowed up. She grinned at me, since I couldn't help but stare. "Happy Nocturne!"

I smiled, and hoped I wasn't blushing. I opened my mouth, but suddenly I had no idea what to say.

"But look at you." She came forward. "Still all in white! Let's do something about that." She tied a ribbon of red cellophane through my hair, tugged it into a bow and stepped back to admire her handiwork. I knew I looked ridiculous, but I could only look at her.

Then it hit me. She was beautiful. That was the word I'd been struggling to find in the months leading up to now, as our conversations got more awkward. She was my friend, and she was beautiful. And she and Isaac were . . . It made things feel complicated, but really, it was that simple. I just had to tell her.

"Isn't it perfect?" she said. "I love the colours and the music. And the food! Come, see!" She took my arm and led me toward the food table, which was busier than the daily marketplace.

But I couldn't think of anything to say. To fill the silence between us, I decided to supply her with news.

"Isaac was here," I yelled. "Nocturne break. He asked after you."

"Oh." Her smile faded. "Thanks for telling me." And the silence got a lot more uncomfortable. She looked down at the end of the food table we'd just reached and didn't pick up a plate. My mouth watered as I glanced over the selection. But as I reached out for a toffee, Rachel grabbed my hand. "Come on! Let's dance!"

"Dance?" It was a different place and time, remember. Dancing meant something. I wasn't supposed to dance with my brother's — whatever she was. I sputtered: "But — what about Isaac?"

"Oh, pfft—" She waved her hand airily. "He's not here. *You* are, and *I* want to dance! Will you?" Suddenly her eyes were on me, earnest and deep. "Please?"

I took her hand, and she led me onto the dance floor among the couples and groups. We skipped to the frenzied beat, sometimes close together, sometimes an arm's length apart. I forgot about trying to tell her what I was thinking. I was happy enough with the dance.

But then Rachel led me off the floor.

"Have you thought about the future, Simon?" she asked abruptly. She gave me a strange look, like there was a particular answer she wanted.

"Well . . . yeah," I managed. "I just heard — I got into the flight academy."

"Oh." Her mouth curved down.

"What about you?" I was suddenly nervous. "I suppose you'll go study at the infirmary?"

"I suppose . . ."

"Rachel, what's wrong?"

She stared into the distance. The music hammered around us. Finally she said, "I want to be somewhere else."

I blinked at her.

"I've heard stories," she said, "about Old Mother Earth. If I were there, I'd still have three years of education ahead of me. More, if I went to one of those universities, before I had to choose what to do with my life."

I nodded. I'd heard the same stories, though I hardly believed them. How could people wait all the way to eighteen for their adult lives to begin?

Rachel went on. "Not here, though. I have to make my choice now. The headmaster wants me to hand in my apprenticeship application. Isaac wants—"

She drew her arms around herself. "I have to decide, and I'm not ready."

"You'll be ready." Awkwardly, I patted her shoulder. "You love nursing. You'll fly through the apprenticeship."

"I know." I hardly heard her over the crowd. "But maybe there are other things I could love." She looked me in the eye again, with an intensity that took my breath away.

I wanted to reassure her, but I didn't know how without repeating what I'd already said.

I squeezed her shoulder. "You'll be a great nurse. I know it. Just make your choice and stick to it. Whatever doubts you have, put them away." I quoted something the headmaster had said in his pre-graduation address. "The future's in front of you. It will work out if you just work toward it."

Rachel looked up at me. I thought she looked disappointed, but she gave me a small smile. I took that as encouragement. "Look, you don't have to worry about this tonight," I said. "How about I brave the food line and get us something to eat? We'll need to build up our strength before we go back to the dance floor, right?"

She looked away. "Yes, Simon. I'd like that very much."

"Good. Wait here!" I got in line for the food. Of course, the line had got a lot longer while we'd talked, but I was patient and made it in time for the cooks to bring a fresh selection up. I had two plates almost full when someone bumped into me, causing me to spill those plates back on the table. "Hey!" I turned. Then I gaped. "Aaron? What's wrong?"

He blinked, as though struggling to recognize me. "Simon? I was in the observation room with my telescope! You won't believe what I saw! Right on the horizon! A *star*!"

I couldn't help but grin. A star? Impossible. "You sure that 'star' wasn't in a bottle?"

"I'm not drunk, Simon! I saw what I saw!"

"Well, what do you want me to do? There's nobody you can report this to; everybody's here. The headmaster—"

He looked at me sharply. "You're right! I should tell the headmaster. Thanks, Simon! He's got to hear about this!" And he ducked into the crowd.

"Aaron, I didn't say you should *talk* to him! Aaron!" But I'd lost him already, and I decided that Rachel and I needed to eat. I picked up my plates, looked back to where I'd left her — and the plates slipped from my hand again.

Isaac stood in front of Rachel. He was talking to her, gesturing, and Rachel was looking nervous. Then he clasped her hand, pulled her closer, and whispered something in her ear. She jerked back, wide-eyed. Then he nodded over his shoulder at one of the exits and gave her a tentative smile. She stayed still a moment. Then she nodded. They turned and walked off the dance floor, hand in hand.

Isaac. He always led the way.

But now, all these months later, he was gone. And I had no idea what to do next.

CHAPTER FIVE
SABOTAGE

After Rachel kissed me, she pulled back, and I stared at her. The moment lengthened, and the silence began to roar in my ears. I had to say something witty that would seal this moment.

"Um . . ."

Then I saw Rachel's cheeks flushing. She was smiling. "I have to go," she whispered. "And right now, you have rehab to do if you want to do a good job for the CommController."

"Um . . ." I said again.

She walked away, but she looked back as she left the Great Hall, and that look gave me all the hope I needed.

•••

Michael's orders were to concentrate on "activities of daily living." I had to practise carrying a cafeteria tray while using a cane. I had to master navigating a flight of stairs. I had to learn how to cope with people staring at my scars.

I do what I'm told, so, over the next couple of days, I went to the quartermaster to get re-measured for a uniform my hardened, shrunken body wouldn't be lost in — one that had a zipper instead of buttons to struggle over. I went to the Housing Commission and gave them my discharge date. My dorm room at the flight academy was long gone and the infirmary bed wouldn't be mine much longer. I went to the galley and had my ration card changed to reflect my less active profession.

I also kept my ears open.

Officially, Iapyx's mass communication system consisted of town criers, newsletters and official handbills in the Great Hall and the galleys. Unofficially, we lived and died by rumours. I'd missed nine months' worth of rumours, and there were some big ones.

The Captain of Icarus Down — our third since our flight from Old Mother Earth — was dying, again. At eighty-nine, he had been dying on and off for a while, but it might be real this time: I could tell by the way people inclined their heads and respectfully refused to speculate before tearing into the political gossip.

The current Captain was from Daedalon; the mayor of Daedalon was a lock to succeed him. No — Daedalon had held the Captaincy since planetfall and it was time for another city to have the chance.

Round and round it went. Our own mayor's name, Matthew Tal, came up a lot. Was he putting together a campaign? Might he be the next Captain?

Then there were the "failures." That's what people were calling them. I walked in the Great Hall, resting on the benches and watching the children play ticktock monsters. People turned their eyes away from my burnscars, and then acted as if I were deaf. I heard tale after tale of pneumatic canisters gone astray. People laughed about lovers' messages humorously misdelivered, or someone ordering a shipment of stem bolts, not getting them, and ordering them again and again, until all the orders suddenly arrived at once.

But there was one man in the galley who was ranting about the CommController. An order to shut a steam valve had been sent, and didn't arrive at the other end. So the pressure built up and up in one of the inspection shafts. No one would have realized if the supervisor who'd sent the first order hadn't had some premonition, and sent the order a second time. This one arrived, and a maintenance crew evacuated in time to avoid getting scalded to death.

Nobody laughed at that story.

But everyone had a theory about what was going on. The CommController was getting old, many said. Perhaps he was going senile. He was hardly ever seen outside his offices.

The mayor's teams were scrambling, others noted, inspecting everywhere.

Looking for sabotage.

That word, too, was whispered through the city. Over and over, I heard it: mothers watching children, steam workers, a pair of battery boys chattering. *Sabotage.*

And they started to talk about the Grounders.

• • •

Since we'd raised our cities out of the fog forest, there had been those who argued that we should lower them again. The Grounders, we called them. We thought they were lunatics.

It must be hard for you, knowing what you know about the monsters in our forest, to understand this. Please try. My people weren't murderers, and we weren't fools. We were — we had been — colonists, civilians, idealists on the run from the Extinction Wars that swept Old Mother Earth after the Great Warming. We set out from Earth with the dream of building a better world, a just world, a balanced world, leaving the mistakes of the old one behind. We went 25,000 light years into the darkness. We spent three generations in space. The only people with military training among us had been the officers of the *Icarus*, killed in the crash, and the advance colonization team, whom we never heard from again.

We had been promised a blue world, an ocean world dotted with islands and broad salt flats, a long lazy year in distant orbit around a brilliant sun. We didn't know what had gone wrong, and when the *Icarus* appeared too close to that brilliance, we didn't have a chance to find out. All the city pods crashed — a controlled crash, because of the sacrifice of our mother ship, but still a crash. No advance team came to meet us. There were no oceans, no salt flats; only a forest so dense that you could hardly walk through it, and a fog that swallowed everything more than three metres away.

Our too-bright sun didn't just leave us cowering from visible light in shadowy canyons. It blasted us with a heavy sleet of electromagnetic radiation. A wire more than a metre long would build a charge and spark unpredictably. Electromagnetic broadcasts were swamped within metres of their source. When our city pods landed, we'd lost our radio instantly, our central power systems within a day, and all but the best-shielded of our computers within weeks.

We did our best. We had limitless solar power, but had to figure out how to move it around without wires. We used steam to send messages by pneumatic tube. We transformed our colony pods into cities, turning the blood-red soil, and prepared our hydroponic seedlings for planting.

Then, one day, a bloodstained and battered man came tottering out of the fog. A man in military uniform. An officer of the *Icarus*! They'd survived!

No. The man told the tale: they had survived,

barely, but after the crash they had been attacked. The fog around us had teeth. There were monsters. Subtle, careful, ruthless monsters. They ticked and clicked: directionless sounds that carried like the snapping of bones. They had slaughtered the crew of the *Icarus*.

I think we only half believed him, this dishevelled, weeping, traumatized man who wouldn't give his name. But then we heard it: the ticking and clicking in the fog. It grew louder, closer. It was all around us, it was everywhere.

And people started dying. Farmers in fields, cartographers on survey — we'd just find their bodies, sliced up, bled out into the blood-red soil. And then, even inside the shelters, at random: there would be one death a night, there would be two. Remember, we couldn't even keep the lights on at that stage. The monsters were glimpsed, here and there: bigger than human; reptilian but moving like apes; talons and teeth. And fast, so fast. Sometimes someone would get a lucky shot and kill one, but it didn't seem to matter. The ticking was constant.

In a long, slow season of terror, one at a time, and at random, hundreds of people died.

We couldn't raise our cities out of the fog forest fast enough.

We drove anchors into the sides of the cliffs, wove cables, and winched our cities as high as we could go, while still staying in the shadow of the cliffs.

The original Grounders had been scientists,

planners: people with expertise in setting up new colonies. They cited "critical populations," "closed systems" and other reasons why raising our cities was a bad idea. They wanted to get our struggling cities closer to the only source of resources. The hard truth, they told us, was that our colony pods could not survive indefinitely in the air.

But our society had hit the steam and clockwork age from the wrong direction, moving fast. We became conservative, modest and obedient — and we frayed around the edges, developing a lunatic fringe of conspiracy theories and alternate histories. Three generations in, the Grounders were broadly considered the most lunatic of the lot.

Nathaniel Tal had insinuated that Isaac might have been a Grounder. And when Isaac told me that Mom hadn't committed suicide, he'd said he'd spoken to some people. Were those Grounders?

Worse, could the Grounders be sabotaging the colony? People had nearly died. My brother would never have been involved with any group that got people killed.

Would he?

• • •

Heading back to the infirmary from another "activity of daily living," I walked through one of the lesser-used corridors. The lights flickered here. I frowned at them.

Two battery boys marched past me, carrying a

ladder between them. They opened the ladder at the light. One boy held the ladder while the other — actually a girl — scrambled up. She snatched the battery from its slot and tossed it down. The boy caught it, shoved it into his satchel and tossed another battery up. The girl snicked it in, and the light shone bright. The girl jumped down, the two swept up the ladder between them and went on their way.

I watched them go. They worked eight hours a day, every day, and this was the plum assignment. Behind the doors of the sorting rooms . . . Nathaniel was right: there were worse things than working at the Communications Hub.

That's when I heard the *whoosh* and *click* behind me. Three metres away, in the middle of a wall, beside the latest inspirational poster from the mayor's office — MEND AND MAKE DO — was a pneumatic message tube. The little plastic red flag flipped up. I stared. This was a public intake area, not an outlet. Who'd be sending a message here?

Another failure, I thought.

I limped over, opened the hatch and pulled out the canister. There was no address label. Should I take it to the Communications Hub? What would they do?

Muttering a silent apology to the patron saint of privacy, I wrestled open the canister and took out the paper inside. It was a single sheet, folded into a square. I unfolded it.

The time has come for Icarus Down to go to ground.

A bang like a hundred balloons bursting at once made me drop the canister. There was a hiss that sounded like it came from a gigantic snake. A thick white cloud billowed through the corridor toward me. People shouted. Someone screamed; I think it was the battery girl. Steam! I pressed myself against the wall. People ran to escape; others ran to help. The cloud washed over everything; over me. Water beaded on my skin and the air heated up. And still the horrible hissing continued. A burst pipe.

Alarms rang. I couldn't see the corridor through the cloud, and I knew that running into it would have been foolhardy. I could hear other people coming, but they wouldn't be here soon enough. The battery girl was still screaming. There had to be something I could do.

Pipes laced through the ceiling. I could see the big pipe that carried the steam from the solar vats to the battery rechargers. Follow that pipe along, down the wall, and —

There! A huge wheel with a handle — a valve. I staggered over, gripped it in both hands and strained. My arms blazed with pain, but I couldn't think of giving up, not when I could still hear the girl screaming. Just as I offered a silent prayer, the wheel shifted. It was the only encouragement I needed. I heaved. It turned. I turned it until it wouldn't turn anymore. Behind me, the *whoosh* of steam ebbed, then stopped. A shocked silence descended upon the corridor.

Then I realized that my hands had cramped. My

arms felt as though I'd broken them. I groaned and staggered back, into the arms of a maintenance worker.

"Whoa!" He looked me up and down. "You all right?" I was breathing too heavily to speak. I just nodded.

He glanced at my handiwork. "Quick thinking, there. I think you saved a few lives."

"Good," I wheezed. "What happened?"

He looked down the corridor in the direction maintenance and medical crews were already running. "Another failure." He looked at me. He looked angry. "Grounders."

• • •

The infirmary was in an uproar when I returned. A lot of people were hurt, and people who had brought the injured were in the waiting area, talking frantically at each other. The message in the canister was in the news — an impressively fast scoop by whoever had first reported it. It put everyone on edge. This wasn't just a steam-burst. The message made it sabotage.

I wasn't hurt, but I was exhausted. I headed to my room and was met by Michael, carrying my possessions in a box. He looked harried and angry, but he brightened when he saw me. "Hey!" He shoved the box into my hands. "Congratulations!"

"Uh, why?" I looked at the box. "What's this?"

"Your belongings. You get to go home!"

"What? Already?" Then I tamped down my protest. "You need the bed, don't you."

Michael's smile was brief. "Yes. Sorry. We're crashed." Which is what the people on Icarus Down used to say instead of buried or swamped.

Behind him, a nurse laid out sheets. It looked like I'd never been in the room.

Michael shook my hand carefully and left. There was nothing else to do. So, lugging my box of possessions, I went home.

● ● ●

What was home, exactly?

When I was small I slept on a purple futon with Isaac. We painted white blotches on it and pretended they were stars. And that was home.

And then Dad died. And Mom . . .

I don't think she jumped, Simon.

Well, however she died, she died. They stuck us in the dorms. I was nine and I had a room of my own, ten centimetres wider than the bed it came with. And that was home. Then I went to the flight academy and got a room thirty centimetres wider than the bed. I stuck a star or two on the wall, along with sketches I'd made of ornithopters. I'd never seen a star, of course, but they still meant something to me. They meant home.

My new apartment was near the Communications

Hub. The rest of my belongings had been sent from the flight academy and were waiting in a box beside the door. I jiggled my key into the lock, shouldered open the door, and nudged the box inside with my foot. Home.

I was moving up in the world. There was room beside the bed for a whole (small) desk. Also, I'd lucked out in being assigned a room with a window. Propping my cane by my bedside, I looked out. The cables of my city laced around me. Below, the chasm stretched out as a white ribbon between black banks. Sunlight glittered off the silica cap, reflecting into the valley, raising jets of steam from the fog — steam devils, the first signs of Solar Maximum, but far enough away to be safe.

An ornithopter buzzed over the clouds. In the middle distance, at the edge of the cables, the gantry spiders were working, swinging hand over hand.

Hand over hand. I shuddered.

My father had fallen from Iapyx when I was five. Though I hardly remember his face, I remember the elevator ride to see him. Iapyx went past us in flashes: the sparks of welders in the factories, people sitting in offices staring at papers, the green pause of the Great Hall. Mom stood behind us, smiling indulgently.

We reached a viewing gallery at one end of Iapyx, where the city narrowed to a point. All around us, a spider's web of cables stretched out to the cliff face, to one of the two great anchors that held us between the chasm walls. The great canopy draped down over us like a blanket, but if I angled my head right, I could see the sunside anchor, punched into the cliffs near the silica cap. Covered in chrome, it reflected the sky, looking to me like a giant teardrop, or a hole cut through the rock.

I pressed my face to the glass and picked out the shapes the wires made around us. Mom knelt beside me. "Can you see Daddy?"

The workers moved along the net of wires, crawling or swinging from one handhold to the next. Suspended over a sea of white, it was as though they were clinging to the only real thing in the world.

Isaac's breath caught. "Mom? Is that—" He pointed.

I looked up. Mom looked up. Her face changed.

There was a flurry of activity along the wires. Workers were running, crawling or swinging their way toward someone dangling awkwardly from a cable.

"No," Mom breathed. It was my father who was dangling.

The workers clambered closer.

"It's okay, Mommy," I said. "If he falls, the clouds will catch him."

Then my father had dropped like a pear from a tree. Against the white backdrop, it looked like he was floating in midair.

The clouds caught him. They didn't give him back.

I looked at the anchor again. It was covered in scaffolding. Workers must be polishing the chrome for Solar Maximum. Life went on.

I opaqued the window. Without another thought, I lay down. I was asleep instantly.

I woke early in the morning. There was still another day before my new job started. I wasn't looking forward to it, but with a day ahead of not much else, I considered reporting early. Instead, I burned some time by unpacking.

I unpacked a uniform — a jumpsuit with no insignia — socks and underwear, and an envelope of ration chits to buy another off-duty suit. Three books followed, placed on the desk. I set my sewing kit beside them.

Then came the map . . .

The roll was heavy, handmade paper. It used a lot of fibre and should have been pulped by now, but no one had come to claim it, and I'd never taken it in. It crackled in my hands as I unrolled it. My hands had changed so much since I'd last touched this. For a moment I imagined my mother's grief had she still been alive: one son burned and broken, the other dead . . . But she didn't get to grieve. That was up to me.

I pinned the map to the wall above my bed. It was of Old Mother Earth, Mom's masterpiece, which had secured her a position in the mayor's office. She'd painted it herself. The lines were crisp and the colours were bright and beautiful. I'd liked looking at that map, trying to imagine being able to live in all that space. I ran my fingers over the coastlines now, picking out the world powers that had existed on the eve of the Extinction Wars: the United States of Eurasia, the Pan-Polar Confederacy, La Federación de las Américas, the IndoChina Empire.

There was a knock at the door.

I limped over, frowning. Aside from the quartermaster, no one knew where I lived.

It was Rachel.

• • •

She was out of her nurse's uniform.

Seeing her this way was a shock. I'd only ever seen her at work and, before that, in vocational school, which had its own uniforms. Save for Nocturne, this was the first time I'd seen her in clothes she'd chosen for herself.

Her white leggings and her tunic followed the shape of her body. She had a capelet wrapped over her shoulders, also in white, but with a pattern of ridged texture that gave a checkerboard appearance of light and shadow.

Her hair was out of its snood, twisted up and pinned, exposing the fine hair that tangled on the nape of her neck.

She stood there looking serious, a dark smudge under her eyes that made her look tired. She also looked a little shy. I stared at her until she said, "Well? Can I come in?"

"What?" I found my voice at last. "Of course! Come in!"

I stepped back so fast I bumped into the foot of the bed. She followed me and pushed the door closed. There wasn't much room. We were standing very close together in that blank and private place. I struggled to think of something to say. The best I could do was, "You look tired."

She sighed and looked away. "Long night at the infirmary. I'm sorry I wasn't there to say goodbye. But this is better. I've got something for you." From her pocket, she pulled out a thin red lozenge, as long as the palm of her hand was wide. She held it out between us.

My father's pocketknife. I took it and looked at it in awe. "How did you—"

"Isaac."

"Oh." I turned the pocketknife over in my hands. It was older than the *Icarus*; it came from Old Earth. I ran my fingers over the edges, and the engraving of a cross on a shield that may have meant something to someone long ago. It was also one of the few things Rachel had left of Isaac. And she'd given this to me.

I looked up at her, feeling a pull at my heart — was it grief? "Thank you. But . . . why?"

"It's as much yours now as it is mine," she said, her voice tight. "And I think maybe you need it more."

Because he was the only family I'd had left.

But Rachel had lost so much as well. "You should keep this." I held it out to her.

She shook her head and looked away, her fingers rising to the betrothal charm. "It helps . . . to give you that. It helps me move on." Her eyes swung back. They were big, dark eyes I could fall into forever and never want a parachute. "We've lost so much. But you can't get so caught up in what you've lost that you lose sight of what you've still got. Things change. Sometimes you just have to . . . move on."

This time *I* kissed *her*.

It wasn't graceful, but I got an arm around her and pulled her closer, and she leaned into the embrace. When we kissed, my bewilderment and sorrow changed to wings. I could have flown. I put a hand behind her head. We held the kiss a long time before we pulled apart.

I was breathless. Rachel looked down, shy. Then her face changed. She looked around, like a pilot gathering her bearings. With one arm still around me, she reached up and pulled the light chain.

Darkness. We were alone in a private room, and Rachel was holding me. "Um," I said.

"Look around," she whispered.

Look around at what? I could barely see the curve of her throat and the uptwist of her hair. There was not enough light to — but then I realized: there *was* some light. With the window opaqued, the door closed, there was still light: a spot on the wall near my mother's map was glowing as faintly as the memory of a star.

"It's—" I turned toward it.

Rachel put both arms around me. "A spyhole," she whispered. Her breath was warm against my collarbone. "I thought they might put one in. Act naturally. I think we're being watched."

"Act . . . *naturally*?" I at least had the sense to whisper. "Rachel, how can I act naturally when there's a spyhole in my room? Why is it there?"

She held me, as if she were comforting me. "It's because of me. It's because of Isaac."

"Isaac—" I began, but she covered my mouth with a hand.

She laughed; a light laugh that echoed around the empty room. "Of all the times for a failure," she said — and turned the light back on. I blinked, stunned into stupidity. We were being watched. Maybe right this moment, we were being watched.

Then Rachel kissed me and my thoughts stopped. I forgot the eyes on me. Her kisses travelled up my cheek, and she whispered in my ear, "There are things you need to know. About me. About Isaac. About your mother. We've got to go somewhere truly private. I'll explain everything. Keep kissing me."

A cover: the kissing was a cover. My stomach dropped. But I kissed her throat. "Okay," I mumbled. "Where?"

She pulled away, clasped my hands, and spoke loudly. "So! What movie are we to see?"

• • •

We went to the Great Hall. Rachel picked out a spot near the top of the grassy amphitheatre, close to the projector hut. We sat among a few dozen other people. From behind the darkened window of the squat hut, the projector started up. The lights dimmed.

The movie opened with scenes of rolling hills and trees. I drew back, struck by the beauty of Old Mother Earth. An *ocean*.

Rachel leaned into my shoulder. "Simon," she whispered. "I'm going to say something you'll find alarming. We're being watched." She gripped my hand. "Don't look around. There are two security officers here. They're in the last row."

I started to stand up.

She gripped my arm. "Don't attract attention."

"Okay," I breathed. The feel of Rachel this close to me, combined with all the secrets, made it impossible to follow the film's plot. Still, we waited until it was over. Then we shuffled up the incline with the rest of the crowd.

"Get ready," she whispered.

We walked close to the projector hut. Then she dodged to the door and pulled me inside. I staggered in the sudden darkness. The room was empty. The projectionist must have stepped out on break.

Rachel locked the door. "This way."

It's hard to be quiet and fast at the same time, especially in the dark. "Where the— ow! What are we doing here? They'll have no problem finding us; there's no back way out!"

"Yes, there is. Mind these boxes."

"What boxes? Ow!"

She guided my hands to a set of what felt like pipes attached to the wall. Rungs, I realized. A ladder. "Watch your step: there's a drop."

My heart stuttered as my feet stepped out over nothing, and then found a rung with ankle-jarring certainty.

"Go down," she said. "I'll follow."

We climbed down to the levels below the Great Hall. Footsteps thumped above me. The doorknob rattled. There was a jangle of keys. A click as a light went on above us.

My feet touched solid ground. Rachel took my hand and led me around towers of film canisters.

"I didn't know all this was here," I whispered.

"That's because you never tried out for the drama program. The trap door to the stage is just past here."

Drama program. She could act. That was good to know.

Above us, the footsteps faded away. Rachel breathed a sigh of relief.

"Why did we have to do that?" I hissed. "Why is there a *spyhole* in my apartment?" My voice rose. "What in sunlight is going on?"

She smiled sympathetically. "What question do you want answered first?"

I stared at her. "Who are you, Rachel?"

Her smile was brief. "I'll show you."

She swung a rack of chemicals away from the wall and pushed on a latch behind it. The whole thing opened: a hidden door.

CHAPTER SIX
THE GROUNDERS

We stepped through and Rachel pulled the disguised door closed behind me. Before we could move, someone pulled on a light chain. I blinked at the sudden brightness, then stared in astonishment. "Aaron?"

He'd gotten a haircut, but his smile was the same as when we'd been at school, back when he was telling me about his dream of becoming an astronomer. "Hello, Simon," he said.

"What are you doing here?"

"Well," he drawled, "would you believe I'm really, really lost?"

Aaron always knew how to make me laugh. "No way."

The room was cluttered with . . . props, I realized. It was a prop room. There were stacked-up chairs, false walls piled six deep, a bust of Caesar that looked more like a potato farmer. It was a big room, jam-packed. There was a little space cleared in the middle, around King Arthur's Round Table — saved from a production of *Camelot* I'd seen years ago — and a single low-watt light overhead. Around the table stood Aaron, Rachel — and Michael Dere.

"Um," I said. "Hi."

Michael looked awkward. "Hi."

"Michael is our newest recruit," Aaron said. "Joined two months ago. He's been a great help finding private places to meet."

Michael grinned sheepishly. "I liked to explore a lot as a kid. Always got into trouble, being found in the service ducts."

"Simon," Aaron said, suddenly more serious. I noticed the quill insignia on his uniform: he'd become a teacher. He was downright Socratic all of a sudden. "You're probably wondering why Rachel brought you here."

I stared at him a moment. Secret meetings, spy chases through the corridors. I realized what Rachel was. And Aaron. And Michael. These were my friends. How could they be involved in something like this? "Are you . . . Grounders?"

Aaron looked me in the eye. "Yes. We're one cell. There are others, but we don't all meet in one place, so we don't attract attention. And you know us, Simon: me and Rachel. We grew up together. That should tell you that we wouldn't do anything to put the colony in danger."

"I'm sorry," I said, "but that doesn't tell me anything of the sort." I was keenly aware that I was accusing him — him and Rachel, and possibly my dead brother — of something close to murder. "You never told me you were Grounders. You didn't trust me enough to tell me, so why should I trust you?"

Everybody stared at me. I was almost used to stares, but from strangers. Friends mostly looked away.

"Look at it from my point of view." I was desperate to break the silence. "I saw a steam pipe burst with my own eyes. Breakdowns are disrupting the city and getting worse. Everybody's saying it's sabotage. And here you are, hiding out of sight of security. What am I supposed to think? Who else could be responsible for all the failures?"

Rachel looked uncomfortable. "Simon, Isaac believed—"

My hand shot up, a warning. "Isaac's not here. And I'm not bringing him into this."

She drew herself up. "Well, I am! Whether you want to bring him into this or not, he was one of us. Isaac was a Grounder."

"And so was your mother," said a voice behind me.

I turned sharply, not only because of what was said, but how it was said. The voice sounded familiar. The face it belonged to was familiar as well. The man behind me was short, balding, in his early sixties, his remaining hair well on its way to grey. In spite of his lack of height and his age, he reoriented the room with his presence.

He was familiar, but I couldn't instantly place him.

He nodded at me, not quite smiling. "Hello, Mr. Daud. It may be a bit earlier than intended, but it's good to meet you at last."

"Simon, meet your new boss, Gabriel Falm," said Aaron.

My jaw dropped. "You're the CommController!"

Well, whatever was wrong with the pneumatic tubes, it wasn't that CommController Falm was senile. His eyes, despite the hint of cataracts, were like steel.

But a Grounder? It made the sabotage theory even stronger.

And then there was what he had said. "You knew my mother?"

Gabriel nodded. "Hagar was a fine woman. She joined us soon after your father's death. She introduced me to you and Isaac when you were both much younger, though we were careful not to talk shop in front of you."

That might be why he looked familiar. "But—"

He cut me off. "Mr. Daud, Ms. Caan says you're smart, and that you've been asking questions. You requested a report on your mother's death. You've accused us of sabotage. Believe it or not, that's good. You know something's not right in this colony."

"How did you know I requested the coroner's report?"

He gave me a smile that was halfway between sympathetic and smug. "Most official communications go through the pneumatic tubes and the Communications Hub."

"You've been reading my mail?" I spluttered.

"Mr. Daud — Simon," he went on, as if I hadn't spoken. "You know these breakdowns are a sign of something bigger. You wondered that about your own accident."

"A faulty battery." Rachel looked bitter.

Gabriel waved her silent. "You're thinking the break-downs might be sabotage. But besides the damage the breakdowns have done, they also start rumours. More and more, these rumours are being aimed at us."

"The Grounders have been around for years," said Aaron. "And yet the breakdowns started only now. We aren't the ones who have changed."

"We wouldn't do anything to hurt this city!" Rachel's voice rose. "Michael and I dealt with dozens of people scalded by that steam burst. We wouldn't wish that on anybody."

Michael was nodding.

I was suddenly surrounded on all sides: Rachel and Aaron earnestly pleading their innocence, Gabriel looking firm, Michael looking awkward. I knew three of the four in this room. It was hard to think of them as saboteurs.

I raised my hands against the tumult. "Then what *do* you want?" In the silence that followed I lowered my hands. "Why are you here?"

Michael looked at the others. "I wanted answers."

Aaron nodded. "I joined because of Isaac. I had questions, and he pointed me here."

"I also joined because of Isaac," said Rachel. "I think he joined because of your mother. He wanted answers, too."

I think she was murdered, Simon.

"Answers," I said. "About what?"

Gabriel laced his fingers together. "The point is,

we ask questions, Simon. You probably know the big one by our reputation," he said. "Why are our cities tethered to the cliffs? Why do we fear the ground?" He raised his hand as I opened my mouth. "I know: the ticktock monsters. But here's a question you don't often hear asked: Why has the ticking stopped?"

I blinked at him.

He smiled. "We're not completely off the ground. As you know, we have the stem, and we have the compound around it to grow enough plant material to make our plastics and our paper, and supplement our fruits. We have people who go down to the surface to tend that plot, protected by the electric fence. Those people say they haven't heard ticking in years. The monsters have gone quiet."

My brow furrowed. "Why haven't I heard about this?"

"Nobody's *asked*." Aaron grinned ruefully. "Except us lunatics, and we're easy to ignore."

"That's one of the questions your mother wanted answered, after your father died," Gabriel went on. "Throughout history, the human race has been at its best when it's asked questions and pushed beyond itself. But asking questions isn't in fashion right now. For the past sixty-two years, the people of Icarus Down have focused on staying alive."

"There's a lot about this colony that doesn't make sense, Simon," Aaron cut in. "We only want to know why. And I think these breakdowns are happening on purpose, to discredit us."

That seemed like the best answer I was going to

76

get. "Okay," I said. "That's why you're here. But what do you want from me?"

"I need your help at the Communications Hub," Gabriel said. "Rachel said you were available, and sympathetic."

I looked at Rachel. She smiled at me, nervous.

"Either way," Gabriel continued, "when I contacted the flight master and asked her to reassign you to me instead of to the battery boys, I wasn't just being kind. I have a job for you."

"The best way to stop these rumours is to figure out what's causing these breakdowns in the first place," said Aaron.

"If we can find that evidence, we can prove our innocence," said Rachel. "Yours too. That spyhole was put in your apartment by the security office."

My mind flashed to Nathaniel Tal, asking me about Isaac and the Grounders. I knew the answer, but I still had to ask. "Why?"

"Because of Isaac. Because of your mother," she said.

And there it was. Because I was a Daud. It wasn't fair.

"So, Simon," said Gabriel. "That's who we are, and that's what we want from you. Will you help us?"

Again they were pressing forward. Wanting this from me. I was in the centre of something, in a way I hadn't been for a long time. It made my stomach clench. Should I say yes and throw my lot in with possible saboteurs? Or say no and disappoint Rachel, not to mention letting Nathaniel Tal pursue her friends for crimes they might not have committed?

"Yes," I said.

Aaron and Gabriel patted my shoulder. Michael shook my hand. Rachel . . . smiled. I valued that more than anything else.

But Michael and Rachel had shifts to attend to, and they couldn't be late without arousing suspicion. The meeting broke up, with Gabriel telling me that I'd see him in his office tomorrow. Aaron escorted me back to the projection room and glanced out the window before letting me out into the Great Hall.

I caught his arm. "How long were you . . ." I glanced around for listening ears. " . . . you know."

Aaron grinned. "You want to know if I was a Grounder the whole time I knew you?"

I nodded.

"No," he said. "I didn't meet them until about two Nocturnes ago. Do you remember the last time we talked?"

I remembered that night, when Rachel had chosen Isaac. I'd bumped into Aaron. He'd looked like he'd seen a ghost. "You'd just been up in the observation booth of the semaphore tower," I said. "You . . . you claimed you'd seen a star."

Aaron grinned. "*You* claimed I was drunk."

"Well, yeah, but—"

"I wasn't drunk, Simon," said Aaron. "I really did see a star."

"But . . . how?"

People passed us on the path, and Aaron looked uncomfortable. "Not here. We'll talk about this later, Simon. I promise. Let's deal with the breakdowns first."

CHAPTER SEVEN
HEATSTROKE

Cane clicking, I arrived at the Communications Hub the next morning.

People were lined up at the public window, holding packages or paper. Two people served them: a man with light brown skin whose nametag identified him as Ethan, and a woman with long, dark hair in a braid down her back. Her nametag said Marni. Above them, along the ceiling, incoming canisters whipped through translucent tubes, disappearing into the wall.

I got in line and waited. Ethan smiled at the elderly woman in front of me. "It's still a couple of days before Solar Maximum, ma'am. This will be off to Octavia long before the semaphore goes offline."

The two turned to me, and their eyes widened slightly — a common enough sight in response to my scars. But Ethan opened his mouth to say something, and nothing came out. It was Marni who said, "Hello, sir. May we help you?"

I cleared my throat. "Yes. I'm Simon Daud. I'll be, um, working with you?"

Ethan lunged across the counter to pump my hand. "Simon Daud! It is an honour, sir!"

Marni looked embarrassed, but Ethan wasn't done. He disappeared into the Communications Hub, shouting. "Hey, Jachin! It's Simon Daud! Hey, everybody! It's Simon Daud! He's here!"

Marni levered up a section of the counter and stepped through to shake my hand, gently. "It's good to have you join us," she said. "Ethan's—" She coughed. "Excited. We don't get much excitement here."

"I can see that," I said.

"Come on! I'll introduce you." As she stepped back to let me in, she paused and looked at me. "Have you seen what we do here?"

"No." I'd been sick the day of the field trip.

"Well, then. . ." With the air of someone sharing a secret, she said, "Welcome to the Communications Hub." She waved me through.

I knew the Communications Hub was one level above the Great Hall. I hadn't realized it was as long and as wide as the cavernous hall beneath it. Only the ceiling was low; I could touch the tangle of pneumatic pipes by raising my hand.

And the place was full of people. Dozens stood at a long table sorting canisters into pyramids. There was a constant rumble as people slammed receptacle doors, juggled canisters, plunked them on tables, or shoved them into intake tubes to be whooshed on their way.

People looked up as Ethan called everyone over, and suddenly I was surrounded, everyone reaching to shake my hand. They pressed on all sides, their enthusiasm like sandpaper on my scars.

"We read about the crash and how you survived it," said Jachin. "It's not every day a hero shows up here."

Another young woman spoke over him. "It must have been terrifying, having to bail over the fog forest."

"Well," I said, and stopped there. I wasn't prepared to think about it, let alone talk about it. Ethan, to his credit, saw my discomfort and looked embarrassed. Marni shoved forward. "Guys! Give him room!"

At that point, a red canister swooped overhead, veered off from the tubes going into the sorting room, and went through the single tube toward the door marked COMMCONTROLLER. Like parts of a clockwork mechanism, the clerks swivelled to watch it. Behind the CommController's closed door, the access hatch banged open and shut.

The clerks scattered, leaving me with just Ethan and Marni.

"It's from the mayor's office." Ethan's voice was low.

"Today's report on the misdeliveries," Marni explained.

Behind the CommController's door a grumble

rose like a steam valve about to blow.

The clerks bent over their work, getting ready to duck and cover.

The door burst open.

And there stood the CommController, as I remembered him from yesterday. His glare cowed the room. Then his steely gaze focused on me. "Who the devil are you?"

For a moment I wondered if he actually had forgotten me, but then I realized that he had to make it look like this was the first time he'd seen me.

I cleared my throat. "Simon Daud, sir. I've been reassi—"

"Walk with me." He jabbed a stubby finger at Ethan and Marni. "You two! Back to work!" They scrambled to comply.

Gabriel strode on ahead while I, cane clicking, struggled to keep up. We walked and walked, Gabriel leading the way through the chatter, barging past dozens who had to stop and duck behind us as we passed. Finally, we reached a wall, and a door labelled FILM TRANSFER. Inside, we walked past ancient video equipment — pre-crash ancient. We detoured around a film camera that was pointed at a screen showing cars racing around a track. It was hard to tear myself away.

"You make the movies here?" I said in awe.

"We lend space to the drama department. They keep the machines going," Gabriel replied. "Bread and circuses, as the saying goes. Personally, I can't imagine Nocturne without the sunset film."

Film — using chemicals to print images on cellu-
loid — is technology from Old Mother Earth, almost
lost until we found need of it when the electromagnetic wash made transmitting video nearly impossible.

We salvaged a handful of video screens at planetfall, shielded them and kept them running as best
we could. We also made films of our own, like the
image of the setting sun that was the centrepiece of
Nocturne. In reality it was last year's sunset, timed
to match the real one outside. A bit of sleight of hand,
but we clung to it. In a world where night comes
once every fourteen months, a sunset was something everyone needed to see.

Gabriel opened the door at the other end of the
room, and we entered a darkened service corridor.
There were fewer people here. He slowed down as
he walked, and the tension eased from his shoulders.

"Welcome to the team, Simon," he said quietly.
"I've been through your record. I expect you're disappointed to find yourself working in the Communications Hub versus piloting an ornithopter."

What was I supposed to do, agree with him? "I'm
hoping to be of use, sir," I said. And found, surprisingly, that I meant it, stiff though it sounded.

"Good," he said. "Good man."

We reached an elevator. Gabriel pulled a lever and,
far away, a bell jangled. I heard the whine of distant and approaching motors. The doors parted. We
stepped on board. Gabriel flipped a switch on the

panel and pulled the lever. The doors closed, and we were on our way. Finally, we could talk.

"So . . . You got a report from the mayor's office?"

Gabriel's expression soured. "Yeah, I did. The stats are horrible. I'm surprised people aren't burning me in effigy. But they have a convenient scapegoat. Ironically, that scapegoat would also be me, if they knew it."

"Sorry," I said.

He took a breath, held it, then let it go. "Whether it's malfunctions, or sabotage, I stand accused, Simon." He glared. He wasn't angry at me, but still, the strength of it made me lean back. "To stand accused with tampering with the pneumatics is to stand accused of treason."

He glowered. "Did you know that, on Old Mother Earth, it was a serious offense to tamper with the mail? A separate offence with its own punishment? It's illegal here, too, but it's rolled in with other acts of sabotage, like breaking a lever off a machine. And that's appropriate, because in this day and age, with so few of us, and the environment so hostile, every breakdown is a potential catastrophe. Sabotaging the pneumatics risks destroying this city, and I will not stand accused for someone else's crime, especially when it threatens me and all I hold dear."

Destroying this city. At the time I thought it was hyperbole, but I said nothing.

The elevator slowed to a stop. We jerked as it

switched direction, going to the right instead of up.

"I'm sure you're wondering why I brought you on board, Simon."

"Yes. I am."

"I need you to conduct an audit of the pneumatic tubes."

"A . . . *physical* audit?" Involuntarily, I looked at the ceiling above us, though there were none of the translucent tubes that ran along the corridors throughout Iapyx. It would mean following every tube, throughout the city. A massive job. Plus, it would mean going into the service tunnels, in cramped and steamy spaces. Had Rachel known this was what Gabriel had wanted? Had Michael? I couldn't see either of them signing off on this. I wasn't sure that I — with my clumsy body, my vulnerability to heat — could do such a thing. "But . . . why *me*, sir?"

"Because Rachel trusts you, and I trust Rachel. And since these failures started, you have been the only person on my staff who hasn't been here. The people I've already sent out haven't found anything, but they don't know what to look for." He leaned forward. "There aren't many of us who are Grounders, Simon. They're good people here, but I haven't confided in any of them. And if these failures are acts of sabotage designed to implicate the Grounders, then I don't know who to trust. I need somebody from outside my department. I need you."

That was a lot to put on my shoulders, but it moved me. After nine months doing nothing but being in a coma and then going through rehab, it felt good to be useful. "Thank you, sir." My voice cracked a little. "I'll do my best."

"Good. We need to find the source of these failures soon. People are laughing now — or, were before the steam-burst — but it's about to get more serious. I had the Power Superintendent at my office door yesterday. He wasn't happy."

I was shocked. The head of the battery boys wasn't often seen outside the recharging rooms. "Why, sir?"

"The mis-deliveries are sending batteries all over the place. Retrieving them is cutting into the battery boys' time."

So this was why the lights were flickering. Why hadn't people figured this out before?

It was one of the first problems we had to confront after crashing here. Yes, we had all the solar power we could want: a column of super-heated salt stuck into the sunlight above each city's semaphore tower. The heat drove steam turbines. But with the electromagnetic wash making a central power system impossible, how could we move that energy without wires?

In sixty-two years, we'd become very good at batteries.

The battery boys, some of whom were not male, and most of whom were not children, ran those batteries from the distribution points to everywhere. Every light bulb, every monitor, every elevator motor, every ornithopter depended on them. Our cities could not work without them.

But the batteries were delivered by pneumatic tube.

If things went wrong, if batteries didn't get to their distribution points, or if fully charged and depleted batteries got mixed up . . .

A faulty battery. Was this what had killed Isaac? But the gauge had said full power . . .

"A quarter of the lights in the upper levels are now without power," Gabriel continued. "The Power Superintendent told me it's faster to run boys up to the stores and bring back the batteries by hand. If these failures keep getting worse . . ." He shuddered. "All we need is something to happen with the elevators, and whole levels will go dark."

Just then the elevator braked, hard. I pitched against a wall, and instinctively, but clumsily, caught Gabriel as he stumbled into me. The press of deceleration ebbed, and we straightened up. We'd stopped. But the doors didn't open.

"What happened?" I said.

Gabriel yanked open a panel in the side of the elevator. It opened to the outside, but showed another panel of wood, like our own. He rapped at it. "Hey!"

The other panel slid open. A woman scowled back. "What?"

"What's going on?" said Gabriel, sharp. "Why are you blocking our way?"

She huffed. "Because somebody else is blocking our way, and somebody is blocking him." She sighed. The frustration eased, and she looked worried. "The signals are out. Apparently, maintenance has been notified. They're sending somebody up to move the elevators manually."

Gabriel looked at me. His expression was grim.

● ● ●

Thanks to the elevator delay, it wasn't until after lunch that I found myself in the service tunnels above the Communications Hub, flashlight in one hand, clipboard in the other, trying to follow the pneumatic tubes along the ceiling without burning myself on the steam pipes. Around me, the workings of Iapyx hissed, gurgled and stank. I hoped my first day at my job wouldn't end with me sounding my emergency locator siren and getting dragged out of some hole by my new colleagues.

On the other hand, that would take care of their hero worship pretty quick.

I did well enough for the first hour. The service tunnels here were bigger than most, which helped me — but more complicated, too, which didn't. I marked the tubes with chalk to keep track of them as they braided and wove. It was hot and humid. I should have been sweating like a cold pipe but I wasn't — I couldn't. Michael had warned me about this: scar tissue doesn't sweat, and without the ability to sweat, I would overheat. I could get heatstroke. I could die.

I could drop the damn chalk again. Which I did.

As I moved into a narrower service tunnels, I was dropping the chalk regularly, and seeing spots. Was clumsiness a sign of heatstroke? Or just one of my body's routine betrayals? It was hard to tell, as I juggled clipboard and flashlight. My fingers cramped as I tried to force them into pincers to reach under a steam pipe and grab the chalk.

The pipe, with no respect for my status as a hero, burned me.

I swore.

I was the worst person in the city to be doing this. *Why* was I doing this?

Because I'd been asked. And I was, above all things, a good follower. Besides, I wanted to believe I could help my city. And I wanted to believe my body was strong enough to serve me.

But I was exhausted, and I could see nothing out of the ordinary from the lines of tubes. Finding a glitch in a pipe among all of the pipes of Iapyx was worse than finding a needle in a haystack. They needed a haystack expert down here, and not a crippled one.

But as I pressed my body flat against the hot floor, I felt a brush of cool air. I frowned, and struggled to sit up. At my knees was one of the master pneumatics, thick as a man's waist, entwined with its neighbour. I ran my hand along its surface. There was a crack in the plastic tubing.

I couldn't look further, the whole thing was covered by a WARNING: STEAM VENT placard, the paint peeling off the canvas. If there was one sign to take seriously on Iapyx —

But there were no steam pipes in that tangle. Just pneumatics.

Bracing myself for a messy death, I pulled the placard aside.

No steam vent was hiding under the clear tubes of the pneumatic network. Just those two big master tubes, twisting around each other. I nudged one of them and . . .

Smooth as clockwork, the pipes twisted out of alignment.

I gaped at them. The pipes were on a pivot. They'd been tampered with to swing so that, with a push of a hand, one pipe could be made to connect with the other, and then back again.

But there was more. Something pushed back as I pushed the pipes forward. I heard the whirr of gears. I shone my flashlight into the gap and looked inside.

The pivot that turned the two pipes was attached to a rope, and the rope to a wheel attached to a squat device that was bolted to one of the steam pipes.

"What the—"

The device hissed, let out a jet of steam, and the wheel turned. Startled, I grabbed the tubes, and managed to stop the section before it swung halfway. Too late, though. A canister shot out of an exposed pipe and skittered across the floor before banging up against a support.

I let the pipes go. The valve vented again and the

pneumatics swung back into alignment.

I lurched over and picked up the canister that had almost been sent off in a random new direction, but was now stuck with me. I fumbled with the hatch and pulled out the paper inside.

URGENT. CLOSE VALVE 13B IMMEDIATELY. PRESSURE OVERLOAD.

It was addressed to the power centre. The turbines.

My breathing quickened. The air felt like mud in my lungs. I didn't need to be a power worker to know that I was looking at the next steam burst. This was it: clear evidence of sabotage. But from who? This was a restricted area. There'd be records of who was through here, surely? They could find out who did this, easy.

But first I had to get this message to the Comm-Controller so it could be delivered. Lives were at stake. The city itself was at stake.

It was hot in here, and it felt like it was getting hotter. I should have been sweating, but I wasn't. Nausea gripped me. Spots swelled in time with my pulse as I looked around, struggling to find my bearings. What were the symptoms of heatstroke again?

I picked a direction in the gaps between the master pneumatics and staggered for the exit. I hoped I was right.

The spots in my vision got bigger each time my heart beat. My head pounded green and purple. But I couldn't pass out. I'd be dead before anybody thought to look for me, and more people would die because of my failure.

I staggered, dizzy, then shouted when I burned myself on a pipe. But the flash of pain gave me a burst of adrenaline that cleared my head. I used that. I turned a corner and saw the exit to the service ducts. Almost there! I staggered forward, muscles cramping

The spots were overtaking my vision again. My ears started to ring. But I was so close to the cool of the Communications Hub that I started to run. My breath came in gasps. I fumbled with the doorknob for several seconds before I realized it was a crash bar. I shoved it and stumbled through.

The ringing in my ears intensified. I saw the Communications Hub in chaos, people running for the doors. I held up the mis-sent canister. "Hey! Somebody! This has got to go—"

Nobody was listening. People were shouting. And the stupid ringing in my ears just wouldn't let up. Why was I still hot? The nausea and the spots in my eyes were getting worse. "Hey!" I groaned. "Hey! Somebody!"

Ethan stumbled to a stop when he saw me. Sweat was streaming down his face. "Simon! We've got to get out of here!"

"Wait!" I thrust the rogue canister at him. "I found it! Somebody sabotaged the pneumatics. This has to be re-sent to the power centre, or there'll be another burst!"

Ethan bobbled the canister, shoved it under his arm, and grabbed me. "Simon, listen to me! We've got to go!"

Why wasn't Ethan listening to me? Why wasn't anybody listening to me? "There's a pivot!" I gasped. "A machine twists the tubes out of alignment. That's what caused the mis-deliveries. That's why people couldn't trace it. Somebody sabotaged the pneumatics!"

"Marni!" Ethan shouted. *"Help!"*

Marni ran up, looking horrified. Something wasn't right. Why was I still hot? Why couldn't I breathe? Why wouldn't the ringing in my ears go away?

Then I realized that the ringing wasn't in my ears.

Ethan and Marni grabbed a shoulder each and hauled me forward. "What's going on?" I mumbled. I tried to walk, but my legs weren't working right.

"Heat alert," Marni gasped. "Something's wrong. They're ordering all personnel on our level to the cold shelters."

We passed an alarm. The clapper blurred as it struck the bell. The flip-display showed the temperature in red numbers.

"Fifty-seven degrees Celsius?" I gasped. It was hotter here than in the steam tunnels. And as I said it, the display flipped to fifty-eight.

"Move! Move!" Marni yelled. "We have to move!"

People shoved through the emergency exits, but they were bottlenecks becoming traffic jams of sweating, panicking, shoving people. And when we managed to stagger through, there were crowds in the corridors to deal with. More bells ringing.

"Stairs?" Ethan breathed.

"Too far," Marni gasped. "We don't know how many levels are affected."

And they were right. Everyone was doing as they'd been drilled to do: make for the nearest cold shelter. You could collapse in the heat if you took too long to find a way out. The elevators wouldn't carry enough people to safety.

Marni and Ethan struggled. I'm not a big man, but I was dead weight, and it was hot. The air was stale, and the two were flagging. Beside us, an old woman struggled — the same one I'd seen at the window when I started work that day. She glared at us when she saw our insignias. "What did you forget to send?" she shouted. "What did you do!"

Her voice was slurring, her eyes losing focus. As she finished her sentence, she pitched forward.

Marni glanced at Ethan, horrified. A message passed through their gaze. Ethan hauled up more of my weight, and Marni let go to pick up the old woman. Now, two exhausted communications workers were hauling two dead weights through the sweltering corridors.

With what remaining strength I could muster, I took some weight off Ethan's shoulder. We stumbled forward faster. I could see the cold shelter ahead, marked by a flashing light, and the people running toward it. A security officer stood by the door, a clicker in his hand, counting everyone who entered. He put his hand on the doorknob.

These things could only hold so many people. And to work, they had to be closed. The last ones were filing in.

"Wait!" Marni screamed.

The security officer looked up, his hand on the doorknob. We were a hundred metres away. One group of dozens in the corridor shouting for help. Ethan tried to pick up the pace.

I'll never forget the look on the officer's face as he shut the door.

We stood, lost, as claxons rang and it got stifling. Marni teetered as she clutched the old woman. Then she looked past Ethan, and pointed. "Washroom!"

My vision was tunnelling. I sensed Ethan lifting me up, and the four of us turning to a wall — not a wall, a door. The women's washroom. Marni shoved open the door with her body. I could hear water running.

There were others here, leaning against each other in the shower stalls, the water running. The air felt cooler. Marni and Ethan dragged us to the last empty stall. They leaned us against the wall. She fumbled with the tap. Cool water sluiced over me as I hit the tiled floor and passed out.

CHAPTER EIGHT
AARON'S STAR

I woke, feeling cooler but still dizzy. I didn't move. I just listened. The water pattered on us, as I imagine rain did on Old Mother Earth. I opened my eyes slightly.

They'd rolled me onto my side. In front of me, I could see that I'd been sick. Today's breakfast was adding its colour to a stream of water running down the drain. Marni and Ethan sat close together against the shower wall, drenched. Marni clutched her knees to her chest.

"You heard the officer," Ethan was saying. "The problem's been repaired. We just have to wait for the temperature to come down a little more, then we can get out of here. The infirmary staff are already here to take the injured."

"But why did she say that?" Marni looked on the verge of tears. She was staring at the old woman, who still lay unconscious. "We didn't do anything wrong. Why did she blame us?"

"She's scared," Ethan replied. "We all are."

"But why *us*?"

Ethan sighed. "Because Iapyx depends on us. And we're letting them down."

Marni shook her head. Her voice quivered. "But if it's sabotage, like Simon said—"

Ethan clasped her hand. "It's still *our* canisters getting sent to the wrong places. It's still *our* tubes that got messed with. From the batteries that got mixed up, to the messages that never arrived, to the records that were lost. If people can't trust the pneumatics—"

Marni shuddered. "But what would cause the fans to fail?"

The *fans*, I thought. So *that's* what happened. Without the huge wood and canvas mechanisms that drove air through the heat exchangers, Iapyx would have become an oven.

But wait — the ventilation?

"The fans?" I mumbled. "The *fans* failed?"

Ethan and Marni looked at me.

"Simon?" said Marni.

"It's okay," said Ethan. "Relax. Help is on its way."

But the fans had failed. No pneumatic tube gone astray could have caused that. No matter what message they got or didn't get, no one would shut off the fans accidentally. No one would shut off the fans *at all*. They were independent. Automatic. Whoever the saboteurs were, they weren't just diverting messages and waiting for things to go wrong anymore. They were attacking the city directly.

Creator save us. The *fans*. The fans, the cables, the anchors, the salt plant, the hydroponics . . . Iapyx was a web of weak points. If it came to active sabotage, the city couldn't possibly defend itself.

I don't know what showed on my face as I worked my way through this. Something. It must have looked like pain. Ethan and Marni called for help. Someone wearing a nurse's uniform came with a sedative. And I was gone.

• • •

When I slipped back to consciousness, I was in an infirmary bed. I heard Ethan's voice, but he wasn't talking to me. He had on a clipped customer service voice, as though he were dealing with a particularly trying client.

" . . . don't think you should wake him, sir," he was saying. "The heatstroke . . ."

Now that I listened, I heard a little tremble in that voice. Fear? I opened my eyes.

Grey. A pillar of smoke. Like a parachutist, burning, falling.

Nathaniel Tal.

"Ah," he said, seeing my eyes. "Mr. Daud. I'm glad you could join us." His metallic gaze flicked to Ethan. "If you'll wait with my officers in the reception area, Mr. Oall," he said. "I'll take your report next." Nathaniel snapped his fingers and motioned to another grey man to escort Ethan out the door.

Nathaniel and I were alone. The colony's chief of security, and me, pumped full of drugs. Swell.

"I wanted to take your report personally, Mr. Daud," he said. "I am sorry to wake you, but it seems the matter is becoming more urgent. You discovered sabotage, I hear?"

Take my report. He must have heard someone — Ethan, likely — talk about what I'd found. Someone must have let something slip about the pivot. Tal already knew.

"It was . . . it was a device."

"You found a device in the service tunnels," he said. "What sort of device?"

"Steam-driven, mechanical . . . It pulled the pneumatic tubes out of alignment, swapped them. It seemed to work at random."

"Ah," he said. "And hence: the failed deliveries."

Wow. He was quick. He'd worked out the implications in about half a second. I just nodded. "It wouldn't take many to disrupt communications throughout the city."

"Just so," said Nathaniel. "But now that we know what we're looking for, it should be easy enough to address the matter."

"But sir," I said. "The fans."

Nathaniel frowned. He looked — uncomfortable? Angry? "You're not a security officer, Mr. Daud. Don't trouble yourself with the fans."

Don't trouble myself!

Nathaniel nodded to me, and left. The door clicked shut behind him.

• • •

Drugs and exhaustion took me again. When I woke up, Rachel was stroking back my hair. She smiled to see me, and I smiled at her. "Hey, you," I said.

"Hey," she answered, softly. Then she looked over at the other side of my bed. Michael was standing there. He smiled at us sympathetically, but Rachel gave him a sheepish look and pulled her hand back.

"You're both here," I said. This was more than just a social call. I struggled to sit up. Rachel came forward to help.

Their uniforms were a mess of stains and wrinkles. Exhaustion was plain on Rachel's face. "Are you okay?" I asked.

"I should be asking you that!" Rachel got me to my feet. She looked angry. "I can't believe the Comm-Controller sent you into the steam tunnels! Your body can't take that sort of abuse. You're lucky you're weren't hurt worse!"

"Don't blame him." Though she was right, I felt a need to defend Gabriel. I think I was secretly pleased that someone of his rank had relied on me. "He needed someone he could trust."

"*I* could have gone in there," she snapped. "Michael could have."

"We'd have no reason to go," said Michael quietly. "We're medical staff, not communications workers. Simon had clearance."

Rachel let out her breath sharply and turned away.

I didn't want to get in the middle of an argument. There were more important things to talk about.

"Nathaniel was here," I said. "I had to tell him about what I'd found. Have you heard?"

"We can't talk here." Michael lowered his voice to a near-whisper. "It's not private enough. Especially if Nathaniel was here. Remember your spyhole."

A bell went off. My heart jumped before I realized it wasn't a heat alarm.

"There's an announcement up in reception," said Rachel. "We're all expected. And since you're officially ambulatory, Simon, you have to come, too."

• • •

The reception area was crowded with medical staff — doctors, nurses, interns, specialists — their clothes limp and crumpled, and some smudged with blood and heaven knew what else. Some of them looked asleep on their feet. Some had been crying. The rehab patients mixed in here and there looked like the picture of health and normality beside these people. I could smell sweat and burn fluids and the high, flowery stink of morphium. Creator save us.

Even the town crier's professionally neutral face wavered as she climbed up onto the reception desk to be heard. She glanced at her timepiece. This was the real deal, an official announcement, to go out simultaneously throughout the city. She watched the seconds. We watched her. Then all at once she looked up and her voice rang out: "Attention, citizens of Iapyx! Attend to a message from Mayor Matthew Tal, on this, the 22,977th day of colonization! Message follows:

"The mayor shares your concern over the mechanical failures that have afflicted this city these past few days. He wishes to assure all citizens that he is taking the matter seriously. The mayor has assembled teams of workers with expertise in maintenance and security to investigate these incidents and identify those to blame. Rest assured, any and all corrective measures will be taken to prevent these failures from happening again. The mayor thanks all citizens for their patience during these trying times, and urges them to cooperate with their neighbours in working toward the safe and secure future of our city.

"In the name of Mayor Matthew Tal, of the Creator of the Stars and the Captains of the *Icarus*, message ends!"

The crier got down from the desk. Muttering started up all around.

"Corrective measures," I said. "What does—"

"The Grounders," someone answered. "He's going after the Grounders."

Michael shook his head, but that word echoed around us. *The Grounders. They did this.* Rachel looked ill.

I took her hand and squeezed it.

At Rachel's order we separated, to meet in the prop room again. Aaron and Gabriel were waiting for us past the secret door. Gabriel nodded at me. "Good work, Simon."

Rachel glared at him. "You shouldn't have sent him into the steam tunnels."

"Rachel," I ventured, "I wouldn't have gone in if I didn't think I needed to."

She turned that glare on me. "Don't talk like a soldier, Simon. I've had more than enough of that in my life."

I stepped back from that glare. Had she meant Isaac? The pilots? Or the Grounders?

"But Simon gave us the break we needed," said Gabriel. "This is the first physical evidence we've found that the failures are acts of sabotage. More than that, there are logs about who goes into the maintenance tunnels — official ones, and the ones I keep in my head. I know who went into those maintenance tunnels, and that included a troop of security officers from the mayor's office. They were supposedly on drill. I think they were doing something else."

Michael looked up. The colour drained from his face. "What?"

Rachel gaped at Gabriel. "You're sure of this?"

"Absolutely," said Gabriel. "It's not enough proof to take public, but it's the first piece of evidence we have that connects the sabotage to the security office."

Rachel clenched a fist. "I knew it!"

"Wait! Whoa! What?" I gasped. At the back of my mind, I'd wondered if this was how Nathaniel had figured out the implications of my find so quickly. But the implications of that were far easier to laugh at than accept. "A conspiracy," I said flatly. "From the mayor's office?"

"It doesn't have to be a big one," said Rachel. "This is a small city. Three or four committed security officers could do a lot of damage."

"But why?" I couldn't keep the scepticism out of my voice. I wasn't really trying. "Why would Tal's men sabotage their own city?"

"They're hiding something," said Aaron.

"Like what?" I turned on him. "People *died* today, Aaron. This isn't a game of ticktock monsters!"

Instead of answering, Gabriel glanced across at Aaron. "He needs to know."

Aaron looked nervous. "Are you sure? This is pretty big stuff."

Rachel pulled a roll of paper from behind a painted backdrop of Verona. "We'd have to tell him eventually. Better that it's now." She rolled it out on the table and held the ends down. "This is what we've been looking for."

It was a map. Right away I noticed three things. First, I recognized the white sphere with lines tracing out from the pole, representing the deep chasms our cities hid inside, like someone had cracked the top of a very round, very white egg. Our thirteen cities were pinpointed in red.

Second, I recognized the handwriting. It was my mother's.

And third . . .

"Notice something different?" said Rachel.

There was more here. Much more. Thinner lines criss-crossed the familiar thick ones, and some extended very far south.

Mom had added to the map.

I closed my eyes, hard, then opened them to make sure I wasn't seeing things.

Why didn't I know about this? Mom had worked at the mayor's office; this map must have been one of their projects. And it had been almost eight years since she'd died. Why hadn't the official record been updated?

There was still more. Mom had drawn red lines from each of the thirteen cities. All these lines stretched south, making a fan that widened out from the planet's equator. I saw a scribbled annotation that might have said "angle of entry" and some calculations. There was a red circle in an area of white farther south than the southernmost city, dangerously close to the line beyond which was written *Danger: Steam*. In the centre of the red circle was a big question mark.

"This is—" I was too stunned to form a question.

"It's your mother's map, Simon," said Gabriel. "Hagar's map."

"I—" I started to say, "I know," then changed my mind. "This — How did she make this? Who surveyed it — this far south, where the fog turns to steam?"

Aaron shrugged. "The Grounders in Perdix cobbled together a couple of robotic flyers to do that, using some parts from before planetfall. That is, until their government found out and shut them down for misuse of resources."

I shook my head. "Why haven't I heard about this?"

"It's not official research," Gabriel replied. "That information has to be vetted and peer reviewed. I can tell you the Perdix discoveries are slowly being added to the official record, but independent verification has been slow. Someone has been throwing up roadblocks, and most of those have come from the mayor's office, right here on Iapyx."

"They're hiding something, Simon," said Rachel. "We don't know what, exactly, but something big."

I threw up my arms and set a stuffed raven swinging, scattering us with dust. It was beyond ridiculous. "You've got theories, though. Tell me."

Aaron cut in. "Simon, remember the star I saw at Nocturne?"

Of course I remembered, but the sudden change in subject stuttered me to silence.

"I know," he said. "We don't see stars here, not even during Nocturne. That's what the textbooks tell us. But it *was* there. I could barely see it past the chasm lip. I know that shouldn't be possible. People laughed at me when I told them. But when I told Isaac, he made an interesting point: the light from our sun is so intense, it drowns out the light of other stars. But light from our *own* sun that's reflected back at us? *That* might have a chance."

He waited, smiling. I tried to make the connection. Reflected back at us by *what*? Then it hit me, hard. "You saw a *planet*?"

He nodded.

"But there *are* no other planets in the system!"

Aaron shrugged. "Again, that's what our textbooks tell us. And that's why I tell my students to think for themselves. I'm not allowed to say what I saw — that's crazy talk — but it turns out the Grounders have been studying this planet for a while, whenever Nocturne gives them a chance. The interesting thing about this planet is that it's about our size . . . and it's blue."

Blue.

We had been promised a blue world, an ocean world dotted with islands and broad salt flats, a long, lazy year in distant orbit around a brilliant sun. We didn't know what had gone wrong.

But it was too big an idea for me to absorb. It had been too big an idea for the original colonists to accept: that we were lost on the wrong planet. We had no way to get off, so what good did this knowledge do? Sixty-two years of thinking about this could drive people insane, so nobody thought about it. At all. My voice shook. "That's crazy. This is *crazy*."

"I agree that we don't have enough proof," said Aaron. "But maybe that's why the mayor's office is so worried. They're worried that we'll find proof we're on the wrong planet."

Gabriel nodded. "I think we may be close to finding where the *Icarus* crashed."

"No way! It's been six decades. The *Icarus* is long gone."

"We don't know that," said Aaron. "And we won't know unless we look. Think of the tech we could recover if we found her. Living could get a lot easier in our cities. And yet the mayor's office is opposed to that."

"No, no, no," I said. "No! This doesn't make sense! Why would they care? How would they even know enough to be worried about what you might find? We don't know if the *Icarus* is out there! There's no one in our cities whose ancestors were aboard the *Icarus* that day!"

"There is, actually," said Gabriel. "You remember that one survivor of the *Icarus* made it back before the ticktock monsters came."

I frowned, but nodded.

"Do you know his name?"

I didn't. I shook my head.

"It was Tal." Gabriel looked at me seriously. "Chief Medical Officer Daniel Tal. Nathaniel and Matthew Tal's father."

I stared at the old man, and again my mind rebelled. "That's *insane!*" My voice edged up. "If Nathaniel Tal's father survived the *Icarus*, we'd have heard about it. The family would trumpet that legacy. Mayor

Matthew wouldn't be leading just this city, he'd be Captain by now!"

Gabriel shrugged. "Perhaps, except that Daniel Tal chose to lie low and bury himself in work — and there was a lot of work to be done securing the cities — before moving to Iapyx to raise a family that never mentioned their father's service aboard the *Icarus*. It's been almost forgotten in the six decades since."

"But — there'd be names in history books. Someone would have found out."

"I only learned about it thanks to your mother. Hagar was our eyes and ears in the mayor's office." Gabriel nodded at the map. "She was working on figuring out where the *Icarus* crashed. She discovered the Tals' secret, and brought it to me. She died soon afterward. I've never been satisfied with the explanation that her death was a suicide."

I shuddered.

"I don't think she jumped, Simon."

"Well, I don't think she flew!"

This was way too much. I couldn't stand to be here anymore. "No," I whispered.

"The sabotage of the pneumatics suggests this is coming from the mayor's office here on Iapyx," Gabriel went on. "The Grounders in the other cities aren't dealing with anything like this. This isn't a government conspiracy, it's personal. So, what reason could they have to keep us from finding the *Icarus*?"

"The Captain's dying," said Aaron. "There's going

to be an election. Everybody knows that Matthew Tal intends to run against the current mayor of Daedalon for the right to ascend. Maybe there's some information on the *Icarus* the Tals fear will derail the campaign."

Rachel took my hand. "Simon, we need your help. Gabriel needs someone he can trust in the Communications Hub. The security office is already following you. You don't have anything to lose."

Nothing to lose. The Grounders had taken Isaac. My mother too. And now they wanted me? Nothing to *lose*? "No!" My voice rang among the pipes, startling even me. I jerked my hand away. "I can't do this!"

They looked at me, shocked, but I couldn't stop. "This is crazy, you know that? Totally crazy! A *planet*? The *Icarus*? A government conspiracy? I can't deal with this! Count me out."

I tried not to see the hurt look in Rachel's eyes. "Simon—"

"Count me out!" I repeated, more quietly. "I want to go home. I'm not going to turn you in, I won't tell anybody about you, but — just leave me alone. Okay?"

Rachel stared at me a moment. Then she turned away.

The silence stretched. Then Gabriel stepped forward. "Fine," he said. "We're not violent people, Simon. Remember that, when more people die. Michael will show you the way out."

CHAPTER NINE
SUSPICION

Michael escorted me back to the projection room and walked off, looking troubled and preoccupied. I went home and fell into bed. I slept until my alarm went off, and then lay there, wondering if I should bother showing up for work.

Then I thought that if the CommController wanted to reassign me, it wouldn't be because I didn't show up. With that rebellious thought in mind, I put on my uniform and headed out.

I'm not sure what I expected at the Communications Hub. An angry mob? Gabriel standing there, reassignment papers in one hand, pointing me in the direction I'd come?

Instead, I found the place as it had been the day before, if strangely quiet. Clerks bustled; pneumatic canisters slipped in and out through the tubes overhead. It was as if the fan failure had never happened.

"Is the CommController in?" I asked as Marni levered up the counter to let me in. I tried to keep the squeak from my voice.

"No, he clocked out a half-hour ago. He won't be back till late."

That threw me. Nobody was going to be ordering me out after all. It was a relief to still have a job, but I didn't like the idea that the confrontation had only been delayed.

"We're a bit short-staffed," Marni went on. "After yesterday, the CommController gave anybody who needed it the day off."

I looked around at the workers moving around, doing their jobs, all in solemn silence. "Why didn't you take the day off?" *And by "you" I mean "everybody."*

Marni shuddered. "And stew at home? No, thank you." She handed me a sheaf of papers. "Here's your orientation papers. Somehow we forgot to give these to you yesterday. Esther will get you started with the canisters."

Let no one tell you that any job is too small or that any person is unimportant. Those Communication Hub workers were heroes that day for showing up. I thought that as I started my last day on the job.

And let me tell you that it was *boring*. Grabbing canisters, glancing at addresses, sorting them so they'd go into the right tube? The job kept me busy, but it was so mindless that my mind started to work on its own. It ran over what the Grounders had told me: Gabriel saying, *"I've never been satisfied with the explanation that her death was a suicide."*

Then, Isaac: *"Did we check these batteries?"*

Someone tapped my shoulder and told me my shift had ended. Marni had left, Ethan hadn't come in yet, so I left, ate dinner at the galley, and kept stewing.

I should have gone home, but I needed to think. I couldn't do that in my apartment, with its spyhole in the wall. I decided to wander.

It was evening, and the people were thinning out. Even though the light shone as bright as ever through the small gaps in the window shields, we kept to the Old Mother Earth clock. There were night workers, but many people went home at the end of the "day." Even in broad daylight, Iapyx slept.

I found myself at the Sunside Point, where I'd seen my father fall. As good a place as any to remember the dead, I suppose. I looked up at the anchor and saw it still behind scaffolding. I was surprised. This close to Solar Maximum, they were taking a long time to shine it.

I looked away and thought about Mom, Isaac, and faulty batteries.

Then, for no reason I could think of, I remembered what Ethan had said to Marni: *"From the batteries that got mixed up, to the messages that never arrived, to the records that were lost."*

Records.

My mind flashed to my conversation with Nathaniel.

"What caused the fault in my ornithopter? Does the white box say?"

"The evidence was inconclusive."

Somebody was sabotaging Iapyx. I could see that. I could also see that, as crazy as the Grounders were, it wasn't them. At least, it wasn't Rachel or Aaron or Michael. So who was it?

And if somebody was attacking the Grounders, had my ornithopter been a target?

The Grounders suspected the mayor's office, its security staff — specifically Nathaniel. That was silly. What reason would he have to do this?

But Nathaniel had known Mom, and Mom had known something about his family history that almost everybody in our colony had forgotten.

It was crazy. I was letting the Grounders' conspiracy theories affect me. But there was one place I could put my suspicions to rest.

• • •

Once upon a time, I learned to work my ornithopter by cleaning it, repairing it and flying it, repeatedly. So, while the flight academy was headquartered in Daedalon, in practice it was split between Daedalon and Iapyx, allowing our training runs to shuttle back and forth between the cities. With space at a premium, we stuck our offices where we could, on either city.

The Iapyx side had the record room. And I still had keys.

I don't know why I'd kept them. Nobody had thought to ask for them. And maybe I'd always hoped to come back.

Though not like this. Not after hours, sneaking like a thief, spinning elaborate murder plots like a Grounder.

We were two generations removed from computerized locks. It was simple to get inside the record room. We were also two generations removed from computerized records, however. The shelves of boxes and books that stretched before me were daunting.

But I treated the challenge like the safety protocols required before launching an ornithopter. My crash had been nine months ago, well short of the two-year requirement that paper be recycled. I went through the shelves, eliminating sections where the reports were too old, or were maintenance records, requisitions, flight manifests, until I found what I was looking for: routine arrival logs.

I scanned the dates, closing in on the day Isaac died . . .

. . . and found a gap on the shelf.

It was small, less than half a centimetre: a sloped space where two volumes leaned against each other. I wouldn't have noticed it, or given it a second thought, except that the logs on either side of this space covered the week before and the week after my crash.

I frowned at the thin space. Somebody had taken the log. Why would anybody take it and not put it back? I couldn't check the sign-out sheets, so . . .

But as I looked around, my eyes fell on a bin in the corner labelled To Be Pulped. There were books inside. On a grim hunch, I limped over. I didn't have to dig very far to come up with the arrival log in question.

I flipped through the pages. The dock hands had been diligent as always: every flight in and out of Iapyx had been logged in careful box script, all well organized. I ran my fingers down the entries until I found the date I was looking for.

There I was: *Ornithopter Flight, Freight Class, Simon Daud Pilot, Isaac Daud Navigator. Left Daedalon 14:00 hours. Arrival Iapyx due 15:02 hours. Arrival: n/a.*

Strange how "Not Applicable" could mean something so disastrous.

Scanning backward, I looked for names I recognized. And I found one.

It was a flight by a passenger-class ornithopter, bearing the mayor of Iapyx and his entourage. They'd paid a visit to the mayor of Daedalon a few hours before my maiden flight; a quick there-and-back. It may have been part of Matthew Tal's undeclared campaign for the Captaincy, but otherwise nothing unusual. Except that the flight back to Iapyx had one passenger fewer than the outbound flight.

Scanning forward, I found that passenger.

Nathaniel Tal had hopped aboard a freight-class flight one hour after my departure, even though there were other passenger-class flights available.

I flipped the ledger closed and leaned against the shelves.

Nathaniel Tal had stayed behind on Daedalon, even though in all the times I'd seen Mayor Matthew Tal, his brother had always been by his side.

I'd hoped I wouldn't find this, much less find it in the to-be-pulped pile months too early. Finding an arrival log in its place without Nathaniel's name would have silenced the whispers in my head that had started when Isaac told me he thought Mom had been murdered. Now I had to wonder: Why had the batteries on my ornithopter failed on the very flight where my brother told me there might be a conspiracy against my family?

Could Nathaniel have sabotaged my ornithopter? Could he have killed Isaac? Could he have killed Mom?

I wasn't going to sleep until I had answers.

• • •

The security office was located in the mayor's offices. They never closed, but I knew I couldn't just walk in and look under things. So my trek took me back to the Communications Hub. The public window was closed, but I was able to let myself in, and found people still working. The pace had slowed, but one or two deliveries shot through the tubes. A handful of workers busied themselves repairing canisters. I followed the wall and came upon a door that I'd passed during my walk with Gabriel. The sign on it read Oversized Deliveries.

It was a large room, with bins on wheels, each filled with boxes too large to go into an average pneumatic canister. Sometimes things just had to be walked to their destination.

One man worked away in a corner, checking address labels and placing packages into the right bin. He didn't look up. Quietly, trying to look like I was supposed to be there, I walked the line of bins, looking down at the labels. I passed packages addressed to the infirmary, the vocational school, the arboretum, before finally finding the bin for the mayor's office. I placed the arrivals log on top and took the handle.

The guy in the corner straightened up and spotted me. "Oh, hey," he said. "Just got the final deliveries ready to go." Then his eyes met mine, and we recognized each other. I was staring across the empty room at Ethan. His brow furrowed.

There was a moment's silence before I tried to keep up the ruse. I shifted the bin. "So, this one's for the mayor's office?"

"Uh . . ." He raised a finger, pointing. "Your shift ended hours ago."

"I'll just take this over, shall I?"

Ethan came forward and grabbed the other side of the bin, blocking me. "What are you doing, Simon?"

"Just doing my job," I said, mustering confidence.

"No," said Ethan. "You're doing *my* job." He struggled for words. "Look, you don't have to do this!"

I was momentarily blank. "Do what?"

"Prove yourself. I mean, in your condition, you shouldn't be pushing yourself like this—"

"Pushing myself? My *condition*?"

"Going into the maintenance tunnel? Getting heat-stroke?" said Ethan. "Pulling two shifts after you passed out and had to go to the infirmary? You're not a pilot anymore; you don't have to be a hero all the time!"

"Ethan, no! It's not about that!" We stood there, on either side of the bin, staring at each other. I'd been sidetracked. How was I going to convince Ethan to stand aside?

Maybe with the truth.

"Look," I said, slowly. "I know I'm not supposed to be here. But I need to get into the mayor's offices, and this bin and my uniform can give me cover."

Ethan's expression grew more perplexed. "The office is always open. Just walk in."

"No." I took a deep breath. "They can't see me. I mean, they can't see me as anything more than a communications worker. It needs to be a secret."

Ethan's mouth dropped open. I wasn't sure if he was getting ready to shout for security.

"It's important," I added, quickly. "There are things I need to know, and they're not going to just tell me. It might tell us who's responsible for the sabotage."

Ethan closed his gaping mouth. For a moment, neither of us said anything. Then he stepped aside. "All right, then. You'd better go."

I smiled as I pushed the bin forward, but then he grabbed the handle beside me. "But I'm coming with you."

• • •

Ethan and I walked through the corridors of Iapyx, pushing our rumbling bin of packages ahead of us. One of its wheels was sticking, and it wobbled and juddered as we went.

I'd expected to feel self-conscious doing this. Having Ethan there, looking at me warily, as if I might make off with the bin, made me doubly so.

"So . . ." he said, carefully. "Why do you think the security office knows something about the failures that they aren't telling people?"

It's hard to explain yourself when you're not sure what you're doing. We boarded an elevator while I thought about my answer. "Let's just say I don't think they're looking at the right target," I said at last.

"What do you mean?"

"Who do you think set the device I found in the maintenance tunnels?"

The question took Ethan aback. "Well, the Grounders, of course! The device was sabotage, and everybody's saying—"

"Is it easy getting into those tunnels?" I asked.

"No. Access points are locked. You have to sign out the keys and—"

"Who has access to those keys?"

His nose wrinkled as he concentrated. "A few maintenance people, I suppose. The people who do the audits. You."

"So, who in the Communications Hub do you think is a Grounder saboteur?" I wondered if he'd name the CommController.

Ethan's eyes widened. "No! Not my friends! No-body!"

The elevator doors parted outside the mayor's offices.

"That's why I want to look here," I said.

We shoved the bin forward and entered the mayor's offices. The night receptionist sat at the front of a large room filled with a squadron of desks, all in rows. A motivational poster had been tacked to the wall behind him: *Stand Firm in the Light — Let Others Take Shade Behind You.* His typewriter clicked and rang as he attacked the top page of a large pile of forms.

Ethan made to push the bin past the desk. "Package delivery."

The receptionist hardly looked up. "You know where to go." Then he gave us a second look. "Why are there two of you?"

Ethan opened his mouth to reply, and froze. I saw his eyes dart this way and that, as though searching for an answer. Silence stretched. The receptionist's frown deepened.

I coughed. "It's my first day."

"Yes!" said Ethan, as if grabbing a lifeline. "I'm showing him the ropes."

The receptionist chuckled. "Sounds like you're learning quickly." He gave me another once-over, then turned back to his typewriter. "Go ahead."

We pushed the bin out of the reception room and into the corridors behind. I had to hold tight to the handle to keep Ethan from running ahead with it.

We passed the security chief's office. The light was on inside, and I heard a throat-clearing sound: Nathaniel, presumably, working late. I wondered if he ever slept. Two doors down, we came to the delivery room.

Ethan breathed a sigh of relief when the door shut. "Oh, thank the Creator!"

The room was mostly bare. There was a row of intake and delivery pneumatic tubes along one wall and, across from that, a table laden with packages too big to fit. Ethan set to work sorting out the incoming packages and putting the outgoing boxes in the bin. It was quick work.

It was also a waste of time. There were no records here. Nothing that screamed "evidence."

That's when another inspiration hit me. My arrival log had been placed in the "to be pulped" bin. That had to be recent. If it had been put there for a reason, maybe there were other things these saboteurs wanted pulped.

I looked at Ethan. "Where do they put the recycling?"

Using the bin as cover, we pushed deeper into the mayor's offices to a door marked Disposal Room. Like the delivery room, the disposal room was small.

Bins of paper lined one wall, full of ancient forms, retired inspirational posters and handwritten notes. Piles of other temporarily abandoned supplies lay where they'd been dumped.

Ethan stared dubiously at the mess. "What, exactly, are we looking for?"

I took a deep breath. "I'm hoping I'll know when I find it."

I sorted through the papers. Ethan tackled the abandoned supplies. I was shoving through forms and records that were two years old when Ethan said, "This is odd."

"What?" I looked up.

Ethan pulled up a tarp that had been lying over a piled pyramid of tubes. The tubes were all short — no more than thirty centimetres in length. They were translucent. Grouped together like that, they reminded me of . . .

The trunk line of pneumatic pipes.

Was this the proof I was looking for? There must be many reasons why a bunch of tube segments lay discarded. "Maybe they were doing some renovations to the pneumatics here?"

Ethan shook his head. "These are mains." He picked one up. "You can tell by the thickness of the material. If there were renovations to be done to the mains, we'd do that." He looked up at me. "We have to keep track of where these things go. We'd have to order the pipes, fit them ourselves, and dispose of the waste."

I turned back to my bin. There were many forms here, all two years old. Except for . . .

I pulled it out. Ethan peered over my shoulder at it. "What is it?"

"A requisition form," I said. My brow furrowed. "Signed two months ago. To the pipe makers of Octavia. The form's not due to be pulped for another twenty-two months."

"Why would the mayor's office bypass the pipe makers *here*?" asked Ethan. "Unless . . ." Ethan was coming to the same conclusion I was, and he didn't like it. Neither did I.

I'm not a brave man, or an idealist. I follow the rules and I keep my head down. But how am I supposed to feel when the people whose job it is to enforce the rules, led by the brother of the man who makes them, don't follow the rules? "We need to get out of here."

We slipped out and picked up our bin. I folded up the requisition and shoved it behind the cover of the arrival log. We turned a corner and almost ran into a phalanx of security officers. They muttered at us as they dodged past.

There were more security officers around now. A lot more, running back and forth, too busy to notice us. I glanced at a clock as we passed. The bustle was odd for so early in the morning. Everybody radiated a sense of purpose that made me nervous.

We pushed the bin forward as fast as we dared, passing Nathaniel's office, which was now dark.

Another group of grey-clad security officers rattled past. These had sidearms. My heart leapt at that. Sidearms? Our security officers never wore sidearms! As we neared the reception area, I could hear the mutters and clatter of a busy crowd.

What was the security office doing, and why was it doing it now? It had been nine months since my accident, and two months since the pipes were requisitioned. For both pieces of evidence to be sent to be pulped *now* felt like tying up loose ends. You only do that when you're about to finish something. Or when you're about to start something.

We reached the reception area. It was full of officers now, moving back and forth. Nobody had any time to look at us.

Ahead, a clutch of guards left a meeting room off to the side of the main entrance. One had a stack of folders under his arm. He stopped, looked at them, then turned back to the room, setting them down on the nearest table. Then he hurried after his colleagues.

"Ethan," I whispered. "I've got to look in that room."

He frowned. "But we're almost to the exit . . ."

"I've got to," I said. "Please. Just take a detour. Make it look natural."

A flash of fear crossed his face, but we turned the bin without breaking stride. Leaving it at the door, we strode into the meeting room as if we had every reason to go that way. Nobody even looked up.

I stopped and stared.

The room was where the security office planned its operations. They were planning something now. There were papers stacked everywhere. Easels holding maps of parts of Iapyx. Schedules plotted out on the whiteboard. Names. Lots of names.

I saw the words *Grounders* and *Arrest Warrants* scrawled in black, and a time, just hours from now. I saw Rachel's name close to the top. I saw a floor plan of Iapyx's residential wards.

"These are plans," I said. My heart beat faster. There were a lot of names. "These are plans for mass arrests."

"Listen to me," said a new voice, as someone entered the room. "I've already told you to forget those names I gave you! These people, they're harmless. There's no reason to go after—"

I whirled around. Standing by the door, staring at me and looking shocked and guilty, was Michael.

CHAPTER TEN
BETRAYAL

Michael, Ethan and I stood frozen. It was a toss-up whether Ethan or Michael's mouth was open wider.

"What are you doing here?" Michael whispered at last.

"The security office is about to arrest the Grounders," I blurted.

Michael looked from me to the list of names. He went pale.

Behind him, a security officer frowned at us. "What are you all doing in here?"

Michael swung around at me. "Run!" he hissed.

We ran. Ethan and I burst through the door, grabbed the bin and shoved it into the startled officer, knocking him over a desk. We rushed to the exit, using the bin as a battering ram.

Behind us, still in the planning room, Michael shouted, "Here! They're in here! Intruders! Saboteurs! In here!"

Which was a brilliant little plan. Officers looked up. Officers ran forward. Officers jammed themselves into the doorway leading to the planning room, leaving us free to escape through the front.

We abandoned the bin in front of the mayor's offices, blocking our pursuers. I managed to grab the arrivals log and the requisition paper before we dashed into the corridor and lost ourselves among the early-morning crowds.

A town crier called out the news. "All citizens attend! It is now two hours before Solar Maximum. The infirmary is on high readiness standby. All non-essential workplaces will shut down in one hour, and citizens are reminded to keep activity to a minimum during the shelter period—"

Her voice was replaced by a babble as security officers poured into the corridor and crashed into the bin. We put on a burst of speed and took several tight corners before my legs and burning chest told me to stop. We made it to an elevator.

"Ethan," I wheezed. "You've got to go. Leave me. Lie low."

He waved at me to follow. "No! If they're going to arrest you, I know the ornithopter schedules. The last flight to Daedalon left a half hour ago, but the last flight to Octavia leaves in fifteen minutes. Everything will shut down for Solar Maximum after that. Security can't get at you if you're on that flight."

It was a way out. I could be on my way to Octavia and security wouldn't be able to touch me for the next few days. They wouldn't even be able to use the semaphore until the sun's brilliance faded enough for people to look. It was a chance to escape, but . . .

I shook my head. "I've got friends, and they're about to be arrested for things they didn't do. I have to warn them."

Ethan looked down the corridor. He looked as though he'd had as much excitement as he'd wanted, and then some, but he put on his bravest face. "I'll come with you, then. I'll help."

"No." I grabbed his arm. This was important. "No!"

I hadn't seen Ethan's name on the list. I hadn't had time to look, but it made sense. He wasn't a Grounder; he'd just been following me. If he followed me any further, he was sure to be arrested.

"Seriously," I said. "Lie low. I don't know what's going to happen next, but you won't do anybody any good if you end up in a cell. If the worst happens, we'll need people on the outside to help. Can you do that?"

He hesitated, then nodded. He straightened up and flashed me a salute. I stared at that. Communications workers didn't salute. Neither did pilots. But I matched his gesture, and that seemed to satisfy him. He turned and ran away down the corridor, leaving me staring after him.

The elevator doors opened, and I stepped in.

Rachel was in her office when I reached the infirmary. She was sorting out pills for patients. Seeing me in the doorway, she gave me a withering glare. "What do you want?"

That look ebbed as I struggled to catch my breath. "I was at the mayor's office," I gasped. "I saw . . . Michael . . . He was meeting with security officers and they were issuing arrest warrants."

"What?" She stared at me. "Are you sure?"

I couldn't answer for a moment. I breathed deep, my hand to my chest. I nodded.

She grabbed a slip of paper and scribbled out a note. "We've got to warn Gabriel. He'll warn the others."

"We don't have time! They chased me. They're coming for *you*."

"Then we need to move quickly!" She pulled a pre-addressed canister from her desk and slipped the paper inside. "I'm sending this to Gabriel. He'll gather the others."

Voices were getting closer. Then heavy footsteps. I grabbed her hand. "We've got to go *now*!"

She shoved the canister into the intake tube and hit the button. We rushed toward reception until I heard other voices and pulled Rachel to a stop.

"Nurse Caan is this way, officer," said a voice. Rachel looked like a trapped animal.

"Is there another way out?" I asked.

She peered around frantically, and stabbed a finger at a door in the far wall, marked EMERGENCY EXIT: ALARM WILL SOUND.

"Well, this is an emergency," she muttered.

We crashed through the doors and the alarm did sound, loudly. But by the time security caught up to it, we were long gone.

• • •

We went to the prop room. That seemed like madness to me. If Michael had been telling security about us, he knew all the rooms. But there wasn't time to find a new hiding place and, we hoped, there were only so many places security could search.

When we arrived, there were almost a dozen men and women arguing in spite of Gabriel's efforts to calm them down. When Rachel appeared, they turned to her, babbling. I couldn't make out any words.

"Quiet, please!" Rachel shouted. She counted the people who were here. "There should be more. Who are we missing?"

"These were the only ones I could contact," said Gabriel.

"Is it true?" said a boy who looked to be about twelve. "Has Michael betrayed us?"

"Simon found him meeting with the security officers who are planning mass arrests," she said. "Then Nathaniel's men showed up to arrest me."

"They arrested my friend," said the boy. "Joshua Ezer."

Rachel turned on him. "He's not one of us."

"Yeah, but he knew me. That was enough."

"That confirms it," said Gabriel. "The security office is moving fast. This is a purge."

I couldn't believe what I was hearing. Why here? Why now? What could these people be on the verge of finding that would require such a heavy-handed response?

There was a frantic knock on the door. Rachel opened it. A battery girl stood there, breathless. "Someone's coming!" she gasped. "Michael, I think."

Rachel whitened. "Is he bringing guards?"

The girl shook her head. "He's on his own."

Rachel's fists clenched. "Let him in."

"Rachel, wait," I said, but I was drowned out by other protests.

"I know what I'm doing!" she shouted. She nodded at the battery girl, who ran off. Rachel pressed herself against the wall by the door. We heard footsteps approach, then hesitate.

Rachel lunged out. "You!" She dragged Michael into the room, throwing him against the table. Michael struggled and pushed her off.

I grabbed her arm and held her back. "Rachel, before you claw Michael's eyes out, get him to tell you why there aren't security officers rushing in after him and arresting us."

"They're not coming, yet," said, Michael, rubbing his head.

"Why not?" Rachel snarled.

"Because I sent them on a wild goose chase. It won't keep them away for long, but it's a start. You need to do something. They have something else planned."

I got a good grip on Rachel's arm. "Rachel, stop! Yes, he was working with the security officers, but he saved me back at the security office. We need to hear what he has to say."

Michael stood up, still rubbing his head. "Thank you."

"You'd better start by giving them a very good reason to trust you," I said.

He took a deep breath. "They've arrested Aaron."

Aaron! Voices rumbled behind me. Michael paled.

"Keep talking," I said.

"But not in the right way," he gabbled. "I saw them, before I sent them on their wild goose chase. They never read him his rights and duties or put him in a holding cell. Last I saw them, they were taking him to Sunside Point."

"Why?" Rachel snapped.

"I don't know!" He looked scared. "I think maybe they're going to use him to implicate you guys in a big act of sabotage, something about the anchor. Look, I'm not out to get you. When that woman from the infirmary hurt her back when the stairwell went dark, I went to security and asked if I could help. Nathaniel said I should join your group and feed him information about where you met and what you talked about. I thought I'd catch you guys in the act!"

He lowered his head in shame. "But you guys *didn't* do anything illegal. And the sabotage continued. And now I hear the Security office might be doing the sabotaging? I picked the wrong side."

"Took you long enough to figure that out," Gabriel snapped.

"I'm sorry." Michael looked at the floor. "But in the next few minutes, you're going to have to decide what's more important: taking revenge on me, or doing whatever you can to stop Nathaniel's purge."

We looked at each other.

"We could go to the anchor," said Rachel. "We could rescue Aaron, and stop whatever it is they're trying to do."

"It could be a trap," said Gabriel.

"They're arresting us already," she snapped. "They don't need a trap."

"We should go to the anchor, though," I said. Then I realized everybody was staring at me. "If they're waiting for us, we'll get captured, yes, but if they're doing something there to blame on us, they'll create whatever evidence they need to jail us whether or not we go. At least we'll have a chance to stop whatever it is they're doing, and get the truth out."

Gabriel cleared his throat. "You said 'us.' I take it, Simon, you've had a chance to reconsider what you said last time?"

I felt a flush of shame, but I looked Gabriel in the eye. "Yes. Whatever Nathaniel is doing, it's wrong. It must be stopped, and I'll help you stop it."

Gabriel turned to the rest of the group. "Simon's right. If I am to be arrested, let it be on my own terms, and not cowering in some hideaway."

A frantic knock rattled the door. Rachel opened it. The battery girl hissed. "Guards! They're coming!"

"Quick!" Gabriel pushed forward. "The trap door to the stage!"

Others followed, but with whispered protests.

"We're sitting ducks! We'll never get out in time!"

"They'll see the stage. They'll see us."

"No they won't," said Rachel. "It will take them long enough to find this place."

Footsteps right above us made us stop talking. Gabriel reached a ladder at the end of the narrow corridor and clambered up.

Behind us, the footsteps continued. They didn't sound like they were giving up this time.

Gabriel pushed open the trap door just as the door to the projection room was flung open. A voice shouted, "Nobody move!"

We clawed our way onto the stage and ran, up the side of the amphitheatre farthest from the projection room. We kept running until we were out of the Great Hall and stumbling to a halt in the corridor outside.

The light from the exterior windows made me stop and squint. The corridor was empty. Solar Maximum was almost here.

I looked toward Sunside Point — where the cables holding Iapyx converged on the anchor embedded in the cliff that received the most sunlight. I shuddered at the thought of getting that close to sunlight again. I also wondered if we could make it there before the security officers found us.

Then I looked back and realized I was part of a

group of just four: Rachel and Gabriel were beside me, as was the battery girl. Everyone else, including Michael, had slunk away.

"I don't blame them," said Gabriel. "Fighting is never an easy option." He looked down at the battery girl. "And it's not one for you, young lady."

The girl spread her hands. "Where else am I going to go?"

Rachel took her hand, and then mine. "Come on."

We had barely taken two steps when voices echoed through the corridors around us. The town criers were out in force.

"Attention, citizens of Iapyx! This is a priority message from the mayor! Investigations have proven that sabotage was behind the mechanical failures that have afflicted our cities. The group seeking to bring our colony to ground, to be at the mercy of the monsters of the fog forest, has been found responsible. Saboteurs have been captured, confessions signed. Security officials are now in the process of arresting known Grounders. All citizens are to give these officials any assistance they require. Attention, citizens of Iapyx—"

We ran toward Sunside Point. The few remaining people ducked out of our way. I heard shouts behind us, and pounding footsteps. Nathaniel's security officers were getting closer. I was running out of breath. But when we reached a junction, it was Gabriel who begged us to stop. He leaned against the wall, breathing heavily. "We're not going to make it," he gasped.

Rachel looked around, desperate. "We'll split up."

"No," said Gabriel. He took the battery girl's hand. "I'll delay them."

I felt the blood leave my cheeks. "How?"

Gabriel squared his shoulders. "I'll consent to be arrested. I'll make sure to take up a fair bit of their time. And I'll make sure that this young lady is treated well. Now, hurry. They have to think that we're on our own."

Rachel stared at him, then nodded. "Okay." Her voice trembled.

"Wait." I handed over the arrivals log and the requisition form. "This is evidence. If Rachel and I are going into a fight, this needs to be protected. It's not much, but it may help."

"I can hide it." The battery girl took the book. "I'm a battery girl. I've been in places the security people haven't even mapped. I'll make sure it gets to the right people who can get the truth out."

Rachel reached out for Gabriel's hand. He looked suddenly a little shy, but he clasped her hand, and mine. "Good luck, you two," he said. "Now go!"

We ran. Glancing back, I saw the battery girl leading Gabriel around a corner, hanging back as the old man struggled to keep up.

When we reached Sunside Point, the observation area was empty and dark. The windows had been opaqued against the sunlight. While I caught my breath, Rachel went to the utility door leading outside and tried the knob. To our surprise it opened, blasting us with the cello drone of the cables. We shielded our eyes against the sudden burst of light.

The furnace wind blew past us. Soon the sun would reach its highest point in the sky, sending light deep into the chasms. The air around us would be at its hottest. If Nathaniel's security forces were at the anchor, exposed, they were risking their lives.

We stepped out onto the narrow platform and shut the door behind us. I leaned against the thin plastic railing, blinking as my eyes adjusted, then wished that they hadn't. I was staring down at a kilometre of open air and cloud. A metre to our right, the platform met one of the cable struts descending from the anchor. Here, a plastic cage ladder was attached, stretching into the latticework above us, all the way up to the anchor, a gleaming block driven into the cliff face, about the size of four apartments, to which the main cables attached.

Rachel pointed. "Look!"

I looked. The scaffolds were off the anchor, now, but it looked weird. It still reflected the sky, but with a bronze tinge. That's when I realized it was covered in reflective mylar — part of the emergency kits found in lockers at the top of the anchor. Above it, a yellow flag flapped in the wind, a signal that the anchor was under threat. It put the whole city on alert. What was happening up there?

I could see silhouettes moving about. There was only one way to find out. I stepped toward the ladder.

"Simon?" Rachel took my arm.

I stared at her hand, then at her.

"There's something I have to tell you," she added. "Just in case . . ."

Tension dug at my stomach. "Rachel, you don't—"

"Simon, please! I need you to know this!" She took a deep breath. "Isaac and I . . . we were thinking of getting married this coming Nocturne."

Why was she telling me this now? Why? "I'm sorry . . . ?"

"I wanted you to know. It's been hard. And confusing. You and him, and how he died. I loved him." She took another deep breath. "But . . ." She pulled me close, and kissed me.

For a minute, I might as well have been hovering in midair. I was only aware of myself and Rachel, and the taste of her on my tongue. Then I remembered what we had to do.

I eased her away. Our gazes stayed locked. "We don't have much time," I said.

She nodded. "Good luck."

"You too."

She got onto the rungs and started climbing. I climbed after her.

CHAPTER ELEVEN
THE FALL OF SIMON DAUD

We half-crawled, half-climbed the rungs stretched between the cables of Iapyx's singing web. The hot wind vibrated the gantry and made my wrists ache. I tried not to look through the rungs at the clouds below. I focused on remembering to breathe.

We emerged from the gantries, and suddenly the web of cables that had surrounded me all my life was below me: we stood on a master cable at the very top layer of the latticework. That *should* have made me feel safer — more stuff between me and the clouds below — but instead it made me feel dizzy and exposed. Hot winds tugged at us. Though we were in the shade of the cliffs behind us, I could see the silica cap at the top, gleaming. If a stray beam reflected through that cap at us, we'd have no protection.

Ahead of us the cable angled up toward the mylar-covered anchor poking out from the cliff face near its glittering cap. The master cable was wide as a gurney, and smaller cables made thin handrails on either side. But just being near the clifftop made me scar-tighteningly terrified of climbing toward that deadly sun.

We were close enough that we could see people on top of the anchor, but nobody looked down at us or shot at us. I just saw the backs of heads and bodies of security officers wrapped in white sheets against the coming sunlight, between the chrome utility boxes that lined the edge.

Suddenly there was a commotion: shouts followed by a scream. Someone toppled off the anchor, hit the master cable and came skidding down it, tumbling over and over until an arm caught a guy-wire and he lay face-up and limp.

Rachel scrambled over to him. I staggered behind her, and almost ran into her when she stopped dead, her hand flying to her mouth.

Because it was Aaron, who'd wanted to see the stars.

Aaron stared between us, focusing on nothing. "He *stabbed* me." His voice was almost childlike at the wonder of it. "Nathaniel. He just brought out his knife." He blinked. "Why'd he do that?" He blinked again, stutteringly, like Morse code.

"Aaron?" I said.

"I don't know why he'd do that. . . ." Aaron's voice was a murmur. His eyes were glazing.

"Rachel," I said. "Can you—"

141

"It's too late." Her voice was taut. I looked from her to Aaron, bewildered. Then I realized that Aaron wasn't blinking anymore. He wasn't breathing anymore. He wasn't anything anymore.

The wind roared in my ears. My hand closed on the handrail, numb and pincer-like. I looked at Rachel as she reached out and shut Aaron's staring eyes. She looked up at me, her face pale.

"Nathaniel Tal," I said, each word a separate breath, "is going to pay for this."

"Ms. Caan! Mr. Daud!" Nathaniel's voice cut through the hot, dry air.

We flinched, then looked up. Nathaniel stood at the edge of the anchor, looking down at us. We both looked back the way we'd come.

"Don't even think of turning around," he called. "I have a clear shot from here."

The master cable gave us only one option: forward. Forward we went, stepping over Aaron's body. We reached the point where the cable attached to the lower side of the anchor. The mylar sheets draped over it rattled and snapped in the wind. There was a small ladder to take us up the last five metres. Straight up, nearer the sun. I could see the silhouettes of men looming at the ladder's top, waiting for us.

At the rungs, I touched Rachel's shoulder. "Did you have any sort of plan for when we got to the anchor?" I asked.

"No. Did you?"

"Come, now, Mr. Daud, Ms. Caan," Nathaniel called. "Don't keep us waiting."

I held out my hand to Rachel. "How about: Don't die, get the truth out later?"

She clasped my hand. "Good plan."

We climbed the final few rungs onto the platform. A guard reached down to help Rachel up, but she slapped the hand away.

As I reached the anchor, another guard reached down, pulled me up and pinned my arm behind me. Not very hard, but it didn't have to be. He knew what my body could no longer do. Rachel's arm must have been twisted harder; I could see pain narrowing the corners of her eyes.

"Aaron's dead," I told Nathaniel.

As if I'd hoped to shock him. There was still blood on his hand. His smile was odd, though. Sympathetic? "He wasn't cooperative. I'm hoping you'll do better. I have confessions to be signed."

A confession? Tell everyone the Grounders had attacked the anchor? No wonder Aaron wouldn't cooperate. I wasn't going to either, and if I knew Rachel, she'd rather die.

Rachel shouted at Nathaniel: "What are you really hiding? What could we possibly be close to finding out?"

Nathaniel turned back. For an instant, I thought he was going to answer. Then he smiled thinly. "There really are some things it's better not to know."

But what were they doing here? What was this

attack they were trying to blame us for? The guards pulled me toward the cliff face, where mirrors stood on easels. Mirrors: that was smart. They could set up mirrors to defend the anchor. And there were two guards laying out the last of the mylar sheeting, too, laying it out over the top of the anchor, pulling it beneath the legs of the easels. All this was good. Other chrome boxes were open, revealing harnesses and escape suits: not much use. A hammer and a wrench lying around —

I was still taking inventory when the sheet of mylar billowed up in the hot wind, tossing me a reflection of the sky.

For a moment I was entirely blind.

In my blindness I heard Rachel yell, then another yell. One of the guards who'd been holding her now clutched his kneecap while she struggled with the other guard. She pulled free and ran at Nathaniel, but the first guard rushed her, arms outstretched, ready to tackle.

I didn't think. A guard held my arms behind my back, but his grip was not strong, and I could move my legs. I stuck out my foot in front of the rushing guard and caught him on his shin. He went flying.

He hit the anchor, hard, rolling across the mylar sheet toward the edge. He grabbed wildly, and caught a fold, but it was no use. He pitched into open air. The mylar sheet slithered with him. There was a terrible tearing sound.

We fell over as though a rug had been pulled out

from under us. The easels crashed. Mirrors smashed. Several pitched off the side. I felt myself rolling until I got hold of myself. I found myself on my back, by the edge, as Rachel, Nathaniel and the remaining guards picked themselves up.

For a moment, there was stunned silence.

And pure horror on Nathaniel's face.

He wasn't staring at where the guard had fallen . . . none of the guards were. They were all looking at the anchor. I rolled over, pushed myself away from the edge, and looked down. I could see the falling guard. He was still falling, trailing mylar like Nocturne ribbons. The sheets over the anchor had ripped away. Tatters flapped in the wind, useless.

Suddenly, a guard pushed past me, knocking me down in his haste, rushing for the ladder. He and another clambered down toward the safety of Iapyx.

"Stop!" Nathaniel shouted. "Come back here!"

I pushed myself back up on my hands and knees, and looked again at the now-revealed anchor. My throat closed.

It was black.

They'd painted the anchor *black*. Without the chrome to reflect sunlight, the anchor would heat up disastrously. The anchor was external shield material. The wires binding Iapyx to the anchor weren't. Nor were the welds. The links would fail if the sun hit the anchor.

The mirrors. The mylar sheeting. They would have kept the sun off, have saved the anchor long enough for the paint to be removed — but they were gone, now. The mirrors had broken, the mylar had been torn away — and it was my fault.

My . . . I couldn't even fit the thought in my head. I was so confused. Why paint the anchor and then break out the mylar and the mirrors? Why try to destroy the city and then try to save it?

Then, finally, I figured it out: Nathaniel wasn't trying to destroy the city. Instead, he'd been trying to implicate the Grounders in a *plot* to destroy the city. He'd brought Aaron here to frame him for that plot, come out here to manufacture evidence for that plot. That failed plot.

Only — it hadn't failed.

It was, in fact, going to succeed.

Nathaniel swung around and punched a button by the chrome box. There was a click and rattle of gears, and a flagpole swung out from a recess beneath the anchor, sending a banner rippling through the air. My heart thudded to see it. I could imagine the reaction of everyone in sight, from the semaphore tower on down; we all knew what it meant. Red flag: *The anchor is compromised. Engage solar defences. Evacuate Iapyx immediately.*

Then Nathaniel pulled a pistol from his jacket and aimed it down the master cable. He fired two shots. The fleeing guards toppled. One of them fell away into space. The other rolled, as Aaron had, thumping down the cable, before an armpit caught on a guy wire and dragged him to a stop.

"Sir!" shouted one of the four remaining guards. "What are you do—"

Nathaniel turned and fired point blank into the guard's chest. The other three guards rushed forward, and Nathaniel picked them off, one by one. They weren't armed.

I shoved myself to my feet and ran at him, but before I reached him, he turned on me, the barrel of his gun poking me in the chest.

He gave me a smile. It was almost apologetic. "No witnesses," he said. Then he frowned. I stared, frozen in fear and shock, wondering what in sunlight he was waiting for. He looked like he was counting in his head. Then he sighed. "Six shots. Dammit."

He tossed the gun aside and grabbed me by the shoulders, hauling me to the edge.

Behind him, Rachel rushed up, swinging the pipe wrench. It cracked against the back of his skull. He grunted and staggered into me. I fell back on the anchor, then rolled, as fast as I could, away from the edge. I scrambled to my feet and stood beside Rachel.

Nathaniel had pitched into the emergency locker. He stood there, leaning heavily on it, clutching the back of his head.

Down below, from Iapyx, a faint wail started up, growing louder as others joined it. Sirens. Above us came the rattle of gears and machinery. Across the canopy of Iapyx, wings of mylar cranked up, blocking the view of the silhouetted cliff face. Angel wings, we called them. Once Solar Maximum came they'd keep the sunlight off the anchor — but they wouldn't last long before they caught fire and disintegrated. They were a last line of defence in case the anchor was compromised, to buy us time. Angel wings to protect us. And angel wings because we were going to die.

Nathaniel straightened up and faced us. I braced myself for another attack. Rachel's knuckles whitened on the pipe wrench.

Just then, a buzzing sound. An ornithopter was flying close. Banking up, it flew level with the dome of Iapyx, dangerously close to the sunline, between us and the angel wings. I couldn't help but marvel at the pilot's daring. I couldn't help but wonder what the pilot was doing.

Nathaniel looked at us. He looked at the passing ornithopter. He looked back at Iapyx, at the smoke already rising from the angel wing that was now in direct sunlight. Then he reached behind him, into the emergency locker, and pulled out a shoulder pack. By the time I realized what it was, he'd already got it partway on.

A parachute.

"No!" Rachel dropped the pipe wrench. She and I lunged for him, but he kicked the remaining parachutes off the anchor and jumped, pulling on the buckles as he fell. By the time we got to the edge of the anchor and looked down, the fabric of his chute ballooned up, and eased him gently into the clouds.

Engines buzzed below us. An ornithopter dropped

from the gantry a hundred metres away. I recognized the plane by its size and the shadowed insignia on its tail fin. The mayor's plane. *The coward's leaving*, I thought. *He's abandoning the city.*

"Oh, Creator," Rachel gasped, her voice so small I hardly heard her. "Oh, Creator! We've got to do something! We've got to—"

But there was nothing to do.

I'd been a pilot. I knew how to read the angle of the sun. We had just minutes before the sunlight burned through the angel wings and hit the anchor. It would eat through the welds. The city would fall.

And there was nothing we could do about it. The mirrors had fallen from the anchor. The mylar sheet was in tatters. There was no way to get all the paint off in time. All the options ticked off toward a horrible certainty. I went to the ladder, but as I did a distant *whoosh* told me the topmost angel wing had caught fire in the sunlight. How long would it take us to get down the ladder and back to the gantries? How long would the remaining angel wings last? No witnesses, Nathaniel had said. He'd done the math.

Rachel started for the cable. "We've got to—"

I caught her arm. "There's no time."

"We have to warn them!"

"They already know."

The sirens wailed. More ornithopters dropped from their gantries and fled away along the chasm. Rachel and I watched them go. People were evacuating. But it wouldn't be enough. Not given the number of ornithopters we had, and the few people each could take, or how long it would take to get everybody boarded.

We both knew this. It wouldn't be the smallest piece of enough.

"Simon!" she shouted at me. "Please! It can't — Not like this!"

I looked at Rachel. I raised my hands, palms up. She looked away, shaking her head in disbelief.

"We're going to die," she whispered. She stared in horror at the light blasting down toward us. "We're going to burn to death!"

Burn to death, I thought. And as I thought this, a new resolve swept through me. I took her hand, and pulled her around to face me. "No, we're not." My voice was steely calm. I hardly recognized it. "We are going to jump."

"Jump?" Rachel stared at me, incredulous. There were no more parachutes.

"Trust me. You really don't want to burn to death."

Amazingly, she laughed at that. Then she wiped her eyes and cleared her nose with a sniff. "Well, I guess if you have to choose." She squeezed my hand.

And suddenly everything was very still. Ornithopters were dropping, one after another. Sunlight was blasting toward us. But in my heart there was a big, open silence.

There were three wings above us now. The top one was on fire.

"Do you remember the first time we met?" I asked. "You were holding scissors."

"You were dripping red paint all over your shoes."

There was a *whoosh*. The top wing was gone.

"Did I ever mention you were a good dancer?" she said.

"No."

She touched my cheek. "You are."

"Rachel—"

"What's it like, falling?" Her hand was tight around mine. "I'm . . . What's it like?"

"Come to the edge."

We went to the edge. Another wing went up in a rush of flames. There was one more left. We had less than a minute. Rachel was trembling so hard it was like she was having a seizure. "I can't do this," she said. "I can't do this."

"Falling's fine," I said. "It doesn't hurt. It's fine."

Rachel whispered: "They say you're dead before you hit—"

"I'll hold on to you. All the way down."

"Okay," she said. "Okay."

The last wing. A huge rush of noise, like every bird of Old Mother Earth taking flight around us.

"Kiss me," I said, and kissed her. And there was nothing between us and the light. It grew. It dazzled. It heated my hair. Above us, the red flag burst into flames.

And I never got a chance to say, "I love you, Rachel Caan," because I was still kissing her when we jumped.

• • •

If there are any manuals about killing yourself, and I really hope there aren't, they should put this warning under the entry about jumping from high places: wind is a fickle thing.

As we left the anchor and started our plummet down the cliff face, a fierce wind whipped up from below. It spun us round and pitched us sideways, into the web of cables stretching out from below the anchor. I hit them, hard. Air left me. Light left me.

Rachel left me.

It was over in a flash. I saw her face. I saw her dangling beneath me. I felt the sudden, shocking pull on my hand. My fingers had only just re-learned how to hold a fork. She slipped from my grip.

And then she was gone.

The vibrating cables shook my chest. I lay too stunned to move, much less try to jump to my death. Again.

Sunlight struck the anchor. And the anchor shone.

Even coated in black paint, it shone so bright the light hit me like a solid thing, blinding me, pitching me back along the cables. My foot caught on a junction between two cables. I struggled, but couldn't free myself. I shielded my eyes and squinted as the anchor turned red, then white.

The last ornithopters flew out, and I heard my city scream. Five thousand voices. I heard them all. The rocks around the anchor sparked. The cables shuddered. And then everything snapped.

Iapyx let out a roar. Cables twanged, faster and faster. Below, a thundering crash told me the stem had failed. The city pitched and bucked. More cables snapped.

Slowly, grandly, the whole city fell.

I dropped. My foot came free and I clutched at the cables, my body overruling my desire to just let go. The gantry holding Iapyx's semaphore loomed and snapped. The gigantic arms, still glowing from the heat of the sun, sliced past. The cables jerked me sideways and I flew in my city's wake. My fingers slipped, and I slid down the cables toward the ends that were still glowing from the melting heat. I hung on, desperate. The foggy floor of the chasm rushed up. I was whipped sideways, speeding through clouds, my vision flipping from clear to white and back again.

Twigs scratched at my back as I skimmed the tops of trees. Then a more substantial branch, poking out of the fog, caught me across the legs. It bent back, slowing me down. The cable slipped from my grasp.

I grabbed the branch as the tree flung me back. Somehow I hung on. Somehow I righted myself. I stared.

From my small island in the shrouded sea, I watched Iapyx sail away from me, carrying everything — my friends, my home — with it, until it crashed into the opposite cliff face. It crumpled like a broken string bag, unleashing a roaring black cloud that cascaded at me. The blast shook my branch again, but I held on. Then all I heard was the wind.

I lay limp in the tree's branches, staring at nothing. In front of me, as the dust cleared, the ruins of Iapyx lay scattered around the base of the cliff like a rockfall.

It was a while before thoughts came back. They came back slowly. They came back black.

I had jumped. I had jumped to my death and I hadn't died. Why not? The Fates had played another cruel joke. I was alive, with no reason to live. I had no home. Iapyx was gone. Rachel was gone. Everything in my life. Gone. What stupid second chance was this? I should just lie in these branches, waiting for death to take me.

I waited.

The wind rustled the branches.

I waited.

Fog shrouded my view of the cliff face.

I waited.

Death didn't come.

I grabbed the branch and hauled myself upright. My mind was too numb to think of anything beyond watching where I put my feet, and maybe not even that.

A branch beneath me snapped.

My hands slipped, and I fell. Again. Twigs and branches broke beneath me. I remember thinking that it wasn't so much that I minded dying, but that it was bizarre that I should do it falling out of a tree. An ornithopter, a city, sure, but a *tree*? It was my one garbled thought before something smacked me in the head.

What I hoped was death took me at last.

THE GIRL OF THE FOG FOREST

CHAPTER TWELVE
NINE DOZEN SLEEPS BEFORE THE FALL

EK-TAAK-TOCK-TAAK:

My story begins far away, nine dozen days before the fall.

It was in the days before I got my current name. Then, I was only known by what my birth mother had named me to the Elder Mother: Small, Fierce-Hearted One — or, as it was pronounced in the Elder's speech, Ek-Taak-Tock-Taak. People find it strange that I have two names. I find it strange, too, though I am proud to have earned the second one.

The idea of days is also strange.

I have been told "days" existed in the world of my birth mother's people. There, a yellow sun would shine and then go away, and once it came back, that would be a day. And it happened often enough that people ordered their lives by it.

But as I grew up, I knew only of sleeps. I ordered

my life by those messages my body sent me, telling me to find someplace safe from predators where I could lower my head and close my eyes. And when I woke, I would be ready to work again, until my next sleep.

So I still feel that my story begins nine dozen *sleeps* before the fall. My story is longer than that, but let me start with when I left home for what I thought would be the last time.

I had gathered my supplies from the huts of my village. The Elder had not said that I could do this, but she had not told me not to do this, either. I also knew that those whose huts I had raided would not complain.

I tied back my hair. I hung my travel pouches over my shoulders, and tied more around my hips. Special leaves to heal cuts, bark to clean water, poison thorns for my blowpipe. Some food for the journey — not much. I would have to get more from the forest itself, but it was enough to start. My best bone knives for . . . later.

Finally, I took the spear I had carved from a branch two sleeps before and tested it against the ground. It would serve as a good walking stick.

I was ready. I left the hut. I stood a while, surrounded by fog, but she did not come to say goodbye. I had not expected it, but it hurt a little. When I saw there was no use waiting, I walked away, on the path leading out of the village.

The Elder's voice stopped me, from out of the fog. « Go then, » she said. « See for yourself. »

I waited, but the Elder said nothing more. I took a step forward.

She called to me. « Safe journey. »

For the first time that day, I smiled. I walked out of my village.

You may wonder how I could fend for myself in a world where I could not see more than ten paces ahead, especially among predators that hunt by smell. But though you cannot see, you can still hear. You can smell, if you practise long enough. I have had a lifetime to practise. I did well enough. I was surprised once by a slink, but I had my hand on my spear. The fight was short, and I ate well afterward.

After many sleeps, I came to a place where the ground rose out of the fog. The plants became few, then none. I walked on rough stone that bit the soles of my feet. The walls of the chasm drew together, and seemed to end here, the cliffs coming together in a tight notch, but I pushed on, and the chasm turned, and continued, though here it was so narrow that I had to walk sideways. I walked several steps more, and came out into a new chasm. Fog stretched before and below me and, in the distance, I caught my first glimpse of one of the invaders' metal hives.

It was so far away that I could cover it with my hand. But even in shadow, it shone so bright I had to shield my eyes. It stretched the width of the canyon, tendrils clinging to the cliff face, sitting above the clouds on top of a thin stem. With the stem and the tendrils, it looked like a giant insect sucking the lifeblood out of the land.

A strange buzzing made me turn, and I saw another of the hives, far away in the other direction. There was a shape flickering from it. What insect was this? But as I watched it come closer, I could see it was no insect.

I ducked behind the fold in the cliff face. From there, I peered out.

The thing was white. Its wings flapped so fast, they blurred. It droned as it approached. It was nothing natural. So, the stories were true: The invaders knew how to fly.

The white insect passed close by, the drone pitching lower as it headed away to the metal hive at the other end of the chasm. I waited until I could see it no more. Then I crept out from my hiding place and walked quickly down into the chasm, into the trees and the fog.

This forest was different from my own. It had the same plants, the same animals; there was the same roar of the slinks, and the hoot and cry of the howler-climbers, but it felt . . . cooler. It was darker, too. Which was strange. The burning time was near. But I had walked so far north, the sun was lower in the sky. Just like the invaders to take the best lands.

But though I was farther north, it was still almost the burning time. I knew the sun could still shine through the glittering cap. I knew what would happen then.

From up ahead came a gust of wind and the shaking of leaves. The breeze that touched my cheeks was hot. I tasted water in the air. A stray reflection of sunlight must have shone through the translucent cap at the top of the cliffs and hit the top of the fog, turning part of it to a whirling column of steam. A boiling wind was coming.

The gust became a bellow, then a roar. I found a bulbtree just off the path and, as the rush of wind rose to a scream, I curled up into as small a ball as possible, and waited.

The air grew dark as leaves were ripped into the whirlwind. A blast of wind, hot as a fire, struck me across the back and got hotter and hotter until I could hardly bear it. I kept my breathing shallow, and willed the whirlwind to pass.

And it did. The wind's screams ebbed. So did the hot blast against my back. When I stood up, my body dripping water, only a tiny breeze pulled at my hair. The scalding pain on my back eased. I gathered my things, and made my way back to the path.

Following the chasm, I went north. Three sleeps later, I came upon one of the metal hives.

I could not see it through the mist, but I could tell by the way the sky darkened that it was above me. I remembered what I had seen above the fog, and pictured it looming above the forest.

Then, beyond the fern fronds, I saw it.

A barrier stretched before me, three steps away, made of metal. Beyond it, on the edge of fog-sight, was the hive's stinger, rising from the ground and widening as it rose before it vanished in the clouds. From a distance, it looked thin enough to snap like a twig. Up close, it was a massive column of stone that seemed to push into the ground, sucking the forest in around it. There was a door in that column, made of wood, but looking no less solid. And I could not get to that door without crossing the web barrier in front of me.

The Elder had told me that touching the web meant death. I was not sure I believed this, but looking at the barrier, it looked so easy to climb. Too easy?

I snapped a thin branch from a bulbtree and reached out with the leafy end. When I was a footfall away, I threw the branch into the barrier. It tangled in the woven links with a rustle of leaves and a snap of wood. Nothing else happened.

I clicked my tongue, satisfied, and reached for the dangling branch.

Before I could touch it, its dangling end touched the ground. There was a flash, *snap*, *sizzle*. I sprang back as flames leapt up. Streaks of blue-white light, not like real fire, lanced up and down the branch before the flames consumed the wood and it fell to the ground in a pile of ash.

I looked from the ashes to the barrier to the stinger beyond.

My will faltered. I had come so far to confront the invaders in their metal hives, but how could I get their attention when I was so small, and the hives were so big? If I touched the barrier, I would die, and they would not even notice me. I had not expected to live, but I *had* expected to get inside.

And the anger that had been building in me all my life boiled over. After all the invaders had done to my people, they should listen to me! I would make them hear! I howled. I reared back and flung my spear. It sailed over the barrier and struck the stone column, snapping in two. The pieces rattled as they fell to the ground.

A crack appeared in the stone.

I stared at it, open-mouthed. Then I laughed. I shouted. I'd hurt them!

But then more cracks appeared, spidered out. There came a distant noise, like a wounded animal bellowing, but an animal huge beyond all reason. Other noises joined it, getting louder, coming closer. The hive's stinger shook. A groan filled the air. Dust billowed out from the cracks. Then the stinger shattered. Stones spewed everywhere.

I threw myself to the ground as rocks sprayed around me. I rolled away, and a great slab of the stinger crashed into the mud where I had just been lying. More and larger pieces fell. I scrambled to my feet and ran for my life. The remains of the stinger plowed into the ground. The barrier leapt up, flashing like lightning. Then a great darkness fell from above.

Wind blew past me as the air itself rushed to get out of the way. Behind me, the body of the hive swooped down like a monster. It swept overhead, the wind in its wake knocking me off my feet. Its tendrils lashed the air. I covered my head. A great mass, glowing white hot, smashed into the ground. The mud exploded into steam. I gasped for air and choked on mud and dust. I stumbled on the shaking ground. Stone and metal kept raining down.

At last I spotted a hollow beneath a fat bulbtree. I dove inside, curled up into a ball, and waited for the hive to crush me.

It did not. Slowly, the rumble died away.

I stayed in the hollow long after the patter of falling things stopped and thought about running home. I did not know what I had expected after travelling nine dozen sleeps to one of the invaders' giant metal hives, but surely not to have it fall and almost crush me. None of my dreams of revenge were so large.

But as the while grew longer and the sounds of the forest returned, so did my courage. I was still alive. The mountain had fallen, but I had not. I would see what had happened.

It was harder to get out of the hole than it had been to get in. I had to let my travel pouches slip off behind me. Pulling loose, I stood up, brushed myself off, and looked around.

And all was changed.

The metal hive was gone, but so was the forest in that place. All that remained was a mud flat with sharp-edged boulders sticking up. The glowing mass lay half-buried, steam rising from the ground around it. With no hive and no forest, everything was open to the sky. I blinked at the brightness. I could feel it warming already. The fog was thinning. I did not like this new feeling of openness. It was like the rocky land above cloud: nothing would grow here again.

I covered myself in handfuls of mud to protect my skin, then pulled on my travel pouches, wrapping them around me like a blanket. That was when I realized I had dropped my blowpipe.

I checked the pouches. Not there. I looked at the mud and the broken stone, and knew there was no hope of getting it back. I thumped the tree with my palm. I would make another, of course, but this one had been a favourite.

Staying in the cover of the forest, I followed the edge of the mud flat, in the direction the hive had fallen, slipping among the ferns, creeping around the bulbtrees, listening to the undergrowth as it rustled, and wondering what could make a hive fall.

Then my foot fell on something that was not dirt or plant. I jerked back and brought up my hands to fight off whatever animal might leap. But I had not been careless. The reason I had not heard this animal in the undergrowth was because it was not moving.

And it was not an animal. It was an invader.

It was a boy.

CHAPTER THIRTEEN
AFTER THE FALL

EK-TAAK-TOCK-TAAK:

Though he was an invader, I was surprised at how much he was shaped like me, and how much his skin was like mine.

He wore that strange woven covering I had heard from the Elder's stories, but had not really believed in. I could not see the sense in it even now. You could carry hardly anything in those coverings, and they were surely too hot to wear.

But . . . I fingered a strand of his hair, and then a strand of mine. I had imagined, through the Elder's stories, that the invaders were hairy all over. He *had* hair, but mine was longer.

Blood ran down his face from a cut on his forehead. I wondered if he was dead, but then I saw his chest rise and fall.

He is an invader, I thought. *He is one of* them. *I should leave him here. Maybe I should kill him. Yes . . .*

I pulled my favourite bone knife from its pouch and raised it, ready to slice across his throat, when something stopped me. What was that smell? I knelt close to the invader and sniffed deep. He smelled . . . strangely sweet. Not like sweat, or mud, though those scents were there. He smelled like . . . flowers. I sniffed again, but that was all I could smell. Curse this inadequate nose!

Still, I had not expected the invaders to smell like flowers.

Parts of his face were very pale, as though he was splashed with colour. I recognized those splashes. He had been burned.

My fingers traced over the lines on his face. He looked a bit like . . .

My brother. Ek-Tek.

He shifted and murmured. I jerked my fingers away. He groaned, then fell still again. The cut by his hairline looked deep. It needed attention.

If I wanted him to live, that is.

After a breath, I put my knife away. I sorted through my travel pouches until I found the leaves I was looking for. *Pointed top to clot blood, fern to bind it.* I wadded both leaves up and chewed them carefully, testing the mix on my tongue. When it was ready, I rolled the wad in my fingers with a small amount of mud. Then I lifted up his hair and placed the ball over the wound, pressing it down and spreading it out. The blood caught in it immediately and stopped flowing.

Just then came a buzzing above the clouds. One of the invaders' strange insect-like fliers, come to see what had happened to their fallen hive, no doubt.

The invader boy groaned and shifted again. His eyelids fluttered. I gathered my things and slid under the cover of the ferns to watch as he recovered.

• • •

SIMON:

I woke to the sound of ornithopters buzzing overhead.

For a moment I lay where I was, staring up at the glowing whiteness. Was I back in the infirmary, under the influence of morphium again? Why else had the ceiling gone fluffy? There was something weird about this, but the mattress hugged me down, and I didn't want to move. If only the ornithopter pilots wouldn't practise their moves outside my window.

Then I thought, *The Iapyx infirmary doesn't have a window anymore. It couldn't have. Not after . . .*

Wait.

I blinked. My eyes opened wider. I shut them as my head began pounding. Every part of my body was in pain. Again. I writhed and groaned and curled up among the plants, retching.

When I opened my eyes again, I stared a long moment at the curling patterns of the fern leaves, wondering what I was staring at and why I was staring at it.

Then it all came back to me in a rush. I stood up, gasping, and immediately staggered and fell back. I jumped up again as if burnt. I staggered around, staring, my breathing ragged, taking in the plants and the fog, feeling the hot moisture bead on my skin.

I'm alive, I thought. After all that, how could I be alive?

It was better than being dead, a part of me said, but the rest of my mind screamed. I was worse than dead. I was in the fog forest.

Around me, vegetation rustled. I heard hoots and cries and snarls in the underbrush. Every foggy shadow hid a monster. I thought I could hear ticking in the foliage.

The Grounders had wanted to colonize *this*? What were they thinking? A fern frond brushed my shoulder and I whirled around, yelling, my fists up.

The voice of my flight instructor echoed in my head: *Get hold of yourself! Here and now, you are alive. The only thing that can really kill you is panic, so that's what you need to get control of.*

I took deep breaths, holding each one for several seconds before letting it go.

Then I thought, *ornithopters.*

Of course! The other cities! They must have seen the semaphore fall. They'd come to the rescue.

In this forest, the only directions I was sure of were down and up, but as another ornithopter passed overhead, I used the sound in its wake to point me toward my ruined home.

I stumbled on the uneven ground, my body protesting every move, but adrenaline pushed me forward. I touched a tender spot on my forehead. A wad of mud and mashed plants came away in my hand. I touched the tender spot again, and my fingers came away with enough blood to tell me I'd cut my head open.

My brain was addled from shock, as well as from the hit I'd taken in my fall. It was hard enough concentrating on staying upright. If I thought about anything else, like Rachel —

No! Don't think about her! Whatever you do, don't think about her!

Then, up ahead I heard . . . yes! Hammers! The buzz of chainsaws! I wanted to shout, tell them I was here, but I was out of breath. I stumbled closer, like a dying man toward an oasis. I topped a ridge and stopped. I heard . . . singing.

Someone was singing. A single female voice, carrying crisp and brittle through the fog. How could someone be singing?

Then I recognized the song, and understood. It was a town crier, from one of the other cities. She was there to sing the Lament.

I'd heard the Lament at Mom's funeral. They may have sung it for Dad's. Now they sang it for Iapyx, while hammers banged and chainsaws roared. I shuddered with sudden cold.

Suddenly a light flooded the foggy air around me. "Who goes there!"

A grey shape solidified out of the fog. I flinched, thinking it was one of Nathaniel's men. But when he came up to me, I could see the hammer and cog insignia on his sleeve. He worked for Daedalon.

He looked at me like he was seeing a ghost. "Where did you come from?"

"Out—" My voice cracked. "Out there."

He stared at me, open-mouthed. Then he holstered his gun. "You're a *survivor*?"

I nodded. A mistake up there with shaking.

He caught my arm as I stumbled, but I pulled away and looked toward the fog-shrouded ruins. "Are there others? Did they get out?"

He sucked his teeth. "A few dozen from the wreckage, so far. And about two hundred people managed to escape beforehand by ornithopter."

The crier sang.

> "What is this that I can't see
> With ice-cold hands taking hold of me?
> Well I am Death, none can excel,
> I open the door to heaven and hell."

Two hundred survivors. Out of five thousand. Of the remainder . . . I thought of schoolchildren, battery boys and girls, pilots and surgeons. Ethan, whom I'd told to lie low so he could stay safe. Marni. Gabriel. My friends . . . Rachel.

My knees gave out and he hauled me up.

"Are you okay?" the guard asked.

I struggled to focus on him, a thousand questions in my mind. For some reason, the first one to come out was, "How'd you get here so fast?"

"Fast? It's been hours. We sent out ornithopters as soon as we saw your semaphore fall." He shuddered as if he'd seen it himself. "Then the mayor of Iapyx arrived. He told us what happened, and we started the rescue and cleanup in earnest. Everybody's in a panic."

"The mayor . . ." I frowned. *Why was that news disturbing?*

But then he caught sight of my insignia.

"Wait a minute." His brow furrowed. "You're a communications worker . . . Are you Simon Daud?"

I have never been smart enough to lie. "Yes."

He stared at me, his eyes all over my face. Then he looked away. "Oh, man."

He was starting to pulse and blur. I realized I wasn't too far from passing out.

The guard shook his head. "No."

"No? What do you mean, no?" Then I thought: Why does this man have a gun?

"You're an accused terrorist, Simon Daud. One of the people on the anchor." He jerked his head back to where Iapyx used to be.

"But — I didn't —"

"I know," he said. "But that's what everyone's saying. The call went out as soon as Nathaniel Tal arrived. He blamed the Grounders. He said you were one of them. If you show your face to any other soldier, you'll be arrested — assuming you're not shot on sight. Tal's orders."

"What?" I shouted. The guard waved his hands frantically for me to keep my voice down. "Nathaniel's *here*?" I hissed. "You've got to help me." I took a step forward. "Please! You've got to tell them the truth!"

He clenched his teeth. I saw his Adam's apple bob. "I can't."

The world dropped from beneath my feet. Again. "What do you mean you can't? You just said you know I had nothing to do with this! You—" The light dawned. "You're a Grounder too!"

"Don't say that!" He jerked around, making sure we were alone. He lowered his voice to a whisper. "They've banned the group! They're arresting the members in all the cities!"

"All of them?"

"Octavia and Daedalon, for sure. The others, once the news reaches them."

"You've got to help me!"

"I can't."

"I can't survive in the fog forest on my own!"

"I'm sorry! If they find out I've helped you, I'll be arrested! My family will be arrested!"

"Please!" I grabbed his arm. "I'll die out here! You've got to listen to me! Nathaniel —"

He shoved me back. "I'm sorry, but you've got to go, or you're under arrest!" He swung up his gun at me, released the safety catch and shouted over his shoulder. "I've found Simon Daud! Come quickly!" He glared at me. "Go!" he hissed.

I could hear heavy boots tramping toward us. I

staggered away, until I could barely hear their voices in the fog. Then I tripped and landed face-first in a clump of ferns.

I froze when I heard Nathaniel's voice. "Sergeant Gaal." I heard the click of a gun. "What did you see?"

"I–I'm sorry, sir," said the sergeant. "I thought I saw something in the fog. Might have been an animal. Guess I was spooked, sir."

Nathaniel grunted. "We're all spooked, sergeant. Keep it together. I'll get your chief to send another guard to keep watch with you. I think we need to double up."

"Good idea, sir."

I pushed myself up and struggled through the underbrush, not knowing where I was going, except away from my home. Away from everything. I didn't know what else to do.

The crier's voice followed me into the forest.

"No wealth, no land, no silver, no gold
Nothing satisfies me but your soul.
I am Death, I take your soul
Leave the body and leave it cold."

The air felt like cotton batting — soft and thick. Black shapes of ferns and trees appeared with every step I took. The heat pressed in on me. My feet slipped in mud and splashed in puddles. All around me leaves rustled and creatures mocked, their snarls and cries like laughter.

When I stepped into water that rose to my knees, I sloshed back, stared around me, and sobbed. I couldn't survive here. There was no way. Though I knew the forest stretched around me endlessly, I felt closed in. I might as well have been buried alive.

I thought again about just sitting down and staying there until death took me, but I couldn't bring myself to sit down. The ground was too wet.

In the end, I turned and walked along the shore of the swamp. I had no idea where I was going. All I knew was that I couldn't go back.

Then something ahead of me roared.

My heart pounded. Nearby, somewhere, something stamped the undergrowth. The creature roared again.

No ticking. Not a ticktock monster. But still very large, very fierce, and probably very able to catch and eat me if it wanted to. The sounds were coming closer.

I could not see myself living much longer. Already, my legs ached with exhaustion. The joints of my hands were tightening up. I had no idea what food to eat or even if the water was safe to drink. But I heard the words of the CommController in my head. *If I am to die, let it be on my own terms, and not cowering in some hideaway.*

I picked a direction, and hoped I was right. I staggered on.

Branches battered me, and I heard the creature roar and smash through the foliage. It seemed to be coming closer. I changed direction. A leafy bush loomed up. I raised my hands, about to crash into its branches, when a small shape shot up beside me, grabbed my arm and swung me back.

I fell backward into the brush. The small monster wrapped itself around me and sat on my chest. I yelled and punched, but the monster grabbed my wrists and pinned them over my head. I shouted and kicked. I would not be some lizard's dinner! I would not!

Then something lunged into my field of vision and let out a ferocious series of snaps and clicks. Brown hair brushed my face. But this wasn't why I froze. I stopped moving because I saw a face staring back at me. It was a human face.

It was a girl.

CHAPTER FOURTEEN
THE GIRL OF THE FOG FOREST

SIMON:

The girl was about my age or maybe a year younger. Her skin was olive-dark and stained with mud. She had on skins or something that matched the olive of her cheeks. Her brown eyes bored into me as she held my wrists down with one hand and stuffed my mouth with her fist. Her eyes flicked up to the forest behind me.

There was a ferocious stamping in the under-growth, then a roar, closer than ever. The girl gnawed her lip. The crashing grew louder. A shadow loomed up in the fog.

She took her fist from my mouth and then, palm toward her, swiped it through the air in front of her lips. I took her meaning and stayed quiet.

It seemed an age, but finally the tramping started to fade. We waited until all we heard was the rustle and smaller cries of the forest. She still pinned my arms above my head with one hand. My shoulders ached, but I didn't dare move.

"Who are you?" I asked.

She looked me up and down with little jerks of her head. Her brow furrowed and her half-opened mouth showed her teeth. Then she opened her mouth, and . . . ticktocked!

My mind flashed to the stories I'd read and the games I'd played as a kid. The ticktock monsters! I struggled against her grip, but I was exhausted and she was wiry and strong. She pushed down on my wrists and clicked loudly in my face.

Gradually, my mind started working again. If she was a monster — and she didn't look like a monster — she wasn't going to attack, at least not yet. I stared up at her, gasping, but calming down.

She opened her mouth and made that strange ticking noise again, a series of clicks. She looked at me sharply, as though waiting for an answer, and that's when I realized she had been speaking to me.

Speaking in the language of the ticktock monsters.

"Um," I said. "Uh . . . I–I'm sorry. I don't understand you."

She jerked her head with obvious contempt. Then she fixed me with a meaningful glare and released my wrists. She crouched there, hands poised while I was careful to lie still. This seemed to satisfy her, and she climbed off me. She crouched down a few paces away and began sorting through one of her bags.

I sat up — with difficulty — and stared at her. Who was she? Where had she come from? She was human, there was no doubt about that, even if she spoke in the monsters' language. She had human hair and human eyes and skin and she was wearing —

My mouth fell open when I realized she wasn't wearing anything. At all. The skins that covered her were nothing more than carrying sacks. The clothing element was accidental. I had never seen women wearing clothes that showed anything more than an ankle. I blushed furiously.

The girl frowned at me. Without a second glance, she pulled off one of the bags and set it on the ground. I looked away.

I pushed myself up. She watched me warily as she sorted through her bags. I opened my mouth. "Um . . ." I had no idea what to say. "Uh . . ." This was worse than speaking to Isaac.

The girl looked up and said something else in her click language — something that required her to snap her fingers twice. I shook my head.

She tried clicking again. I shrugged. She flinched at that, looking bewildered, so I tried holding out my hands, palms up, miming bafflement.

She turned away with a click. She went to the bush I'd almost run into. Her face lit up and she let out a happy squeak, tapping her knuckles together. She stepped forward, opening one of her bags, and began pulling off leaves.

I staggered to my feet and stared at her. "What are you doing?"

The girl glanced at me over her shoulder, said nothing, and returned to her work.

Around me, the animals hooted and cried. In the distance, I thought I heard the crash and roar of the creature the girl had saved me from. I took a step toward her. Then I staggered, and clutched the stalk for support.

The bush she was pulling leaves from — the one she'd stopped me from crashing into — was round as a globe and a metre tall. Nearby were smaller, spiny globes. Even in a forest full of plants I'd never seen before, these were distinctive. What oddly shaped leaves! I reached out.

The girl batted my hand away. Her click language wasn't much good for shouting, but she managed it.

"What?" I rubbed my wrist.

She chittered at me and pointed at the bush with her index and middle finger. I looked at the bush and back at her. I shrugged. Her brow furrowed at that and after a moment of silence she clacked at me again, and pointed again. Then she tapped my chest with her fist and did a two-finger point at the ground. *Stay there*, I thought that meant. Well, I could do that.

She stepped into a swampy puddle, wading toward a thin-leaved, long-stemmed plant. After a brief struggle, she pulled the long stem from the ground and held it like a javelin as she waded back to me.

She reached with this pole and eased the leaves of the globe plant aside. She looked at me, clicked, and tilted her head toward the opening.

That's when I saw the animal skeleton trapped within, thorns lacing through the bones. I felt the blood drain from my cheeks. The world swayed. Then again, that was probably just me.

The girl clicked twice. Using the pole, she eased me back. Dizzy, I eased myself back on the ground. She stepped to the plant.

"What are you do—"

She snapped off thorns. She worked fast, but expertly, shoving the thorns through little holes in one of her carrying bags — one of the thickest and most heavily padded, I noticed. She also took care not to get scratched.

Then she walked back to the stiff-stemmed plant and snapped smaller twigs off, peering down the length of them and tossing them aside until she selected two. The larger of these was hollow, and she used the smaller one to clean it out, blowing through it occasionally to test.

"What are you making?" I said. But the girl kept cleaning out that tube of hers.

She picked up the carrying bag she'd set down and put it on. She looked at me, her gaze running me up and down. I felt myself thoroughly appraised. Then she clicked and nodded over her shoulder. The meaning was obvious, especially when she turned to go.

I hesitated. Did I just get up and follow her? Yes, she'd saved me from that animal, but . . . who was she? How could she *be* there? And speaking in the language of the ticktock monsters? How could I possibly figure out who she was if I couldn't even talk to her? Could I trust her?

Suddenly, there was a crash of vegetation, and the air beside me went black. A lizard — possibly the same one the girl had rescued me from — leapt with a roar, its claws outstretched.

In one smooth moment, the girl pulled out her hollow twig, shoved a thorn inside it, brought the twig to her lips and blew. The thorn zinged past my ear and struck the creature in the chest. Its roar turned to a screech, and it crashed to the ground at my feet. I leapt aside.

The girl let out a wordless cry of triumph — clearly she could make sounds other than ticking — shoved her new blowpipe back into its pocket, and knelt by the creature. It was breathing, but just barely. The girl wrapped her arms around its neck and gave the head a sharp twist. There was a crack, and the creature's stiff limbs relaxed. I stood there, my face frozen in a grimace of shock and horror.

She hefted the lizard onto her shoulders like a big sack, and stood up. She looked at me, clicked twice and nodded over her shoulder. She turned away without another word, slipping through the underbrush.

I cast a glance at the impression the creature had

left in the soft ground. Before the fog shrouded the girl from sight, I turned and followed her.

• • •

EK-TAAK-TOCK-TAAK:

I did not know what to expect when I got to the invaders' metal hives, though I imagined many things. What I had not imagined was that I would find an invader boy and make him my responsibility.

But once I had decided to let him live, he became my responsibility. He would have died otherwise. Even if he had been in good health, he was not prepared for the dangers of the forest. And he was not in good health. He walked slowly, stiff and limping, leaning on anything that could offer support.

The strange invader boy followed me as I made my way up the slope toward the side of the chasm. He stumbled back, startled, when the cliff face emerged from the fog. He was that hopeless.

The gurgle of water told me I was close. A few steps later along the rock wall, I found a cold stream pouring from the cliff face. It had cut a hole into the rock large enough for me to step inside without lowering my head. The air smelled clear. No animal had made the cave its home.

I turned to the invader boy. « In here. » I tilted my head at the cave to make my meaning clear. It seemed to work. He followed me.

The heat left me after a few steps. This was the one

thing I hated about these caves. Though shelter and shade were welcome, there was too much of it here. I would need to build a fire. But the cave opened up as I entered. It looked large enough to handle a fire and — here! — was a dry spot where I could put the slink down and lay the tinder.

The boy looked around and took deep breaths. He seemed to like the cold. I left him as he fell to his knees beside the stream and ran his hand through the water.

I took off all my carrying bags and set them around me. That was when I heard a splash. The boy had fallen into the stream. He sat, staring at me, the water coursing over his lap. Then he looked away quickly. I could not stop myself from laughing — he looked so silly — but I had work to do. I went outside, returning with an armload of sticks.

The boy had pulled himself up beside the stream and sat, twisting water from the fabric that covered him.

At the centre of the bank, I shifted a large stone so it was flat. Then, from one of my pouches, I pulled out the round container of firepills I had taken from a hut in my village. There were not many left, but I was in no mood to build a fire from scratch.

The boy stared as I took the firepill from the container. Again he spoke in that howler-climber language of his.

I placed the firepill on the stone and whacked it with a stick. Flame leapt up. I held the stick over the flame until it caught. Then I piled on more sticks, making a fire gather.

The boy crept forward, his eyes on the shiny canister. I let him take a few more steps before I put the canister back in its pouch. I pulled out my second-favourite bone knife and went to work on the slink's sinewy flesh. The boy backed away.

Soon, two hunks of meat were sizzling on the stone. The smell made my mouth water. Looking up, though, I saw the boy draw back, a look on his face that was not quite fear, more like disgust, with a touch of sorrow.

The boy pulled himself to his feet, limped to the cave mouth and stared out at the fog. He walked as though he was in pain. That should not be surprising. Given that he had fallen out of his hive, I was surprised he was not hurt more. But this pain looked old. Maybe it had to do with his burnscars.

Soon our meal was ready. I placed the meat on large leaves that I had brought in from outside, and I held it out to him, « Here, take this. »

He hesitated when I held out the leaf-wrapped meat, staring at it as though it were still alive. I frowned at that. Surely he should be hungry?

But he took the meat from my hand and took a bite. We sat by the stream, the fire between us, and started to eat.

I stared at him while he ate his meal. It was clear that whatever I had thought I was going to do when I got to the invaders' hives was not going to work.

But I had seen a hive fall. This boy had landed at my feet, and his people would not let him go home. That meant something. Maybe he knew why the hive had fallen. Maybe I could ask him. But how, when his language was so different from mine?

Perhaps this was a question best answered after sleep. I ate my meat, washed my hands in the stream, and got up. The boy looked up from his half-eaten morsel.

« I will come back, » I said, and stepped outside. I returned with my arms full of fern fronds. The boy stood up as I entered, wincing as he did. I measured out half of my bundle and tossed the fronds on the ground in front of him. He looked at the leaves, and then at me.

How could he not see the meaning? I began arranging my fronds on a flat area in a corner of the cave. As I worked, I glanced back. I saw the boy pick up his ferns. He looked at my work and began spreading them around where he stood. He worked clumsily, but he worked.

Finally, I placed a leaf-wrapped stone where I would lay my head and stepped back and looked at what I had done. It would serve.

Then the boy called me. He stood beside his pile of leaves. He pointed to it with one finger and squealed something.

I tilted my head. My shoulders ached at the thought of how his shoulders would ache when he woke from sleep — if he did find sleep. But I was tired and in no mood to help him rebuild his nest, or gather more ferns to help him pad it.

Then I looked again at the strange fabric that covered his body. That might do for something soft to lie on. « Try that, » I said, pointing.

He looked at my fingers, then at his chest. He did not understand.

« These! » I pulled at his sleeve. « Use these. That will make you comfortable and you can sleep. »

He pulled away at my touch. I could not believe it. He wanted to keep these things on!

« These are silly. » I gripped the fabric that covered his chest and pulled. « You cannot carry anything in them, and they will make you too hot. Use these as padding and get a good sleep! »

But the boy jerked back and pulled the covering tighter against himself. The fabric was surprisingly strong.

« Fine, » I snapped at him. « Be like that. Silly thing. »

I stomped to my side of the cave, angry with myself as much as with him. Why should I care that he wanted to keep his silly coverings on? He was an invader boy; it was not my concern. I sat down in my nest and speared him a glare. Then I rolled over and lay down my head for sleep.

I sensed the invader boy's gaze on my back for a while before finally I heard him settle into his nest. As I had expected, he rolled around and mumbled a lot, but he must have been more tired than I thought. After another little while, he was asleep.

I thought about what I would do next. I thought long, because there were no answers. Sleep found me first.

And in my dreams, I returned to my mother.

Her nest had been laid out by the Elder herself, but Mother had slumped against the side. Her eyes, which had so recently gone white, stared out at nothing.

I settled beside her and stroked her cheek with the back of my hand. Softly, I began to murmur the comforting sounds she had murmured to me when I was sick; sounds she had learned from *her* mother many sun-turns before.

Her head jerked. « Daughter? »

« I am here. »

« I am not, » my mother replied. « I feel myself fading. Tell the Elder. It is almost time. »

« Do not go, » I begged. « Please. »

« I cannot help it, » she replied. « I am spent. This place takes away my life, just as it took away your father's life, and your brothers'. »

« I do not want to be alone! »

My mother shifted. Her voice changed. « The Elder tells me you plan to go to the invaders' hives. »

I hesitated before answering, but I could not hide the truth. « Yes. »

« Do not be a fool. »

« The invaders need to pay for what they have done to us! »

« Daughter — »

Suddenly my mother cried out. I flinched at the sound. « Mother! I will get the Elder — »

« No! » My mother rested her fist on my arm. « No. I need — I must tell you — Please . . . »

She took a deep breath, though it seemed to hurt. Then, though she was blind, she looked right at me.

« Daughter, » she said. « Tend to your ancestors' graves. »

My jaw tightened. « I cannot. Do not ask me to. »

Her words cut me: « The invaders are your people, too. »

Then she died.

I woke with a gasp. The cave was cold. The fire had burned to embers. On the other side, the strange invader boy lay curled up in his hollow, snarling in his sleep.

I glared at his back. « I am not like you, » I snapped. Then I settled back in my nest and fell asleep again.

CHAPTER FIFTEEN
BURNSCAR

EK-TAAK-TOCK-TAAK:

The boy's mumbles and squawks made for a fitful sleep. « Be quiet, » I snapped.

Then he screamed.

His cry jerked me out of my nest to look for the lizard that had gotten into the cave and was trying to eat us. But there was no lizard. There was only the boy, screaming in his sleep.

I stomped over and grabbed at his arms. They were crossed across his chest and would not move aside. I shook him. « Wake up! » I clicked. « Wake up! You dream too bright! »

The screams stopped, and he stared at me in bewilderment and fear. Some expressions your body knows ahead of your mind.

I could feel his heart thumping against my

fingers as I held his arms. I felt his beat slow as he calmed down.

Then he began to gasp for air.

He pulled back against my grip. He gaze went up toward the ceiling. His arms stayed across his chest.

That's when I realized he could not move his arms. He could not move anything.

My heart sped up. I had only seen so much pain once before.

I eased him onto his nest, carefully unlocked his arms and pulled them to his side. Every move seemed to make a wind-blow of pain. When he was flat and straight, I gathered the ferns from my own bed and stuffed them under him, making him more comfortable. But still his breath came in short, sharp gasps.

What had happened? If it had been the fall that had done this to him, he would not have been able to follow me here. What were his coverings hiding from me?

His coverings were cut through with a line of metal teeth. There was a handle at the top of this line. Curious, I pulled it down, and the teeth gaped apart. I pulled the flaps of strange hide aside, and found another covering, this one without the line of teeth. The only way to remove it would be to pull it over his head, and I could not do this without causing the boy pain.

But his gasps continued. I had to do something.

I got my pouch of bone knives and picked a sharp

one, with a handle that curved away — for fitting under things and slicing up. I went back to the boy and raised this knife in the air.

He stared at it, wide-eyed.

« Come now, strange boy, » I said. « If I wanted to kill you, would I have saved you and fed you? »

I brought the tip beneath the covering, and sliced it open. I pulled the new flaps aside.

Great Mother of the Sky! His chest was almost all burnscar.

How had he walked this far? How had he even survived?

But I knew now why he could not breathe. I knew how to ease the pain.

« Stay, » I told him. I poked the embers of our fire until flames leapt up from it, then added wood. I placed large, round stones the size of my fist around the fire, and I stepped out of the cave, returning with the fat, meaty leaves of the bowl-plant. I draped them across the boy's chest. He looked down. His eyebrows arched up.

Finally, a leaf in my palm, I picked up a stone near the fire. It made the leaf hiss steam, scalding my palm, but I wrapped the leaf around the stone, and turned to place it on the boy.

Fear came back to his face. He squawked something. He did not want this, but he did not know that it would be good for him. I could only show him, and he could not stop me.

He cried out as I placed the hot rock on his

shoulder. Then, almost instantly, the cry became a groan. The muscles of his chest relaxed, and he breathed deeper.

« As I told you, silly boy, » I said, softly.

I placed a second leaf-wrapped stone on his other shoulder, and a third on his chest. Even his tightly clenched fingers relaxed.

His eyes drifted up. He murmured something I could not understand, but it was soft, grateful.

Before I realized it, I started murmuring my mother's sounds of comfort, a soft, soothing rhythm, with tones that flowed up and down.

And the boy . . . sang it back. He was half conscious, but I saw his mouth moving. As I listened, I heard the same rising and falling tones. His noises were different; fuller. Were these words in the boy's howler-climber language?

The boy's eyes fluttered closed. Within breaths, he was asleep.

I put on my travel pouches, grabbed my spear and left the cave.

Outside, I looked at the cave mouth and thought about what I should do to hide it. I would be tied here for days as the boy recovered. If I left on a hunt, he would be easy prey for the first slink to nose its way in.

And when he got better, what then? I thought about leading him anywhere with his slow, limping gait; helping him over logs. He would slow me down. And in the forest, slow was dead.

But he was an invader boy, cast out by the invaders. He was my best hope for revenge.

And . . . I had seen burnscars like that before. My brother, the one nearest to me in age, had been caught in a boiling wind and horribly scalded. He had survived, but his injuries had made him easy prey. We tried to protect him, but there were not enough of us, and eventually someone . . .

Eventually I made a mistake . . .

I closed my eyes against the memory. My hatred of the invaders burned. They had cast out a boy who had been injured worse than my brother. The boy could not survive in the forest. How could those people be so cruel?

I was also angry at myself. Had I known he was this badly hurt, I would have helped him build his nest.

But I could help him stay alive.

I snapped off branches and long stalks, and whittled these down to points. Across the mouth of the cave, I wove a low fence, the points of the branches sticking up and out, ready to impale any slink that dared to cross.

The boy slept. I decided he was safe enough for me to look at the ruins again.

The fog had disappeared where the metal hive had clawed out the forest. The sky was open. I flinched from the brightness of it, then pulled back under the cover of the forest edge as one of the mechanical insects roared overhead. The ferns crunched beside me. The leaves here were brown and brittle like the edges of a scab. I wondered if the forest would ever heal. The forest around my village had not, fully.

More flying machines buzzed overhead, and I watched as they settled on the ground near the fallen hive. People in white or grey coverings climbed over the carcass like scavenging mites. The ones in grey, I saw, had wrapped themselves in white to hide themselves from the sun. I clicked my tongue. What a strange people.

I followed the edge of the gouge, heading toward the ruins. As I approached, I heard machines and voices as they worked on the carcass. Stranger still, I heard someone howling . . . not howling. There were words in the noise, like the boy's voice. There was music in it too.

I pressed as close as I could and found a place where the ferns were thick. I pushed through and peered out at the wreckage.

They had cut into the fallen hive. The area was littered with things that had once been smooth and were now twisted, and strange machines that the white-covered people surrounded and looked over. Some of these were loaded onto one of the flying machines, at rest, now, on the mud flat beside a new lake.

On a rise at the other end of the clearing, a woman in white stood with her hands at her sides. The strange howl came from her.

I looked back at the invaders, some less than fifty

steps in front of me. I had almost despaired when I had come to the death-dealing fence, but here were my targets. I might never get a better chance than this for revenge.

I pulled my bone knife from its pouch. It wasn't my favourite, but it would do. Behind cover, I clicked at them. « *Tik-tik-tik-tik*. Hello, invaders. I am coming for you! »

Two invaders, carrying something from the ruins on a board between them, looked up at the noise. It was as I had been told: The invaders were afraid of our voices. « Yes, be afraid! *Tik-tik-tik-tik!* »

The invaders screamed, dropped the board they were carrying, and ran. More invaders shouted. The wailing woman stopped her voice. I tightened my grip on the bone knife and prepared to pounce.

Then I saw what was on the board they were carrying. They had pulled it from the wreckage, but it was not a machine. They had covered it with something white. It was —

Oh.

Farther along the mud flat, two invaders walked to the edge of a hole they had dug in the ground, tipped their board, and let the body fall in. They looked up when they heard the shouts.

A shout caught my attention — a tall man calling to the people clambering over the wreckage. Of those wearing the grey coverings, he alone did not wrap himself in a cape of white. He was all grey, even his hair, like smoke. I peered out from behind the cover of a bulbtree for a better look, and put my hand on a branch. The branch snapped and fell into the dry ferns with a crash.

The grey man turned and stared at where I was. He pulled a tube from his belt and pointed it. The tube sparkled.

Suddenly the trunk of another bulbtree burst out in little holes, as if blowdarts were whipping past.

I ducked behind the bulbtree and curled into a ball. The whistling and the snapping of the leaves stopped, and voices came closer. I struggled to my feet and looked for a place to hide, but saw that running was better. I ran into the forest. The voices faded behind me.

I returned to the cave, stepped over the fence, and found the boy where I had left him, snarling in his sleep. I set my travel pouches around me, pulled my knees to my chest and thought about the events of the past few sleeps.

I had lived longer than I had thought I would, but it was clear my plans were useless. On the other side of the leaf, Father Fate had given me something I had never expected to receive.

I looked at the sleeping boy.

I had made him my responsibility, but what else was he?

How could he help my future?

CHAPTER SIXTEEN
PEACE OFFERING

SIMON:

The mysterious girl sang to me.

My next few days were an echo of my time in the infirmary, this one spent in firelight instead of a bright hospital room. I could do little more than sleep, while this dark-haired stranger slipped into and out of my dreams. But I was sure her song wasn't a dream, because I had to work to recognize it.

> *Rockabye baby, on the treetop.*
> *When the wind blows, the cradle will rock.*
> *When the bough breaks, the cradle will fall,*
> *And down will come baby, cradle and all.*

She wasn't singing the words. I only recognized the tune, an ancient song from Old Mother Earth that I remembered from my childhood. It struck me that she could sing as well as click.

The tune was comfort, especially after the nightmares.

The girl tended to me, rubbing chewed-up leaves on my chest, applying more hot rocks to my sternum. Slowly, my cramped muscles unclenched, and the ache of my burns receded.

Then one morning, I woke with a gasp and found I could sit up. A blanket of leaves (an echo of my hospital robe, I guess) fell off me as I looked around the cave, lucidly, for the first time in days. The girl wasn't there; probably off hunting. The fire had burned down to embers.

My communications uniform had been piled into a makeshift pillow. Thinking of the girl coming back and seeing me in nothing but a blanket of leaves brought me to my feet, albeit slowly, wincing as the rocks bit into the soles of my feet. I picked through my clothes. My shirt was cut in half, but my tunic was fine. With a struggle, I dressed myself.

As I was doing up my tunic, something poked me in the side. I fumbled through the pocket and brought it out, then let out a sound like I'd been punched in the stomach.

Isaac's pocketknife.

Rachel had given it to me to help me mourn Isaac's death, and to move past her own grief. Now she too was dead.

See? Rachel's voice echoed in my head. *Life goes on.*

I gulped. The grief that had been bottled up inside me, corked by shock and pain, bubbled out. Rachel. Life hadn't gone on for her. It wasn't fair.

Fair won't keep your flight level, cadet, Isaac had said.

Isaac. I sat down on the stone, hard. I covered my face and cried for a good long time.

Finally, when I had no more tears, I pulled my head from my hands and looked up at the cave ceiling. Rachel's voice echoed back at me again.

What are you going to do about that? Give up?

I took a deep breath, then let it out slowly. What *was* I going to do?

I had wanted to die, but the Fates had kept me going. Here and now, sitting on a stone in a dark, cool cave, I didn't have the stomach to think of new ways to kill myself.

I frowned at that thought, but it was true. Something in me wasn't ready to die — something that hadn't been there when I had to choose between burning and falling. And wondering why, I realized that dying meant letting Nathaniel Tal win.

I looked at Isaac's knife, resting in the palm of my hand.

Nathaniel had destroyed my city. He'd killed thousands of people. He'd left Rachel and me to die. He'd killed Aaron. Maybe Isaac. Maybe even Mom. He'd killed them all, and unless I did something, he was going to get away with it.

My hand closed around my brother's knife. *No.*

No, he was not going to get away with it. Not

while I still had life. I had the truth, and I would bring him down.

I brought Isaac's pocketknife to my lips. "I swear," I whispered to it. "In the Creator's name, I swear. For Isaac. For Rachel. For Mom." I lowered my hands. "For everybody."

• • •

But how?

I couldn't go to the ruins of Iapyx. I'd be shot on sight. Perhaps I could go to one of the other cities, where the guards were less trigger-happy. If Nathaniel had any say, I'd have little time to tell people what I knew before I was conveniently shot trying to escape. But Nathaniel couldn't be in all the cities at once. He and Matthew seemed to have fled to Daedalon, so I would walk to Octavia.

Walk. To Octavia. Through the fog forest. An hour's flight by ornithopter translated to . . . what? A week's journey by foot? A month? It was madness. Even if I was healthy, I couldn't make it.

I did have an ally — or, at least, I thought she was an ally. She'd fed me, and nursed me back to health. She knew the forest in ways that would take me years to learn. I wouldn't have survived without her.

But she spoke in the language of the ticktock monsters — even the fact that the ticktock monsters *had* a language was a revelation.

Could I ask her to take me to Octavia?

Maybe I could start small, by trying to be useful.

And so I learned that though I didn't understand her language, I could get a good sense of her expressions.

Like the time I tried turning over the meat while her back was turned (I thought it was in danger of burning), burnt my fingers and lost the meat to the flames. She turned at my shout, stared blankly at the empty stone, and then her eyes narrowed and she glared at me.

Or the time she caught me fiddling with one of her bags, fortunately stopping me before I scratched myself on her poison thorns. Her sigh and the shake of her head were easy to translate.

The next day I tried to follow her as she left the cave. She turned sharply and planted her fist on my chest.

I pushed forward. She pushed me back, harder, and said something. The meaning was clear enough.

"I'm fine," I said. "I mean, I'm getting better. I can't stay in this cave anymore; I'll go nuts. I want to see my city—"

But the girl poked me with that two-finger point of hers, pointed at the fire, and then at the wood. She stalked off into the wilderness.

I slunk back to the cave. So the only job she thought I was capable of was fire-stoker. I added a stick to the fire. The worst thing was, she was right. I still couldn't walk far without a break. In the forest, I'd be a drag on her. Of course this was the only sensible place to be. It didn't make me feel any less useless, however.

I glanced at the latest carcass keeping cool in the stream. There was not a lot of meat left, and what remained had been dead a while. We could use a fresh kill.

And as I thought about that, a resolve grew in me. I would show her I wasn't completely helpless. I'd watched her as she moved through the forest toward this cave. I'd already learned some of the plants to avoid. More than that, I already knew of a plant I could use to hunt.

I stepped over the protective fence and followed the gurgling stream until it emptied into a pond. A quick but careful search revealed one of the plants with the long, tough stems. I gripped one and pulled. It was harder than it looked, but finally the shoot came free.

I tested the thing in my hands. It was as long as I was tall, but light. And though it was hollow, it wouldn't bend. The end, however, was smooth and round. This wouldn't do.

Back in the cave, I looked for a stone to carve the end of the stalk into a point. My eyes fell on the bags the girl had left behind. Picking through them, carefully avoiding the one with the thorns, I found one that housed the bone knife she'd used to cut up the lizard. Actually, six knives, all of bone so white they almost glowed in the dark, their blades at least fifteen centimetres long, curved and sharp.

I flipped the bag closed and put it back where I'd found it. Now that I thought about it, I didn't like the idea of how she'd react if I touched her knives. The fact that she had six didn't mean she wasn't attached to them individually. Six knives. Yeah, I would be leaving them alone.

But my hand fell on my pocket and I felt Isaac's pocketknife there. All this time and I hadn't realized that I was holding a tool in my hand. A tool to make other tools.

I set to work whittling the end of the stalk into a point. The stalk snapped twice before I was able to work it into something that could pass for a spear. Finally, I tested the point against the palm of my hand, hurt myself, and was satisfied. This should bring down small game.

I hesitated as I stepped to the protective fence in front of the cave. Was I being foolish, imagining myself a hunter? But what choice did I have? If the girl hadn't found me and shared her food, I'd have had to do this by myself. Enough moping in the safety of a dark cave. I stepped into the forest.

It was at least a week since Solar Maximum, but the day was still bright and hot. As I pushed past the ferns, keeping the water on my left as a guide, I heard Rachel's voice in my head. *What are you doing, Simon? Hunting? With a sharpened stick?*

"What does it look like I'm doing?" I started to mutter, then stopped. A rustling ahead of me sounded promising . . . it suggested something not too big.

You're going to hurt yourself, said Isaac.

Rachel's voice: *You should be asking questions.*

"Why should I? The answers led me here!" My voice caught. "I hate this place."

Well, keep on asking questions, said Rachel. *Maybe they'll lead you out of here. We're Grounders, Simon. We believe that if we stop asking questions, we die.*

"You died anyway," I muttered. "And I wanted to die."

Wanted, said Rachel. *What about now? You have to be curious. Who is this girl? How could she be here? What language does she speak?*

"How do I even begin to answer that?" I snapped. "She's not using words I understand!"

Try, said Isaac. *Just because you haven't tried doesn't mean it's impossible.*

I stopped. "Wait a minute. Should I be hearing you in my head like this?"

Good question, Michael joined in. *And I'll point out that one of the symptoms of heatstroke is hallucinations.*

His voice echoed. I snapped back to reality, though I wasn't sure if I'd ever left it. The heat . . . The heat was oppressive.

I looked at the water, set my spear aside, and knelt down to splash water over my head and neck. That helped clear my head.

Around me, the forest animals chirped, grunted and cackled. I heard stamping in the distant foliage that I knew I needed to avoid. But then a bleat near-by made me stop. I listened, and the sound came again, to my right, and near the ground.

There were ferns in the way, and twiggy branches. I didn't see any thorns. I pushed the plants aside and crept through, as quietly as I could.

That's when I saw it — a little lizard, less than half a metre long. Kind of scrawny and slightly helpless looking. Rather like me. I raised my spear high.

The creature looked up at me and bleated. I stopped my spear halfway through its arc.

The creature was small. Just a baby, really. What in the Creator's name was I doing killing a baby animal?

But we needed food, and I wasn't going to rely on some wild woman of the forest to take care of me. Never mind about my dignity; if I didn't start pulling my weight, she might abandon me as the useless burden I was.

I hefted my spear again. "Sorry, little friend," I said. "It's you or me."

The creature bleated once more. I hesitated again, and not in a tender-hearted way. It was a baby.

Babies have . . .

The giant lizard hit me from behind so hard, I sank into the ground where I landed. I struggled to get up, to turn around, but the creature bashed me into the ground again. Then it rolled me onto my back and sat on my legs. I stared into a snout full of many sharp teeth. Hot air beat against my face. Behind it, the little creature bleated incessantly.

The giant lizard batted at me. Its strike caught me

on the jaw. I saw stars, but amazingly I didn't feel myself bleed, or any skin rip away. As the creature raised its forelegs, I saw its claws emerge. It snarled and drew back for a slashing blow. I struggled to free myself, then closed my eyes.

Suddenly its weight was off me, and another voice snarled. I opened my eyes. The girl was standing above me. She'd picked up my spear and was fending off the giant lizard with fierce stabs and lunges. It backed up, but roared and lunged at her.

The girl struck twice with the spear, but then the creature batted at it. The spear snapped and fell from the girl's grip. She glanced at her bare hands, but quickly lunged forward, snarling, baring her teeth. She crouched, her shoulders and back arching. She stamped her hands on the ground.

Though the creature was twice her size, spitting, and making short lunges at her, she stayed where she was, hissing, snapping and then roaring when it got too close. Finally, it turned away, gently picked up its baby in its teeth, and crashed into the forest.

The girl snatched up the pointed half of my spear and pulled me upright. Her eyes were wide and her cheeks pale, and she took several glances behind her while she shoved me forward. We didn't stop running until we reached our cave. That's when she knocked me into the wall and chittered at me in that language of hers. I suspected she was saying, "What in sunlight were you thinking?"

For a moment, I couldn't figure out how to answer

her, but her eyes drilled into me. So, I took my broken spear from her hand and mimed stabbing with it.

The girl turned away with a snort and crackled something else. The campfire had burned down to embers again. The girl shook her head and set to building it up. I tossed the spear to the ground and sat in my makeshift bed, feeling like a scolded child.

The girl got the fire going, then sat a long moment, staring into the flames. Her gaze fell on the remains of my spear. She uncurled herself and picked it up, testing it against the palm of her hand. Her eyebrows flicked up at its sharpness, then she angrily grabbed up the bag of bone knives she'd left behind. Her anger ebbed as she fingered their blades. She must have realized that they were still sharp and that I had not touched them.

I could see the wheels turning. She looked at the point of the spear, and then at me. She said something, and I realized to my surprise that she was asking me a question.

"You want to know how I made that?" I ventured.

She clicked at me, mimed striking with the spear, then pointed at the tip.

Yes, she did, I thought.

I fished out the pocketknife, flipped open the blade, and held it out to her.

She took it, fingered the blade, then jerked her hand away, sucking back a gasp. She turned the blade over in her hands, looking at the way the firelight reflected off the shiny surface.

Had she never seen metal before? But, of course she had. She had that canister of firestarters. But her own knives were handmade from bone. She'd never worked metal; didn't come from a place that knew how. So, where had she got that canister? Could she have stolen it from one of the other cities? How could she have sneaked in?

She picked up the remains of the spear, brought the blade down, and drew it over the shaft, raising a strip of wood. She held up the knife again, open-mouthed. I could tell she was impressed. I couldn't help but smile at that.

She pushed the back of the blade, was surprised to see it move, then pushed some more. Her eyes widened as the blade swung back into its slot. She turned the red lozenge in her hands a long moment, then held it out to me. She clicked something.

"You can have it, if you want," I said. And took a breath of surprise. I'd cried, seeing it. It was my link to Isaac, to Rachel, and now I wanted to give it away?

The girl frowned as I didn't take the knife. She held it out again, but I gently pushed it back.

"No, seriously," I said. "I owe it to you, because you're the only thing keeping me alive out here. I owe you a lot more, but except for the clothes on my back, this is all I have. It's the only link I have to my home and my old life. It's precious. Take it."

She looked thoughtful. Then she stood up and held out my pocketknife. I didn't think I'd be able to push the knife back again. I took it.

Then she handed me the pointy half of the spear. She pointed to it, and then to herself.

"You want me to make you a spear?"

She stepped out of the cave, returning a few minutes later with two long, hollow stems. She held these out. I took them, juggling them with my knife.

"You definitely want me to make you a spear," I said. "All right." Maybe I wasn't as useless as I'd thought.

I set one of the stems aside, took the other one, opened the blade of my knife and started whittling.

She settled down across the fire from me, and clicked something. And, this time, I listened — really listened — to the click. There were differences here; each series of clicks was a word. « *Click, TAK! Tiktik!* »

It was a safe bet that she was thanking me. I wondered what the clicks were for "You're welcome."

Try, came the distant echo of Isaac's voice.

I couldn't imagine how to say "You're welcome," so I repeated what she said to me. I opened my mouth partway, as I'd seen her do it. I tested a few clicks with my tongue, then went for it. « *Click, TAK! Tiktik!* » Maybe repeating "thank you" might convey what I meant.

The girl blinked at me. She opened her mouth. I watched her tongue move. « *Click, TAK! Tiktik! . . . Clock, took?* »

Thank you . . . for the knife? Or for the spear? I

tried again. « *Click, TAK! Tiktik!* » Then I held up the pocketknife. "Knife." I said, enunciating, letting her see my mouth move. "Kniiiiife."

The girl looked from the knife to me, and back again. She pointed at the knife.

Clock, took? I worked my tongue. « *Clock, took.* » Then, "Knife."

The girl opened her mouth. I could see her moving her tongue, uncertainly. Her first sound came out as "ugh!" Then "nuh." I smiled and she tried again. "Nniiiiiffe. Nife."

I nodded. « *Clock, took.* » "Knife."

The girl smiled. So did I.

CHAPTER SEVENTEEN
THE NAMES OF THINGS

EK-TAAK-TOCK-TAAK:

With patience and hard work, we began to talk to each other.

The boy's screeching, ear-grating speech offered more sounds to name things than my own collection of clicks, ticks and snaps. In fact, the boy's words seemed to fit my mouth in a way I had never expected. Once I learned some of his words, it was easier to teach him mine. We did make mistakes. Like the time I tried to teach him to count, and he thought I was naming different stones.

But we kept teaching. We kept learning. We named things as soon as we got up from our sleeps and while we ate our meals. We named the meats and the bones I used to cut them. We named the spear the boy whittled with his impossibly small metal knife. We named the walls, and when we sat by the fire, we named the flames.

Then the boy put his hand to his chest and said, "Simon."

I sat up straight. He had named himself. But then I thought, everything we have picked up here has two names: his and mine. Except for us.

The boy patted his chest. "Simon."

I frowned. How could he hiss like that? There was a wetness to it; not just a breath of air. Not quite a whistle. I tested my own tongue, and blew. "Hhhhhhh . . ." I tightened my tongue against the roof of my mouth, and ended up spraying him with spit, but then I suddenly had it. "Sssssssss." I pulled back. I sounded like a snake! "Ssssssssssiiiiiimon. Sssimon. Simon."

"Simon!" he said, grinning. "Yes. Simon!" He looked as happy as if he'd just killed a huge slink.

"Simon," I said. Then I thought, *What was my name for him?*

I clicked, « *Clok-Taak-Tock-guh.* » Silly Strange Boy. As a name, it seemed appropriate.

He stared at me. I tapped his chest. "Simon," I said. Then, « *Clok-Taak-Tock-guh.* »

He blinked. I think he understood my meaning. He opened his mouth and curled his tongue. « *Clok-tuk-Tock-guh.* » "Simon."

« *Clok-TAAK-Tock-guh,* » I corrected.

« *Clok-TAAK-Tock-guh,* » he replied, grinning. "Simon!"

He *understood*! I smiled. Then I took his wrist

and pressed his hand to my chest. He tried to jerk it away, but I held it against me, and said my own name. « *Ek-Taak-Tock-Taak.* » I looked at him expectantly.

He nodded, and pulled his hand away. « *Ek-Taak-Tock-Taak.* » He smiled, and said something I did not understand. It sounded like "nise."

I said my name again. « *Ek-Taak-Tock-Taak.* » I waited.

He said something, but it sounded wrong to be a name. A question?

Growling, I took his hand and pushed it to his chest. « *Clok-Taak-Tock-guh.* » "Simon." Then I put his hand to my chest. « *Ek-Taak-Tock-Taak!* » Again I waited. « Come now, Silly Strange Boy, I named you. »

He worked his tongue. « *Ek-Taak-Tock-Taak.* » He pulled his hand away and looked at me. "Hmm . . . Eliza?"

I frowned. "Ee-la? Ee-la?"

"Eliza," he said again. "Eeellliiizzzaaa."

Open mouthed, then tongue on roof of mouth, strange whistle, then open mouth again. "Eeellliiiiss-saaa." How did he make that buzzing? "Eelliisszaa—" Wait! "Elisza . . . Eliza!"

"That's it! That's great!" His smile was wide and bright.

I stood up and tapped his shoulder with my fist. "Simon." « Silly Strange Boy. »

He reached for my hand in a strange ritual way. « *Ek-Taak-Tock-Tack.* » "Eliza."

How strange it was to extend fingers as a gesture of friendship. Clearly, it must have been a while since his ancestors had claws.

• • •

Many more sleeps passed. The fallen hive had been picked over. Simon's people left it, after a solemn ceremony that I felt uncomfortable watching, but the mechanical insects kept flying, as though they were looking for something to blame.

As Simon and I stepped over the little fence at the mouth of our cave, another mechanical insect buzzed low. Though we could not see it, we frowned up at it through the fog.

« What do they look for? » I asked.

Simon's brow furrowed as he translated my words. After a breath he said, "I don't know."

I looked at the sky two breaths longer, then hefted my spear. "Come!" I marched into the forest. He clasped his own spear, and followed.

Simon clung to the strangest things, like the white coverings on his body. I saw even less sense in them as the sleeps passed. They picked up dirt. They were little shield against the plants and none against the heat, but he would not take them off. When I came upon him while he was washing, he would pull the coverings on quickly, once falling over in his haste.

But while Simon was silly, he could learn. His new spears were even better than the first one. I could trust him to turn the meat now. He was eager to get out of the cave to learn. So I decided to teach him, starting with how to hunt.

It was not long before I saw signs of our prey. « Look here, Silly Strange Boy. » I pointed.

Simon looked. His brow furrowed as if that would help him look harder. No understanding lit his eyes. How could he not see it? But I reminded myself to be patient.

« Look, » I repeated, trying to chop my words short so he could hear them better. « Track. Prey. We follow. »

I hated doing that. I sounded like a hatchling, or a hatchling mother. I was neither, and Simon was not my child.

Then he pointed, with one thin finger, at a leaf. It was still attached to the plant, but it had been pressed into the muddy ground by a foot. He looked up at me, hopefully. I smiled, then drew my hand across my mouth for silence. He followed me into the underbrush.

It was not long before I smelled the prey. Then I heard it growling as it brushed against a tree. I looked back, and saw Simon focused on following me. Had he heard the quarry at all? I nudged him, and told him to look ahead with a jerk of my head. He looked confused. Then the slink let out a growl that even someone underwater could have heard, and Simon understood.

But I was not finished with the lesson. « Smell, » I

said. I gestured at my nose. He frowned at me, then breathed deep. He breathed deep again. Then he raised his shoulders at me, his I-do-not-know gesture.

Patience, I thought. How long had it taken me to learn how to sense the forest by smell?

I pushed two fern fronds apart, and there it was, a two-stride-long slink rooting along the forest floor.

It stopped and raised its head. I stiffened, and imagined myself a tree. Simon did the same. After a dozen-breath of listening silence, the creature lowered its head and plodded forward.

I smiled at Simon, then gestured: watch, learn.

I sized up my prey. I gripped the spear. Then I lunged from the bushes with a roar.

The slink had no chance. It was not full grown, and my spear was strong. The fight was short. I struck the killing blow and stood back as the slink flopped to the ground. I turned to Simon, flicking blood off my hand. I felt proud, strangely proud. I have hunted for as long as I could hold a spear, why should I feel so much happier about this kill?

Simon, however, looked uncertain. His pulled his lips back as he stared at the blood on my hands. It was the same look he made when he smelled the meat cooking. Then he looked up, and spotted a pulpfruit, hanging low from the tree. He pointed at it. « Eat? Safe? » he asked.

I frowned at him. « What? Do you have someone kill your meat? »

He blinked at me. « What? Not safe? »

I took a breath, then let it out slowly. « Yes, » I said. « That fruit is safe to eat. »

• • •

The boy may not have liked the idea of hunting, but he helped carry the slink back to our camp. We tied it to his spear, which we carried between us, and he put the fruits he had gathered in a carrying bag slung over his own shoulder. I led the way back to our homesite.

As we approached, I heard something wrong. I stopped, listening hard.

Simon, who was not paying attention again, ran himself into the butt of the spear. He rubbed his leg. "What's wrong?"

I shot up a hand. Could he not see that I was listening? But then the voices got louder. Simon stiffened.

" . . . Something . . . Over here . . ."

Somebody else. " . . . What . . . ?"

« They are in our cave, » I warned. But Simon did not understand me. How would his words go? "Cave," I said. "People. In."

Simon nudged me, pointed to the lizard, then at the ground. We set the slink down and I led the way forward.

We knelt behind the cover of ferns. Closer, the voices became clear. It sounded like a man and a woman, but unlike Simon, neither of them was speaking slowly so I could understand.

"Someone . . . here," said the woman.

" . . . animal?" said the man.

"Fire," said the woman. " . . . fence."

Simon leaned forward, listening so hard he almost fell through the cover of the ferns. I grabbed him back, making the plants rustle. We froze, but the voices did not change. The people had not heard us.

I heard a babble of sounds from the man. I heard "ticktock," "them," and "on the ground."

Then the woman said something that ended with "Tal," even as her voice drifted further into the fog. Simon stiffened.

The man followed her, grumbling. " . . . into . . . Daedalon . . . sudden . . . charge . . ." His voice also faded.

« What are they saying? » I asked.

He looked afraid. « People look, » he said. « Find cave us. »

It was as I thought. But I knew how to deal with this. I brought out my blowpipe and put it to my lips.

He grabbed my wrist with an open hand. "No!"

I yanked my hand away. « Why? »

He bit his lips. This was important, I could tell, so I waited for the explanation. He spoke slow and soft. "If we attack, they will know we are here. If they do not report back, others will know. More will come looking."

I did not understand "report," but I saw his point.

These people were from one of the invaders' hives. If they never came back . . .

But the two were circling back. The man spoke somewhere near the cave mouth. "What . . . do? Wait . . . ?"

" . . . long wait," said the woman. "Can't . . . like that idea . . . ?"

I understood "wait." Were we going to have to stay out here, hidden, while these two stayed at our camp? Looked at the carrying bags I had left behind? Touched my knives? I gripped my blowpipe tight.

Simon closed his fist and tapped my back gently. He had learned that this gesture soothed. I lowered myself behind the cover of the ferns and tried to soothe my anger. It was hard. "Why, no?" I whispered. "They cave. Hunt! Us! Danger!"

"More dangerous to kill them," he whispered back.

I let out my breath. He was giving *me* hunting advice?

"And," he added, "we don't know how many—"

"Crew!" called a new voice, deeper in the forest. "Sound off!"

"One!" Yet another new voice.

"Two!" The man.

"Three!" The woman.

Numbers rang through the forest. They reached six. They were all around us.

"I *thought* there were more than two on patrol," Simon muttered. "Six seems like overkill. We need to hide." Then he looked at me. « Hide. »

Hiding was wise. I motioned for Simon to follow.

We crept through the undergrowth. Simon tried to place his feet in my footsteps, keeping the rustling to a minimum. Fortunately, the forest was full of the cries and calls of other animals. The people did not hear us.

But I almost did not hear the man before it was too late. As his shape hardened out of the fog, I ducked down and pulled Simon after me. His face hit the mud and he spat dirt, loudly. He struggled to push himself up, but I pressed down on his back. He took my meaning and raised his head carefully.

It was a man, taller than Simon, dressed as Simon was, but in grey, not white. We were so close I could see a picture on his upper arm, of a notched wheel and a heavy stick. He also had a weapon that fired bigger blowdarts.

If we could see him, he could see us. Fortunately, the luck of the Elders held. He was not looking at the ground and there were many plants around to hide us.

Simon shifted. The rustle caught the man's attention. His head snapped round. He stared in our direction, at the air over our heads. He took a step toward us.

He did not have to see us to find us. Stepping on us would do the same. Moving slowly, I brought out my blowpipe. This time, I looked at Simon. Surely I should use this now?

He shook his head. We waited.

The man took another step.

Then the first man's voice carried through the fog. "Guys . . . going back. Log . . . location . . . next group . . . okay?" I only understood some of the words, but it seemed like he was ready to leave.

The other searchers muttered agreement. The man — so close I could have stabbed his boot — turned and moved through the underbrush toward our cave. Soon, the voices — all of them — vanished into the distance. Simon let out the breath he was holding.

I got up and strode to our cave. The embers of our fire were scattered, but my travel pouches remained in the corner. Stepping over, I saw that they had not touched my knives.

I looked at Simon. Anger tightened my chest. This may only have been a campsite, but somehow it had become like a home to me. The invaders had ruined it.

In Simon's eyes, I saw that anger reflected. And fear.

He looked at the scattered kindling and the tossed ferns. Then he looked at me. « We must go. »

We did not say anything more. We gathered our things and got ready to leave.

CHAPTER EIGHTEEN
LEAVING THE WORLD BEHIND

SIMON:

We struck out, in a grim mood.

I was relieved that Eliza had listened to me and not shot the security patrol with her blowpipe. That would have brought more search parties down on us. Besides, what had those guards done to us, really?

If Nathaniel had been out there, I might have snatched Eliza's blowpipe and used it myself. But he hadn't been out there. He had, however, sent them. Those security patrols might have been from Daedalon (I recognized their hammer and cog insignias), but they'd been talking about Nathaniel. Grumbling about him, actually, while they debated whether the cave belonged to ticktock monsters or Grounders.

"Ticktock monsters or Grounders, what are we doing looking for *them*?" the man had said. "If these are the monsters, they won't like us invading their home.

If these are Grounder terrorists, they can have this cave. Makes sense, doesn't it? They want to be on the ground, let's leave them on the ground."

"Well, you can tell that to Tal," the woman had drawled. "I'm sure he'll appreciate your constructive criticism."

The man followed her. "He barges into Daedalon and all of a sudden it's like he's running the place."

So, Nathaniel had convinced Daedalon's security office to send officers out here. But what for? Was Nathaniel looking for *me*? That didn't make sense. He had no reason to think I was alive. Yes, Sergeant Gaal had said he'd seen me, but once I'd run, he'd said he'd been tricked by the fog. Even if Nathaniel thought that I was alive, why waste resources looking for me? For all he knew, all he had to do was wait for the forest to do me in.

So, maybe Nathaniel was looking for something else. But what? The security guards themselves weren't sure.

Eliza was deep in thought. As we stopped in a clearing so I could catch my breath, she turned and made a "pay attention" click. She worked her mouth as if she had something hard to say. "You," she managed. "You, no home."

It sounded awfully final, put that way. I glanced aside. "Yeah. I have no home."

Her eyes echoed the sadness, but mostly she looked — as she often did — frustrated with me. "You . . . no *go* home?"

I shook my head. "I can't go back. Nathaniel's there. I'd be put in prison. Possibly even shot, if Nathaniel got his way."

She frowned. "Pri-son?"

"Yes, prison—" I stopped. How could I possibly explain prison? "It's a . . . place . . . They put you there. A small place. Like a cave."

« A homesite? » she clicked.

"No." I bit my lip. "Like a cave, but . . . but you can't get out."

Her eyes widened. « Why? »

"Because they won't let you out."

« Why? »

"Because they don't want you to."

She cocked her head. « Why? »

I dropped my head against a tree and closed my eyes. "It's too hard to explain. I'm sorry."

Eliza paused. Then she repeated: "Sorry."

That was a word we knew.

Sorry: You, no home.

Above us, carrying in the fog, came the buzz of ornithopters. I looked up. "They're looking for something. If they find me . . . It's not safe here. I need someplace to hide, until I can go back." I looked back. "Where can I go?"

Eliza only looked at me, and waited. She knew the forest, but what good was that? I couldn't tell her what I —

On the other hand, I was a map-maker's son.

I took up my spear and cleared some ferns away

with my foot, baring a patch of red mud. With my spear, I scratched lines in the mud. Soon enough, I got caught up in it. I could even feel my tongue press at the corner of my mouth — just as my mother's used to do.

Eliza came closer, stooping over the map.

"Iapyx was here." I used the spear butt to push in a dot, though it was like marking a grave. "Nathaniel's here, in Daedalon." I pointed at the dot some distance from the other side of the gouge Iapyx had torn out of the forest. "I think I need to go here —" I pointed at the third dot "— to Octavia. I might have a chance to tell my story before Nathaniel comes. But —" It was a ridiculous plan; it was much too far. "I don't know. I'm not even sure where we are." Then: « Ek-Taak-Tock-Taak, where . . . we? »

Eliza looked at my map, then reached out a foot and tapped a spot with her toe, near where the tip of my spear was hovering. I nodded, pleased. I hadn't been far off.

She looked at me. « What do you need? »

I wasn't even sure what to ask. Finally, I said, « Help. They hunt. I not safe. Where I go? Stay safe? »

Her eyes narrowed thoughtfully. "Hide," she said. "From Na-than-i-el? He tall? Big man fire many blow-darts?"

That sounded like Nathaniel. Had she seen him back at the gouge? « Yes. »

She looked at my map a moment longer. Then she reached out with the tip of her spear and traced the air above the line representing one of the cliff faces. She brought it down on one of the deeper notches. « Here. »

"The niche?"

She looked at me, and tapped the spot again. « Here. »

"But —"

She poked the map again, in the same place. But I knew the niche was a mistake, a dead end. Everybody knew that. It would be just another cave to hide in and be discovered. « No go, » I clicked. « Nothing. »

Eliza smiled. She pushed the tip of her spear into the ground and started drawing, extending the line into the cliff, keeping it thin, and then turning it through a sharp bend.

My mouth dropped open as she kept going, widening the line into another chasm, and extending the chasm far south, until she ran out of ground near the edge of a pond. Finally, she pressed a dot at the end, just like the dots I'd used to mark my cities.

She pointed at the new dot with her spear. « There. We go there. »

• • •

Eliza marched ahead, across the chasm toward the niche. I kept my hand on my spear and followed her.

That was the way we walked together. She led and I followed. She pushed through the fog forest, confident. I tried to ignore the plants that lashed at my trousers. I was glad she knew where she was going, because I was lost within minutes.

And we never held hands. That's important to know. At one point, I tried to take her hand in order to step over a stream that was a little too wide, and I caught her unawares. She jerked up and pulled away from me, and I fell in. Quickly, she clicked an apology and helped me to my feet . . . by putting her balled fists under my armpits and hauling me up by her wrists.

That was one of the many strange things about Eliza. To her, an open hand seemed to be an aggressive gesture, and a closed one was one that soothed. She only grabbed me with her fingers when we had to move quickly, but that was something she had to think about.

How did a girl get to be like that? Where had she lived?

I'd hardly believed Mom's expanded map of my planet when I'd seen it, but this new chasm Eliza had drawn hadn't been on it. Everybody, including Mom and the Grounders, knew that the niche was a blind alley.

Still, I began to hope. Eliza had put a dot on that map, just like Daedalon and Octavia. It couldn't be a lost city; we still had all of ours from planetfall, but it could mean something similar. Eliza's home. A village. Maybe more people like her. All talking in the language of the ticktock monsters.

That was another mystery. But maybe there weren't ticktock monsters. Maybe there'd never been. What else could explain how this strange girl was here, and no monsters other than speechless, crawling lizards that loomed out of the fog? Maybe Eliza's people were outcasts.

We didn't have executions on Icarus Down. That was one of the shames from Old Mother Earth that we sought to leave behind. Banishment to the fog forest was our severest penalty, which amounted to the same thing, but not nearly so direct.

If this was a colony of banished settlers, they might be criminals or descendants of criminals. That made me nervous but, still, they might be able to help. They certainly would have no reason to co-operate with Nathaniel if his men came to kill me.

Eliza clicked at me to keep up. I picked up the pace and followed her.

Eliza's trek led up and up. The forest thinned out. The animal cries became more distant. Then, with a start, I realized that I could see farther than I had in days. A few minutes later, we climbed above the cloud.

I blinked while my eyes got used to the sudden bright clarity. We were on an outcrop of rock high up the cliff face, and I could see for kilometres. The sky was a smooth white sheet, blinding in its brilliance. The ground was a soft white river between two stone walls. The air was so dry, it sucked the moisture from my tongue. Far away, near where the chasm turned, I saw cables and the gleam of mirrors from another city — Octavia — perched on the vanishing point. I thought of Iapyx, and a lump formed in my throat.

Eliza called out, « *Cloc-Taak-Tock-guh,* » then, "Simon?" but for a moment I could only stare.

I heard the rocks skitter, then Eliza was beside me. She tapped a fist against my arm. I started to say something, but she cut me off. « I know it is hard. »

And that was all. We stood, staring at the gleam of Octavia, while the hot wind blew around us.

Then I looked away.

Eliza looked at me. "Come?" she said.

"Yes." Then, « We go. »

With Eliza in front, we climbed a scree of fallen stones, into a cleft in the cliff face. The rock walls closed in around us.

The gap was about ten metres wide. A hundred metres in, it narrowed further, until we had to walk sideways, and then it made a hard left. Beyond here, everybody thought the chasm came to an abrupt end. But as we reached the turn, and the wall to my left fell away, I found myself staring down a kilometre-long gap, sloping down at an easy angle. Most of the gap was rock and shadow, but in the distance I saw cloud. I looked behind me at the narrow gap. I couldn't imagine any pilot getting through here. No wonder the Grounders hadn't found it.

Suddenly I understood the value the Grounders placed on curiosity. *I'm the first person to see this*, I thought. Imagine what my people would say once I told them what I'd found. Would they name this chasm after me?

Then Eliza entered my field of vision, and I realized how arrogant I'd been.

She looked concerned. I'd just been standing there, breathing heavily, leaning with one hand against the cliff wall. « You need rest? » she asked.

I gathered my breath. My legs ached. But as I stared out at the long stretch of rocky ground before this gap descended into the clouds again, I could still feel the pull of curiosity. I was a Grounder after all.

"No," I said. "Just a little farther, okay?"

I walked forward. Eliza smiled, and walked beside me, as step by step I left the known world behind.

● ● ●

ELIZA:

My thoughts were a mixture of nervousness and excitement as we followed the chasm back to my village. It had been nearly half a sun-turn since I left. I wondered what had changed.

I had missed the burning time. I should have been grateful, as I hated hiding in caves and covering myself in mud to keep cool. But instead I felt a strange ache to know that my village had gone through a burning without me. It was a time of being close, of telling the stories of the foremothers, except now there was no one to tell the stories to. Had the Elder missed me? How would she react when I showed her Simon?

We walked. We ate. We nested in caves or wherever we could when our bodies needed sleep.

And I noticed strange things about Simon.

We bathed whenever we found a clear pool. I showed Simon a leaf that smelled nice and was good for removing dirt from skin, and he was grateful. But he always bathed alone. He also once tried to cut the hairs off his cheeks and chin, using the small metal knife he used to carve our spears. I thought a lizard had attacked him and gnawed his face. I gave him a shard of glass that had fallen from a clifftop. That, at least, worked better.

But his desire to bathe alone bothered me and it made me notice something else. Once, we made camp in a spring-cooled cave. While Simon started the fire, I took off my carrying bags and stretched. I pushed at a crick in my neck.

I looked at Simon and saw him looking at me. Or through me. He was half in thought, but his eyes were on me. Then, suddenly, he seemed to realize what he was seeing, and looked away, quickly. His cheeks turned pink.

"Why you do that?" I asked, crouching across the fire from him.

He looked up. "Do what?"

"Turn head away," I said. "When I take bags off, you turn head away. Why?"

I had been my mother's only daughter, the rest had been sons. Other than my mother, I was the only woman I knew. I had no idea what sort of woman I was. And if Simon always had to turn away from me . . . Was there something wrong with me? In that cave, I found I had to ask the question.

Simon reddened as he struggled to answer. "It's just . . . I —" He glanced at me, then quickly averted his eyes.

I jumped up, my hands pressed to my sides. « Look at me! » I clattered, so sharp that Simon jumped. He looked me in the eye.

I tilted my head. « Is there something about me you do not like to see? »

He did not know how to answer that. I saw his eyes trace down me, then back up again. There was no disgust there. Just . . . embarrassment. Maybe a little shame. Why shame?

He took a deep breath. "We are . . . dressed differently, where I come from," he said at last.

I chuckled. « I have eyes, Silly Strange Boy. I can see that. »

"I mean . . . women are dressed differently."

« That does not surprise me. What does that have to do with anything? »

"I'm not . . ." He struggled for the right words, even in his language, " . . . used to . . . being with a woman . . . dressed as you are, right now."

« I am not . . . » This was a strange word that did not translate. I used his. "Dressed."

« Yes, » he said.

We stared at each other across the fire, as I thought over this answer that Simon seemed to think was adequate, but was not.

« It has been a long time, » I said. "Why not used to it?"

He let out his breath. « It be other way . . . all my life. »

I began to understand. Though Simon had learned well since dropping from the invaders' hives, he still had much to learn. He had even more to unlearn.

« I sorry. » He struggled for the next words. « I anger you. I not mean to. »

I leaned back. After a breath, I sat down. It was not me. I began to feel foolish that I had worried. But at the same time, it felt important.

"No turn away," I said, looking across the fire at him. "See me. See the other. Be who we are."

He nodded and looked me in the eye. « Yes, » he said. Then, "Promise."

• • •

Simon grew stronger as we walked. Often, I had to make him stop to rest, as he pushed his body too hard. He would let out a relieved groan as he sat.

As language came easier, he also told me stories about the invaders' hives — cities, he called them.

« You are bragging! » I snapped at him.

He looked hurt. "No!"

« You make drawings move? » I looked hard at him. « You shine them on wall to see? How? »

"It's . . . a thing we know," said Simon. "Look, it can't be so hard to believe. It's like shadows on a cave wall."

"Shadows not drawings," I said.

« Same idea, » he said. "You know how we can see through thin glass? Imagine drawing something on thin glass and shining light through it onto a cave wall."

My brow furrowed. He tried again.

« Thin glass. You draw. Shine light. » "We do it every year," he said.

"What 'year'?"

We walked. We talked. Gradually, misunderstanding happened less and less.

What he did not talk about was how his cities came to be. Instead, he told me of wonders lost. His people had machines that could shine moving pictures on walls, but they were not as good as machines his foremothers had known. They had pulled their cities into the space above the clouds, but they had come from a place far, far more distant than that.

"Why your cities up?" I asked, at last.

He looked at me, frowning. « Because monsters. »

I stiffened. « Monsters? »

« Monsters hunt. Monsters in fog. Monsters kill, but . . . » He looked around at the trees and the fog. « Here — no monsters. »

He looked confused. So was I.

"Monsters kill hunt eat?" I tried his words. "Slink lizard."

He shook his head. « No eat. No slink. Monsters. »

"Monsters kill. Why?"

"I don't know." He looked away, his brow wrinkling. "I don't know what happened. I don't know where the monsters are. They're in all the stories: the ticktock monsters, the sounds in the fog."

And at once I knew what the monsters were. I stared at him. He did not know. How could he not know?

« You are lying, » I said.

He looked at me blankly. We knew "joking." We knew "bragging." But between us we had not got to "lying." He did not know the word.

"You know," I said. "You know. Why monsters kill."

He shook his head. "I don't," he said. "I don't know, Eliza. Maybe they weren't even real."

How did he not know?

Should I tell him?

As I thought about it, for a countless time, sitting in a cool cave around a small fire we had set up to cook our meal, I realized I did not want to tell him because I did not want to accuse him of being a murderer. Because I knew he was not. He was a man, in the way my father had been a man. And if Simon was not a monster, who in the invaders' hives were?

I saw my mother's blind eyes staring at me. *The invaders are your people, too. Tend to your ancestors' graves.*

I had not. I still did not want to.

So I kept it unsaid. For now. I told myself I still had time. We could learn more of our languages. I could wait until I was ready to speak.

Across from the fire, Simon looked up at me. « Where you come from? »

I suddenly felt the boy was learning too fast for his own good. "My village. We go. You safe there." I hoped. "You meet Elder; talk more."

"But where did your village come from?" Simon's brow furrowed. "This far from the cities? Where could the people have come from? For sixty-two years, we've only known thirteen cities. That's all that came on the *Icarus*. How did we miss you?"

He looked at me, hard, in a way that made me feel shy.

"And you are *so* different," he went on. "You're human, but you sleep differently, talk differently, and when you point, it's always with two fingers. Where would you learn those things?"

I held out my arms. I did not know how to explain.

He asked. « What your village called? »

« The village, » I replied.

He pinched the top of his nose. I felt bad that I could not give him the answer he was looking for.

Later, as we prepared for sleep, he spoke again as he lay in his nest. "Good night, Eliza."

I smiled. It was not night, but it was what he said. « Good sleep, Silly Strange Boy. »

He rolled onto one elbow and looked at me. I looked back at him across the fire.

"I may be strange, but I'm not *that* silly, am I?" He grinned.

I rolled away. "Is your name now. Nothing I can do." I added, "Simon."

Three sleeps later, half a sun-turn since I had left, we arrived home.

• • •

SIMON:

I still don't know how Eliza knew the way. When we pulled away from the cliff face and walked along the forest floor, I lost all sense of direction, but she homed in as though she had an internal compass.

The air had been getting hotter over the last week, even though the sun was halfway toward setting for Nocturne. I thought back about how long we had walked. How much farther south could we go? Not much farther, I thought.

Then, as we walked, the fog brightened and the air got even hotter. I realized with a jolt that the shadow of the cliff face had fallen away. We weren't in direct sunlight, but . . . Feeling the hot wind, and blinking from the brightness, I figured the chasm had turned, or branched. It ran parallel to the sun's rays rather than perpendicular to them. I shuddered. That would bring the sun's light low. At Solar Maximum, the fog would surely turn to steam.

« You *lived* here? » I asked.

Eliza frowned at me. « Yes. »

« But the sun! How? »

She looked at me a long moment, perplexed. « There are caves. »

I ran my tongue over my teeth, "Was it hard?"

Her brow furrowed. "It was home."

She pushed on into the fog forest. I picked up the pace to follow her. Then the first hut loomed out of the fog.

I say it was a hut. It was really just a metal box, with rusted sides, although someone had piled more metal on top for a roof, and made an effort to polish it. I ran my hand over the corrugated sides. The box looked familiar.

It looked like a storage container, sunk halfway into the mud. Vines were clambering up the sides, but it had been used recently. One side looked as though it had been pulled and twisted open. But it was empty.

How could this be here? Eliza's people didn't know how to work metal.

The next box I nearly ran into was also empty. So was the third. Suddenly I realized that the shapes in the foggy shadows that I'd taken for trees were other storage containers, also empty. The wind rustled the leaves above us, whistled over the yawning openings, and rattled loose pieces of metal. Banished outcasts would not have brought this much metal with them.

A new theory formed in my head. Remember, a year before our arrival, the *Icarus* had sent out preparation teams in smaller, faster ships to make the landing sites ready. These advance teams never met us after the *Icarus* crashed. We'd wondered where they'd gone. Was this where?

And, if so . . . "Where is everybody?" I asked.

The look Eliza gave me made me shiver. « There is nobody. Except me and the Elder. »

Lead filled my stomach. Had I come all this way for nothing?

"Where did they go?" I asked.

She looked away. « To rest. »

The ruined huts lay all around us. I sensed she wasn't even sure that the Elder was here.

One girl alone in the fog forest. How long had she been alone? I gnawed my lip.

Eliza called out a hello. In her language, it came out as « *Tik-tik-tik-tik.* »

No response. She called out again. « *Tik-tik-tik-tik?* »

I peered into the huts. Some looked like they hadn't been used in years. Some looked like they'd fall apart if I touched them.

Eliza vanished into the fog. Around me, her calls filled the air, like it was the only sound in the world. « *Tik-tik-tik-tik? Tik-tik-tik-tik?* »

We approached the centre of the village — at least, I think it was the centre. Here, the boxes had been arranged in some kind of order. I walked along the fog-shrouded paths, with only the wind and Eliza's lonely call for company.

Eliza emerged from the fog. Somehow, she'd ended up behind me. She looked around, her frown deepening, fear building in her eyes. « *Tik-tik-tik-tik?* »

Then, finally, an answer.

« *Tik. Tik. Tik. Tik.* »

It was lower. Octaves lower.

And it was — I didn't even want to think it, but it was, surely it was . . .

Eliza relaxed. « She is still here. Follow me. I shall show you to her. »

She pushed forward into the fog.

CHAPTER NINETEEN
ELIZA AND THE ELDER

ELIZA:

When the Elder spoke out of the fog, I breathed relief, but a new nervousness took me. I had come back, but I had not come back alone.

Still, I pushed forward, eager to see my Elder Mother for the first time in half a sun-turn. The buildings of my village felt a lot less empty, now I knew she was here. I walked to the Elder's hut. At the entrance, I pulled off my travel pouches and set them on the ground.

Simon stepped up behind me, about to enter, but I put my fist to his chest. "No," I said, keeping my voice low. "Wait. I call you."

He understood, and held back as I stepped into the cool dark.

I smelled the musk of the Elder, but could not see her yet. « Elder? » My heart stuttered. Had I imagined her greeting? « Elder? Are you there? »

The Elder rasped, and rose from her nest. « *Ek-Ta-ak-Tock-Taak?* Is that you? »

Did I imagine it, or did she take longer to heave herself upright? But her shape was so familiar, a liquid warmth ran through me.

« Elder! I am here. I have been to the invaders' hives. »

The Elder stepped forward. She put an arm around me and tipped her forehead to mine. I turned my face up and touched my nose to hers. For a heartbeat, everything was as it should be. I felt small and protected, like a new hatchling.

The Elder stepped back. « So, you have seen for yourself. What have you learned? »

« Much, » I replied.

The Elder drew back, shocked and proud. « How? Did you get inside? Were you captured? Did you escape? » Her voice dipped lower. « Did they hurt you? »

« No, » I replied. « I did not enter, but I watched. I heard them speak. »

« You did well, Fierce One! You are a good hunter. »

I allowed myself a smile.

Then, at the edge of my sight, I saw Simon silhouetted against the entrance. The wind picked up and rattled the broken metal of the huts. I looked up at the Elder.

I had to do this. I had walked half a sun-turn to the invaders' hives and back. I had come to understand something the Elder did not, and Simon deserved to know, too.

In front of me, the Elder coughed.

« There is more, » I said. « I have brought someone for you to talk to. »

The Elder tilted one eye at me, then the other. « You . . . what? »

« A boy, » I continued. « From the hives. » And I gestured toward Simon.

The Elder looked. Her breath rattled. « You . . . bring . . . *them*! »

I had a choice then to try to calm the Elder, or tell Simon to run. I tried to calm the Elder. « No. Just a boy— »

It was a mistake.

The Elder roared. She leapt for the entrance, knocking me down in her haste. I scrambled after her. I leapt onto her back, but she was on top of Simon, bellowing into his face, her talons gripping his chest, threatening to crack his ribs. Simon looked so small, and so scared.

« Stop! Stop it! » I strained against her bulk. « He is my friend! You need to talk to him, and you must not kill him! Please! He is my *friend*! »

Somehow, my words got through to her. She stopped bellowing. She glared at Simon, snout to nose, her protruding eyes jerking to focus on him. For a minute, in that silence, we all stared.

Then Simon tried to smile. It looked far more like a grimace of fear. He tried to say something, too, but all that came out was a squeak.

I gripped the Elder's shoulders, hard. « Get off him! »

The Elder snorted at Simon, then straightened up. I jumped from her back and helped Simon to his feet. I wanted to tell him I was sorry, but I did not think it wise to say anything to him in front of the Elder, just yet.

The Elder swung her face at me. « You fool. »

I started to fold my arms across my chest, but stopped when I realized that was a Simon gesture. Instead, I pressed my hands to my sides and faced her. « We must talk. »

She snorted again, then stomped inside her hut.

I eased Simon to the wall. He fingered the cuts the Elder's talons had left in his chest, through his stained white coverings. He was breathing heavily. His hands trembled.

"Are you all right?" I whispered.

"A ticktock monster," he muttered. "A real, live, ticktock monster! And I'm still alive!"

I snapped my fingers in his face. "Do not call her that!" I did not have to tell him why. I tapped his shoulder with my fist. "Wait here."

Sure that Simon was safe, I faced the Elder's hut again. I breathed deep, and marched inside.

The Elder was stomping around the back of her hut. Her breath rasped. She swung at me as I approached, but now was not the moment to back off. I pushed her, hard enough to send us both stumbling back. She caught herself on the metal wall with a crash. Her breath rattled in shock and anger.

I was shocked that I could have pushed her so, but I was not through being angry. « He is my friend and you *attack* him? »

« He is one of *them!* » she snapped. « They kill! They steal! They drive us to extinction! »

I drew my breath in at that. The Elder did not know Simon. She had judged Simon by the shape of his skin — a shape I mostly shared. The sudden sense that I shared this guilt felt like a body blow. It was not fair that Simon should be so judged. But then, had I not done the same with Simon's people? With Simon himself, at first? That realization hit with a second body blow. My anger flared.

« He is no different from me, » I snapped back. « *I* do not kill or steal! »

The Elder snorted. « *You* were brought up right. »

That was a silly answer. Simon had also been brought up right.

« He does not know, » I said. « He is good. He does not know what happened. »

The Elder snarled. « He will betray us! »

« He has not! He *will* not! »

The Elder brought her voice low. « You want to mate with him! Your judgment is suspect! »

« Oh, find a mate and lay eggs out of season! » I snapped. The Elder growled, but said nothing. Anybody else, she would have clawed. I looked her in the eye. « All I have said is true. Silly Strange Boy is good. He does not know what happened. He will understand when we tell him. »

The Elder looked at me. « Silly Strange Boy? »

« That is his name. Nothing I can do about that. »

Her talons flexed. She coughed again. I frowned at that. Finally, she said, « You know their speech? »

« Yes, » I replied. « The boy taught me. »

« Speak it! »

What was I to say? But after a breath's thought, I tried. "I speak the invaders' speak."

« Stop! » the Elder snarled. « It sounds horrible in your mouth! »

I winced at that.

Then she exhaled and settled onto the ground, slowly, as though there was pain. « Bring the boy forward. We will talk. You will translate. »

I nodded, then turned to where Simon waited. I let out the breath I had not realized I was holding. I had convinced the Elder to set aside sun-turns of anger and talk to Simon. That was a relief. But a new fear rose: what were Simon and the Elder going to say?

• • •

SIMON:

Eliza emerged from the shadows. "Come," she said. As we stepped inside, she added beneath her breath, "Careful. No speak like me. Anger her. I speak for you."

"Yeah, I wouldn't want to *anger* her," I muttered.

Gradually, my eyes got used to the darkness. The shade was welcome, even if the air smelled of damp, musk and slightly of rot.

The Elder sat in one corner. She was much larger than a human. Her legs were thick and muscular, but curled up into her body. Her scales gleamed blue-green in what little light came through the door. She had slender arms with claws — two wide fingers and a thumb — at the end. The inner joints of her fingers had fearsome claws of their own, as did her palm. No wonder Eliza touched me with her fists, and not an open hand.

In front of the Elder, a dozen rounded pebbles lay scattered. She scooped these up into her taloned palm and poured them out again, studying the patterns.

She looked up at me.

For a moment, we stared at each other, myself keenly aware that I was looking at the first intelligent alien I'd ever seen. Emphasis on intelligent. Emphasis on alien.

Then the Elder leapt up on her haunches and lunged at me. I flinched back, but she didn't claw or strike. Instead, her nostrils flared and she sniffed deep, while her snout did a pass of the air in front of my torso.

She settled back and chattered.

Eliza took a deep breath. "You afraid."

I stumbled to put together an answer. "N–no."

Eliza clicked the word back, and the Elder chittered again. Eliza translated. "Wrong word. I smell fear. You people full of wrong words. Spring from mouth like water from mountains."

Wrong words. Lies. Full of lies.

"All right, I'm afraid!" I licked my dry lips. "But I don't need to be, do I?"

The Elder clattered.

"I kill you," Eliza translated, and I dearly hoped she'd missed a "could."

"But you won't," I said, fervently. "Yes, you're strong enough and you have sharp claws, but you won't kill me because you haven't, yet. You're willing to hear me. You're good enough to give me a chance."

The Elder rattled. Eliza didn't translate this. I looked at her and saw her grimacing. I looked back at the Elder. She shook with the noise. To my horror, I realized she was laughing.

The laughter continued a long moment while Eliza and I waited in fearful silence. Then the Elder looked up at me and spoke.

"Good," Eliza translated. "You right — I good. I tell you true self. I give-you-a-chance." Eliza said it as if it were one word. "I give-you-a-chance. Again. I *wrong* give-you-a-chance before."

This wasn't going well. Desperation drove me forward. "Look, I don't know you. I've never seen any of your kind. I mean you no harm."

The Elder let out a snort, then fired questions and accusations at me so fast, it was all Eliza could do to keep up. "You not *harm*? You harm *all*! No more for harm."

"I don't understand," I said. "I've never seen you before."

"Your mothers. You people. *You* do this."

"Do *what?*" I said, bewildered. "What did we do? You attacked us! You were the ones who attacked my colony when we first set up, over sixty-two years ago!"

The Elder snarled. "Yes," said Eliza.

"But why?" I said. "Why would you attack us?"

The Elder spoke. "Because *you* harm," said Eliza.

"What harm?" My voice edged up in alarm. "Landing here? We didn't know this was your planet—"

The Elder's laughter cut Eliza off in mid-translation. For a moment, I could only stare as the Elder laughed long and hard. I lost my temper and shouted. "What's so funny?"

She looked up at me and snarled.

"Not our place," Eliza translated.

I tried to parse this. I couldn't. "What?"

"This. *Not* our place," Eliza said again. I noticed she hadn't translated my question. She must have thought I'd misheard.

"You were here—"

The Elder clicked and snarled. Eliza's calm voice provided the words. "*This. Not* our place. *You* bring us. Through sky."

I blinked. "Through the sky?"

More clicks. "You. Your people."

"But . . . how—"

The Elder clicked furiously

"*Our* place," Eliza translated. "Clear skies. Many islands. Great water. Our place. Our *place*. Our home. You kill us. Take us to this bad place."

Planet, I realized with a shock. The word Eliza was rendering as place. It was *planet*.

I took a step back. "No . . . That's not possible."

But: Oceans. Islands. We'd been promised a blue world. An ocean world dotted with islands and broad salt flats. We didn't know what had happened, and that question had lingered uneasily in the back of our minds all these years.

This didn't make sense. And what the Elder told me next filled me with horror.

"You came," Eliza translated. "You fall from sky. You make us great sickness. We died and we died. Then us — so few, us! — you bring us. Here: bad place. All of us. All of us die."

I stared at the Elder as I finally understood what this meant. "But that's . . . that's *genocide*!"

Just saying the word made my stomach lurch. It was a word we hardly said on our colony, but which all of us knew. "It's from the worst days of Old Mother Earth. We swore, when we fled, never again! We would never do that again! Not to *anybody*! Ever!"

The Elder chirped something, but Eliza didn't wait to translate. "You did." She looked at me, grim-faced. "Your people did, Simon. See here. Look here. We here. Only us. Only us here."

I stared at her, stunned. It was horrifying and confusing at the same time. I stood accused on behalf of my people of destroying an entire civilization.

Eliza and the Elder stared at me. Eliza had that same look on her face as when she'd woken me from my nightmares about Rachel. The Elder cocked her head. She leaned forward and sniffed deep. She said to Eliza, « He does not know. »

« I said so, » Eliza replied.

« How could he not know? »

« They did not tell him, » Eliza said. « Perhaps they did not tell themselves. »

The Elder leaned back on her haunches. « Then we must show him. »

Eliza kept her eyes on me. She started to say, « I do not think this is a good— »

« Take him! Show him! »

« I do not want— »

« Show me what? » I said.

Then I realized my mistake.

The Elder hissed at me. Eliza looked horrified.

For a moment we said nothing. Then the Elder stood up, slowly, shakily. Eliza looked alarmed and rushed forward, helping the Elder to her feet. The Elder waved her off, then lumbered to the door, her heavy feet hitting the metal floor with a fleshy smack. She paused at the doorway, and did not look back at us.

« Show him. » Then she vanished into the fog.

Eliza didn't look me in the eye. She started for the door. "Come, Simon. You see."

I grabbed her wrist. She flinched.

"You knew this," I said. "Why didn't you tell me when you found me?"

She turned slowly to look at me. "You not speak me."

I didn't let go. "But what about when I learned

how to talk to you? You knew — when I asked about monsters, you knew."

She hesitated. She took a deep breath. "I not want. Tell you truth."

"Why?"

Her eyes bored into mine. "Because truth make you monster."

She yanked her wrist free and walked out of the hut.

I followed her into the village. We came to another hut, which had also been kept in better repair than most. As I stepped to the opening, the Elder emerged and, for a second, we were face to face again, with me staring right into those teeth. The moment froze. Then the Elder stepped aside and extended her claw toward the darkness within.

I took a moment to prepare myself for the unknown, and ducked inside.

I couldn't see right away — it was so dark — but the smell hit me immediately. The place was full of something. The musky odour of the Elder was thick here.

Nothing moved. I started to pick out shapes among the shadows. There were small mounds evenly spaced across the floor, like row upon row of lumpy kickballs. I could see patches of white, now. First I thought that the mounds were actually piles of spheres, then I realized they were slightly oblong, carefully stacked, surrounded by cobwebs . . . no, pouches. They looked like . . . eggs.

They were eggs. Dozens of them. But why were they here?

But then I thought, if there are eggs, why aren't there babies?

Behind me, the Elder spoke and Eliza translated. "These . . ."

She didn't know the word.

"Eggs," I said.

"Ekkz," she said, then tried again. "Eggs. All eggs laid in this bad place. Put here."

My mouth went dry. "They don't — why don't . . . ?" I switched languages, afraid the Elder would kill me, but needing to know. « Where young? Eggs dead? »

« We keep them dry, » the Elder replied. « They will not die if they stay dry. But they will not — »

That word must be *hatch*. I missed something here, and waited for Eliza to catch me up.

"They need great water." She said. " Special place."

A special place. A hatching ground. We'd taken these people from their hatching ground. We really had killed them all.

I could feel bile rising in my throat. For a moment, there was just the breeze whistling past the empty openings and rattling the loose roofs. Genocide. The most complete form possible. The evidence was right here.

The Elder chirped, but I didn't really need Eliza to translate. "What you say now? When you see this. Here. What you say?"

I took a deep breath and opened my mouth. Then I closed it. Finally, I said, "Nothing." I swallowed. "Nothing. There is nothing I can say."

The Elder spoke again. I translated it before Eliza said anything: « He understands. »

The Elder lumbered away. Eliza looked from her, to me, then back again. Finally, she followed, leaving me alone.

I stared at the eggs a while longer, then pushed away. I stumbled past the abandoned huts, picking a direction at random. I needed space to think. I didn't look where I was going, and so, being me, I hurt myself. I stubbed my toe on a metal strut.

I jumped around, grunting, clutching my toe. Frustrated, I gave the strut a kick, which did the opposite of help. Then, after I'd massaged the pain away, I knelt by the strut. I ran my fingers along the rusted surface.

It was bigger than I'd expected, big as a tree trunk. One end was buried deep in the ground, and the other rose up at a forty-five-degree angle, losing itself in cloud. With the size and the weight of the thing, I imagined it stretching up until it rested against the chasm's cliff face.

The ship, maybe, the deportation ship that had brought the Elder's people here. Clearly they'd had some human tech to scavenge. But it didn't make sense. If we'd stolen their world and sent them to this too-bright, fog-bound hell, why were we in hell ourselves?

The *Icarus* had crashed almost instantly on jumping to this system. When would we have had time to organize a . . . genocide? It was undeniable, but it made no sense.

Then I remembered the advance force. They'd come ahead of us. They had smaller, faster ships. Some of those ships could have brought the Elder's people here, and maybe the Elder's people had salvaged what they could from these shuttles and their storage containers to build their village. Okay: that was a viable explanation. But if we'd stolen the Elder's world, why hadn't we claimed it?

I was finally asking questions. Rachel would have been proud. I flinched at the memory, but I held it. What did she say I should do next? See where the questions led me?

I tapped the strut. I tapped it again. Then I stood up and walked deeper into the village. I ran my hands along the sheet-metal huts. Some of these were cobbled together, but some of them weren't. Some were pieces of machinery lying abandoned. I came upon a rocket booster, half buried in the mud. I kept going, walking until the cliff face loomed out of the murk.

But it wasn't the cliff face. It was metal. And it was as big as a city.

Above me, the painted-on flag had blistered with heat, and faded with time, but I could still see its white olive branches on the blue background.

I ran my fingers along the scorched metal surface and looked up. "Great Creator," I breathed. "I've found the *Icarus*."

CHAPTER TWENTY
THE FALL OF THE *ICARUS*

SIMON:

I followed the hull until I came to the airlock door. Around it were mounds of dirt, each twice as long as it was wide. There were far too many and they were far too regular to be natural. They stretched into the fog.

An airlock was still on its hinges, stuck mostly open. Black vines were using its struts as a trellis.

I stepped inside. The only light was at my back, filtering in from the outside. I stood a moment, letting my eyes adjust, and history swam into focus.

The *Icarus* bridge.

I'd seen it many times in picture books, paper crackling in my teacher's hands. Walking into it was like walking into a dream.

It was tilted, and thick with dust, and so quiet

. . . But it was real. There was the captain's chair on its raised dais, facing the front viewing screen. To the left of the viewing screen was the science station, its computer panels smashed and the white surface blackened with soot and dust.

I stepped deeper into the room, through what must have been an emergency airlock, moving quietly, as though I didn't want to wake a crew who might only be sleeping. I ran my hand over the navigator's console, fingering the depression where he must have placed his hand —

Lights on the console flickered to life.

I jerked my hand back. There was a flash. A screen fuzzed briefly with static and then everything faded and died.

I tried touching my hand to the spot again, but nothing happened. I tried again. My hand came away black with dirt. Using my sleeve, I wiped down the console as best I could, then placed my hand on it again.

The console lit up. The screen flickered to life. The display was dim, and the screen responded sluggishly to my touch, but it responded. The *Icarus*. The *Icarus* was alive.

The screen solarized, resettled and flashed: *Touch here.*

I stared at that message. Not only was the *Icarus* alive, but it had something to tell me.

I touched.

• • •

A video began to play.

I know you've seen it: it's now the most famous video in the world. But I'm told that a person's reaction to news is almost as important as the news itself.

So, here's how I reacted: I stared.

There was a man on the screen. I knew the greying hair, square jaw and creased face: the second Captain of the *Icarus*. I might not have been able to pick out my father from a lineup of photographs, but this man, I knew.

He looked tired; he needed a shave.

"Ship's Log." The Captain picked up a plastic notesheet and peered over his glasses at the text. "Day 26,298 of our journey from Old Mother Earth." He looked back at the camera. "The advance force leaders are due back tomorrow. They'll have the first reports from our new home. After seventy-two years in deep space, anticipation is high. I've reminded everybody that we still have work to do, but I can't help feeling excited myself. I think the thing I'm most looking forward to seeing is what a sky is like."

"The duty—" Then, as if the film had been snipped in the wrong place, the scene crashed to black, and something new spliced in.

" . . . this report." the Captain said. He had different clothes on — a different day? — and a binder in his hand. "My clerks have examined every paragraph, and my security people have debriefed the advance force personnel. None of them can find anything amiss, but Tal's people are hiding something, I know it." He tapped his desk.

Tal, I thought.

"They used far more fuel than was budgeted, and Navigator Salk won't look me in the eye." He slapped the binder onto the tabletop. "But what can I do? Turn this ship around? Not a chance. If nothing else, I can't leave behind the people we still have on the planet. Maybe when we get there, I'll see what really happened during Tal's year-long trip."

He stopped. "Mark private," he commanded, and his thumb loomed into view . . .

Again, a clumsy jump, and something new started. This wasn't random; someone had assembled this.

"Ship's Log, day 26,303," said the Captain. "The final jump is scheduled for fourteen hundred hours. Navigator Salk is due to supply me with the jump coordinates.

"Earlier today, he slipped me a note, asking me to make the report drop a private meeting. Clearly, he wants to tell me something, and he doesn't feel safe telling me in the open. I think I may be closer to figuring out what CMO Tal is hiding from me.

"It's frustrating, though," he added, "on the day of our final jump to our new home. If Salk has information that will scrub this mission, I'm not sure how the crew will handle the disappointment."

Behind the Captain, there was a knock at the door.

"Mark private," he said, hastily, and reached for the switch.

The next picture was of the bridge, as seen from over the Captain's shoulder. Crew members bustled from panel to panel. The uniforms shocked me. So much colour, compared to our colony's bleached-out clothes, so many dark blues and bright yellow insignias. They'd soak up light, those colours: they'd catch fire in minutes.

The Captain signed a clipboard and passed it off. The viewscreen showed a sea of stars. The babble of voices ebbed. Officers turned from their panels one by one. It had the feel of a ritual.

"All colony pods report ready, sir," said a woman.

"Acknowledged, Lieutenant Dere," said the Captain.

"Engines report ready, sir," said a man.

"Acknowledged, Lieutenant Oall."

Another man turned from the science station, and I flinched. For a moment, I thought it was Nathaniel. But then I realized that I was looking at Nathaniel's father, Daniel.

"Bridge crew reports ready, sir," he said.

"Thank you, Officer Tal," said the Captain. "Navigator Salk?"

A young man looked up from the navigator's station. "Sir. We have green board."

"Punch up the final coordinates and display them on screen."

The man the Captain identified as Salk looked nervous as he touched the control panel I now hovered over. On the viewscreen, a series of numbers popped up. Beside it, the image of a blue planet turned.

"Coordinates entered," said Salk. "Ready to jump at your mark." His hand hovered over a green square on his console.

The Captain cleared his throat. "Not that one, Navigator. The other coordinates. The ones you told me about earlier today."

Salk blinked at him. "Sir?"

Daniel Tal and the other bridge officers looked confused.

"Just do it." The Captain's voice was like steel.

Daniel Tal stepped forward. "Sir? What is going on?"

Salk tapped his console. The numbers changed, and the spinning blue planet vanished, replaced by a gleaming white one. The planet of Icarus Down, though it wasn't called that back then. It had the designation V4647 Sgr-b. The green square flashed on his console.

"Recognize those numbers, Daniel?" the Captain said. All eyes were on the Captain and the Chief Medical Officer, now. "You should. From what Navigator Salk tells me, the advance force is intimately familiar with that location."

Daniel Tal straightened up, his face grim. "Sir?"

"What Salk tells me explains a lot," said the Captain. "Your excessive use of fuel, and the medical supplies. Please tell me what happened with the indigens was an accident, and you didn't engineer the virus yourself."

Daniel Tal clasped his hands behind him. He said nothing.

"Shall we pay that planet a visit, Tal?" The Captain nodded at the white sphere on the screen. "Have a look at your handiwork?"

There was a twitch in Daniel Tal's face. It might have been a smile. "That would not be wise, sir."

"I shouldn't think so," the Captain snapped. "I have to commend your pilots on their flying abilities, to navigate through enough solar radiation to kill the *Icarus*. But, really, Daniel? After all those indigens faced, you left them to burn?"

Daniel Tal said nothing.

The Captain lifted his chin. "Well, our pilots are going to have to be exceptional again. We *are* making the final jump to the blue world to meet the advance team. The pilots will go to the bright planet, rescue the indigen survivors, and put them back where you found them. Then we're heading on our way."

"Where do we go from there, sir?" said Daniel Tal.

"We'll figure that out after we leave."

"Seventy-two years in deep space, sir," said Daniel Tal. "How much longer will you have our people wait?"

"That does *not* give you the right to commit the same mistakes we left behind!" the Captain shouted. "Chief Medical Officer Tal, you are dismissed. Hand over your weapon and leave the bridge."

Daniel Tal stood there, his face impassive.

"Officer Tal, I have given you an order!"

Tal didn't move.

The Captain's jaw clenched. "Lieutenant Dere, escort Officer Tal from the bridge."

The officer looked up from her station. She looked from the Captain to Tal, distressed, but she didn't move.

"Lieutenant!" the Captain snapped.

"Navigator Salk," said Tal calmly. "Re-enter the final coordinates and initiate jump."

"Belay that, Navigator!" The Captain leapt from his seat. "This is my bridge! I give the orders here!"

Tal shook his head. "I'll follow no orders that lead us back into the darkness."

Another officer pulled a gun and pointed it at Tal's head. "You heard the Captain!"

More guns were pulled, and suddenly there was a tense silence, as everybody realized what they were doing, and what would happen if somebody made the slightest mistake.

The Captain took a deep breath and spoke, his voice low. "Everybody, what we need to do right now is calm down. No one make any sudden moves—"

Someone grabbed Tal from behind. There were shouts. There was a melee of bodies. A gunshot rang out. Navigator Salk clutched his shoulder and fell backward onto his console.

The engines roared. The bridge shuddered. On the viewscreen, the stars became streaks of light.

The bridge crew froze. Everybody looked at the screen.

"Navigator!" Tal shouted over the engines. "Which coordinates did you enter?"

Salk was working frantically at his station,

one-handed, even as blood from his shoulder made his dark tunic even darker. Sweat beaded on his forehead. "The bright planet, sir!"

The bridge crew looked in horror at the display showing the coordinates, and the white sphere of Icarus Down, still spinning.

"Arrival at jump destination imminent," Salk shouted. "Arrival in five . . . four . . . three . . ."

"All hands . . ." The Captain struggled into his seat. "Brace for— "

The air flashed white. I shielded my eyes with a hand. On the speakers, people yelled.

"What the hell?"

"I can't see!"

"Get the shutters down! Get the shutters down!"

"They *are* down!"

"Lieutenant Dere!" the Captain shouted. "Status!"

"We're being bombarded by intense electromagnetic radiation," Dere shouted. "Hull temperature rising! Four hundred Kelvin! Six hundred Kelvin!"

"Helm!" the Captain yelled. "Point us toward the sun. Get the colony pods in our shadow, *now*!"

Though it hardly seemed possible, the blaze of light intensified. Shouts turned to screams.

"Navigator Salk," the Captain shouted. "Abort landing. Prepare to jump back— "

"We can't, sir," Salk shouted. "The radiation has killed our jump engines. It's a marvel our computers still work. We can only move by rockets, sir, and not for much longer."

"Sir," Lieutenant Dere shouted. "Hull temperature is at a thousand Kelvin and rising; we are rapidly approaching melting points. We have damage reports coming in from the colony pods! We can't take much more of this!"

Lieutenant Oall yelled, "Sir, scans confirm the planet has an oxygen-nitrogen atmosphere; it can protect us from the worst of this, but we have to deploy, now!"

There was a pause then all there was, was shouting. Through it all, the Captain was silent.

"We have no choice, sir," Daniel Tal shouted. "We have to deploy the colony pods, or we'll have casualties."

Another pause.

"Sir!" Lieutenant Dere yelled. "Sir! What are your orders?"

"Do it!" the Captain shouted. "Keep us aligned to the sun. Keep the pods in our shadow."

I knew my history. This was the death sentence of the *Icarus*, flying it backward into the planet, taking the full brunt of the sun. But what I hadn't been taught, what had been lost to history was this: they all knew.

I saw it on their faces. They knew they were going to die.

But no one questioned the order. What had been a babble fell to near silence as the heroes of the *Icarus* got to work. The only one speaking was Lieutenant Dere. "Launching colony pods now." Her voice shook.

She read out the litany of names, the cities they were dying to save. They came slowly. Too slowly. "Daedalon . . . Iapyx . . . Octavia . . . Perdix . . . Talos . . ."

A pause. I could hear them breathing. They were sweating, too: the ship must be heating up. In the pause, I shivered and pushed my hand hard against the console, as if this weren't a settled matter, as if to urge them on.

Dere started to speak again. "Cocalon . . . Ariadnon . . . Theseon . . . Ovid . . . Latona . . . Scylla . . ."

Another delay. The light was too bright, even through the shields, even over three generations of history. I squinted. My hands hurt.

The pause went on. They'd launched eleven pods. There were thirteen.

"Herculon." Dere's voice rose to a shout. "Telamon! That's it! Final colony pod away and in the atmosphere, sir!"

"Helm! Navigator," the Captain shouted. "Plot course for the planet's umbra; get us in its shadow—"

"Can't, sir! Our engines are burned out. Our fuel is gone!"

"We've been caught in the planet's gravity well," the Lieutenant shouted. "We can't control our descent."

"All hands," the Captain yelled. "Brace for impact!"

There was a noise. A moment's darkness.

The recording stopped.

They died, I thought. *That's how they all died.* I bent my head.

And the screen snapped back to life. I jumped, startled.

The recording was dim and staticky. It showed the Captain in his quarters. His face was scarlet with flashburn; there was a bandage over his eyes, like a blindfold. "Ship's log, UNS *Icarus*. Seven days since planetfall. The crew of the *Icarus* — let the record show that one hundred thirteen members of the crew of the *Icarus* gave their lives in the effort to save our colony pods. The balance of us: we are working to repair the ship."

"We finally have internal coms back. We have not made contact with the colony pods. Radio transmissions are impossible, and we've not been able to send out reconnaissance teams. Conditions outside the ship are . . . difficult. It's impossible to see more than three metres." A faint, ironic smile, under the blindfold. "I'm told."

He took a deep breath. "Chief Medical Officer Tal and his supporters are still serving under my command. We need all hands to repair the ship, contact the colony pods, and try to find some way — any way — to get back into space."

"I can't help but wonder if our citizens in the colony pods realize what's happened," he added. "Are they setting up their cities? There's no way to know. And what choice do they have? Until they find us, or we find them, we won't have the resources to leave this planet."

The screen flickered, then resumed.

"Ship's log, ten days after planetfall," said the Captain. The blindfold bandage was gone, but his eyes were swollen and blinking: it gave him the look of a man who had been crying. "The indigens have found us. Security crews have reported shadows in the fog and strange noises — snapping and clicking. Today Lieutenant Dere disappeared." He shuddered. "We found her body two hours later, torn to shreds."

"Initial reports confirm Tal's analysis," he added. "These are intelligent creatures; there's forethought here. They're scoping out our defences — doing everything I would do if I were planning an attack. All attempts to communicate with them have been . . ." He grimaced. " . . . rebuffed."

He took a deep breath. "Frankly, I don't blame them. But my first duty is to the safety of this crew and this colony. I've opened the weapons locker and our officers stand ready. I don't hold out much hope. Our supplies are limited, and the fog is a defender's nightmare. Salk is working on plans to negotiate our surrender, but I don't think it will help. These creatures aren't interested in talking. If they attack in force . . ."

Behind him, someone pounded on the door. "Sir! Come quick! Scouts report movement! There's dozens of them!"

The Captain's jaw clenched. "Coming," he shouted. He looked back at the camera, opened his mouth to say something, then closed it. Taking a deep breath, he let it out slowly. "Mark public," he said. "Mark public all."

The screen went black.

The screen stayed dark for a long moment before it flickered again. A new video appeared of the Captain's quarters, but now Navigator Salk stared at the screen. The camera was tilted badly, and he appeared almost sideways. His arm was in a sling, and blood trickled down his face from a cut above his eye. Behind him, I heard shouts, clicks and the sound of gunfire.

"I . . ." he said. "Um."

He struggled to get his breathing under control. "My name is Joshua Salk."

He turned sharply at the sound of a woman's scream. Then he turned back to the camera and spoke quickly. "I'm just the navigator. But the Captain is dead . . . Tal is missing . . . I guess . . . I guess it's me, who has to tell this."

His hands loomed up and straightened the camera. "If anybody from the colony finds this record, there are things you need to know. About why we're here." He took a deep breath. "We *are* on the wrong planet. I know this because I pushed the button that brought us here."

He took several breaths before continuing. "I'm sorry. I'm really, really sorry. I was shot. It happened so fast. I wanted to show the Captain, I wanted him to see — but I never meant to —"

He closed his eyes and composed himself before continuing. "Now that we're here, given what's out in the fog, you need to know what happened during the advance expedition."

"We got to the right planet," he said, "the blue one, and we found a civilization there. Don't ask me how we could have missed knowing it before, but there they were: a race of lizard-like people building their first cities.

"We were devastated," he went on. "To come all that way . . . But then things went wrong. CMO Tal initiated contact with the indigens, to try to buy a place to land. I told him it was against protocol, but he said that Earth law meant nothing now that we were twenty-five thousand light years away. Most of the advance force agreed with him. We met with the indigens' leaders. We tried to talk . . . and then the indigens started getting sick."

Salk looked up at the camera with haunted eyes. "I've heard about what epidemics could do — what they did back on Mother Earth, but until you've seen it, you have no idea. Their civilization collapsed within a week. They turned on each other. They would have turned on us, except we were safe in orbit. And when it was done, there were less than a hundred left."

His jaw tightened. "That's when CMO Tal decided to take the planet for our own."

Behind him there was a crash, more shouts, a few gunshots, and the sound of chittering.

"We promised them help," said Salk. "We gathered them together in one place, and then we boxed them. We put them on shuttles and sent them to the system's other planet, the one we're now on.

Our reports indicated that life existed there, even though that planet was on the inner edge of the Goldilocks zone.

"I protested," Salk added. "But Tal had the support of the advance force. Even back on the ship, they watched me — I thought they might even kill me. Finally I got a secret meeting with the Captain. Even so, I was afraid Tal had enough support to mutiny if he had to. And I was right. Tal was going to take over the ship. He was going to get away with genocide. I had to —"

He faltered. Then he looked up at the camera. "So, we're here, on the bright planet, not the blue one. But there's still hope if someone from the colonies gets this. The people need to know what we did. Maybe then we can make peace."

The shouts and clicks were closer now. Salk spoke quickly. "I've altered the security protocols. Automated the playback. I've downloaded the advance force's logs, this video, everything. The proof is in the black box. If anybody from the pods finds this, tell everyone, please! Tell people what we did!"

Behind him, the shouting stopped.

Salk looked behind him. Shadows moved beyond the doorway. There were clicks and ticks and the sound of heavy footsteps getting closer.

"They're here," he breathed. He looked back at the camera. "This will be the last transmission of the *Icarus*." He closed his eyes. "I don't blame them. I really don't."

He sat there, his eyes closed, as the noises got closer. I found myself breathing in time with him, and counting our breaths. Four . . . Five . . .

There was a click, startlingly close, like a bone breaking. I translated what Salk couldn't. « There's one in here! »

"*Icarus* out," said Salk.

A flash of moving darkness. Then the screen went blank.

•••

After the video stopped playing, I stared at the blank screen a long time, hardly breathing. I felt dizzy. Aaron had been right. Gabriel had been right. The Grounders' suspicions had been right. This colony, the planet, our place here . . . it had all been a lie. We were on the wrong planet. Worse than that, we didn't deserve to stand on the ground. Not on this planet nor the other one.

But as I thought about this, another part of my mind spoke up. If I didn't do something, this would stay a lie. Aaron died for nothing. Joshua Salk died for nothing. Rachel . . . Rachel died for nothing. Daniel Tal would get away with genocide, and Nathaniel Tal would get away with destroying Iapyx to protect that secret. I was the only one with the truth in my hands.

Well, not *in* my hands, yet.

I felt around the screen, and my fingers fumbled open a compartment full of grounded wires and outlets. I searched until I found it: the black box.

I turned it over in my hands. It was like the white box on our ornithopters, only smaller and sleeker, and, of course, black. It could fit in my pocket. We weren't able to make things as small as they used to, but the connection looked compatible.

Light gleamed off glossy black embossed against the matte, showing the Seal of the Captain of the *Icarus*. I saw the letters in the circle (*"Relinquamus vias veteres"* — we leave the old ways behind) around an insignia of a man wearing wings of flame.

I slipped the black box into my pocket and walked toward the airlock, my footfalls echoing across the broken display panels and the fallen chairs. I paused at the door and looked at the busted consoles. For a moment, I thought I heard the ghosts of voices from long ago.

I wondered if I should do something, to show respect for the dead. Did they deserve respect? After all that had happened?

Then I looked out the airlock door, and saw the mounds of dirt, stretching out from beside the airlock door, vanishing into the fog, each twice as long as they were wide.

They'd buried them, I realized. After the Elder's people had defeated the *Icarus* crew and killed everyone, they'd buried the dead, and someone had tended to the graves. They'd decided that the invaders deserved that much respect, at least.

I faced the bridge.

Yes. The crew of the *Icarus* deserved respect, as long as the truth came out. Navigator Salk had tried to get that truth out. The Captain had wanted to make restitution. If I helped, maybe as a people we'd find some measure of redemption.

I saluted the empty bridge. Then I walked back into the fog, toward the centre of Eliza's village.

CHAPTER TWENTY-ONE
SIMON AND THE ELDER

ELIZA:

After leaving Simon behind, I followed the Elder through the village. She was tall, and at her normal speed I had to hurry to keep up. But she was not walking at her normal speed. She was stooped forward further than I had remembered. She walked with a limp.

She stopped at the edge of the village. For many breaths, she did not look at me. She was rasping. There was a catch in her throat I did not like.

« Elder? » I called.

« Fierce one, » she replied. « Your mother would be proud to see you. »

I was always proud to hear the Elder say how proud she was of me, but this felt different. As if this was the last time she could.

« Elder, » I began.

« I am glad you can fend for yourself in the forest, » she cut in. « And take care of someone else as well. It makes me hope for your future. »

The words were meant to be comforting. They made me afraid.

« Elder, » I started again.

« Why did you come back, Fierce One? » The Elder looked at me. « What did you hope I could tell you? »

I had no idea. The anger that had driven me across chasms to the invaders' hives had ebbed now that I had met Simon and seen how he reacted to the truth. Perhaps I did not need revenge to make things right.

« Come with us, » I said. « Simon needs our help. There is a bad man who has hurt many people. We help Simon, he can help us. »

She tilted her head at me. « What happened to your plan to make the invaders pay? »

I sucked in my breath. « It . . . changed. »

The Elder looked around at the shadows of the forest in the fog. « After living this long, I have found that rage only takes us out to deep water. It does not help us swim. And so, in many ways, it takes us too far. I am glad you have learned this before you drowned. »

« Come with us, » I said again.

The Elder chuckled, a rumble in her chest that was touched with regret. « I cannot. »

« But — »

The Elder began to cough, a high, chirrupy sound

that made no words, only made me wince in pain. She bent over so far, I dropped my spear and grabbed her shoulder, though I had no hope of holding her up. Indeed, as she came forward, I feared I would be crushed. "Simon!"

A second pair of hands grabbed the Elder. Simon grunted as she pitched into him. His feet slipped on the mud.

The Elder was too heavy for both of us, but together we were strong enough to ease her fall to the ground. She lay a moment, then rolled onto her back, her breathing shallow.

I knelt by her. Simon knelt across from me.

« Elder? » I swallowed. « Elder! »

She brought her breathing under control, and took one, slow, deep breath. « Fierce One. I cannot go with you. I am going nowhere in this world. »

Her words were another punch in my chest. « Do not talk that way! You live! »

« Not for much longer. »

« No! »

She reached out a fist, then uncurled a talon which she gently drew down my cheek. « You are a good child. You were raised right. You saw the invaders' hives and you learned their language. There is much you can do if you only try, but you cannot stop time. »

The horror of what she told me filled my mind. I looked at the days ahead, with no Elder watching over me. No one who understood me. « I do not want to be alone! »

The Elder chittered softly. It was laughter. I frowned at her.

« You are *not* alone, » she said. Her talon reached up, then tapped Simon on the chest. He looked from the Elder to me, bewildered.

She took a deep breath and turned to Simon. « Did you find . . . what you were looking for? »

He looked at her, then back at me, asking permission. I tipped my head, *yes*.

He looked down at the Elder. « Yes. I did. »

« You have questions, Strange Boy? » asked the Elder.

Simon thought through his words carefully, then worked his mouth. « *Ek-Taak-Tock-Tack* . . . How here? »

The Elder took another breath, then another. Finally she said, « There were . . . hatchlings. Seven. Three small, four much younger. Five males. Two female. »

Simon thought about this. « Your people . . . raise them? »

« We do not kill children, » the Elder replied.

The words stayed in the air between us. The Elder's people did not kill children. Simon's people . . . did. Simon looked at the ground. I held my breath. The Elder's breath rasped.

Finally, Simon looked up and said, « I sorry. I make this right. »

Another pause. The Elder asked, « How? »

« I . . . » Simon licked his lips. « I not know. I try. »

She started to say something, but another fierce coughing spell wracked her body.

« Elder! » I grabbed her shoulders. I felt so powerless.

The Elder got her breathing under control. She eased me aside and looked at Simon. « You want to make this right? »

Simon nodded. The Elder stared at him. I leaned close. « He says yes. »

« The truth, » she said to Simon. « Bring it back to your people. »

Simon licked his lips. He looked pale, but he nodded. « Yes. »

« The eggs, » she chittered. « The eggs are your responsibility. Protect them. »

Simon nodded again. « Yes. Promise. »

She took another shuddering breath. « *Ek-Taak-Tock-Taak.* »

I leaned forward. « What, Elder? What? »

But she was not talking to me. She was looking at Simon.

« Yes? » he asked.

« She . . . your responsibility . . . too. Take her home. »

« What? » I snapped. « Elder? »

She looked at me, but her eyes were looking through me. Like my mother's had. I felt suddenly colder.

« You are not alone, Fierce One, » she said. « Go to your people. »

« *Them?* The invaders are not my people! »

The Elder looked up at the sky. « They are all you have left. »

Then she died.

• • •

SIMON:

The Elder went still. The colour seemed to seep out of her. It took me a moment to realize what had happened. That realization hit at the same time as it hit Eliza.

« Elder? » She touched the Elder, then shook her. « Elder! »

The Elder didn't move.

« No! » she clicked. « No! » She grabbed the Elder and started sobbing. Her cries echoed across the empty buildings as the wind rattled the roofs.

I sat there, numb from what I'd learned from the *Icarus* log, and numb from the responsibility placed on my shoulders. I couldn't think of what to do. I stared at Eliza as she wept.

And it struck me that she was now truly alone. Earlier, I'd imagined her as one girl alone in the fog forest, but the truth was she hadn't been alone. She'd had the Elder back home, waiting for her. But no longer.

I reached out and touched her shoulder. "Eliza . . ." I began.

She flinched and shoved me back. « Do not touch me! »

I quailed at her fury. "But—"

« Do not talk to me! » She leapt to her feet, her hand swiping up her spear. I brought up a hand, as if that could hold her back, and for a second I thought she would run me through. Instead, she yelled at me in her click language.

« Do not talk to me! You bring death! Death follows you! Death follows wherever you people go! »

« *Ek-Taak-Tock-Tack,* » I pleaded.

She turned away with a howl, and threw her spear at the air. It vanished into the fog. A second later, a rooftop rang from the impact.

She stood a moment, breathing heavily. Finally, she swiped the air between us with an open hand. « Do not talk to me. » And she walked back into her village.

The invaders are not my people, she'd said.

I struggled to my feet and followed her, keeping my distance, as she strode back to the village square. Outside the Elder's hut she fell to her knees, covered her face with her hands, and wept. I kept watch, making no sound.

She stopped crying at last, and looked up at the sky.

Finally she stood up and began looking through the huts and pulling out supplies. She sorted these into piles, keeping her eyes on her work, not looking at me.

Not knowing what else to do, I leaned against one of the buildings and stared at the ground. I felt the *Icarus*'s black box in my pocket and I pulled it out. It gleamed in the foggy light, perfectly preserved after sixty-three years.

The same could not be said about my uniform. It was ruined after all the time we'd spent walking here: mud-stained and full of holes. Useless. And suddenly, I didn't want to wear it anymore.

We do not kill children.

The invaders are not my people.

I unzipped the tunic, yanked it off and threw it to the ground. I stared at it. Then the emotions that had been building in me poured out. Daniel Tal had reduced the Elder's people to nothing. And to hide this, his son Nathaniel had haunted my life. So many people had died: Rachel, Aaron, Ethan, Isaac . . . Mom. Iapyx, all of Iapyx. It was a travesty.

I pulled off my shoes and threw them as far as I could, yelling with each one. They bounced off a distant metal roof with satisfying clangs. My trousers followed. A wind rustled the burnt branches and rattled the twisted metal. It cooled my bare back.

Eliza stopped what she was doing. She stared at me.

Kicking the last piece of clothing off and stomping it into the ground, I stood up, feeling air all round me. I felt like I could finally breathe. For a long moment I did nothing but breathe.

Then I walked to where Eliza waited and began sorting out supplies and putting them in bags, ready to carry. I slipped the *Icarus*'s black box into a pouch. I looked at her.

She didn't look angry anymore. I couldn't tell quite how she looked, except serious. She stood up. I stood up with her, our gazes locked.

"I know the truth," I said. "I know what we must do." Then I asked, « Will you come with me? »

She looked at the empty huts, the ruined roofs. Then she looked at me, her gaze firm.

« Yes. »

CHAPTER TWENTY-TWO
THE VOICE OF GRIEF

ELIZA:

Much as I wanted to, I could not leave right away. We had to prepare the Elder's body.

We moved the Elder to the edge of the swamp outside the village. I sent Simon to gather wood. He moved about, while I stood solemnly over her body, as I had seen others do for their dead. They said no words until the time was right. I wondered, though, if they thought about the whiles spent in friendship. I thought about that.

I also thought: She looks so much smaller in death than in life.

Simon finished stacking the wood and he came to stand beside me. He looked at my face, then at the Elder, and matched my silence. Our fingers brushed and he took my hand. And, for once, I did not take my hand away.

But soon it was time. I gathered the bits of wood and wove the most flexible ones into a nest that float-ed on the swampy water. I motioned for Simon to help me move the Elder onto her death nest. When it was ready, I grabbed an edge and pushed into the swamp. The water lapped up my legs and over my waist, but I kept going.

Then the current pulled at the nest, and I let go. The Elder slipped through a gap in the trees. I watched until the fog veiled the nest from sight.

I stood with Simon, up to my waist in water, and began the Grief Song.

« *Go to waters beyond.*
And the rewards that wait there.
Justice. Joy.
Your time has ended.
The fight against pain.
Against hunger and need.
Is over.
Go beyond, to your well-deserved . . . »

I stopped. I bit my lip in frustration. I could not say the last word. My eyes stung. I could not say it!

• • •

SIMON:

I stood in the silence a long moment before I looked up, wondering what was wrong. Eliza was staring ahead. She worked her mouth, but no sound came out.

From listening to the earlier words, I guessed that the word Eliza wanted was "peace." I realized then that we'd never spoken it. We'd spoken around it, using words like *rest*, *quiet* and *no more fighting*, but none of these would have fit as well.

Then I realized that the Elder had made other sounds when she'd been speaking to Eliza — sounds I couldn't mimic, much less begin to translate. My mouth hadn't been built for it.

Eliza's mouth hadn't been built for it either.

So the word remained unsaid. Her jaw tightened. Her eyes glistened.

Then she let out a wail. It rang across the roofs and the water, rising and falling in pitch. It was more than just grief. There were no words in it. It was just Eliza's voice, singing the Elder's way to the Creator.

As Eliza let out her mournful wail, I found my thoughts straying. Back to Iapyx and all the people I'd left behind — who had gone before me. To Aaron. To Ethan. Marni. Rachel. I hadn't had time to stay for the Lament. So I sent up a solemn prayer from my childhood, one that had been spoken at my mother's funeral. I said it for them, and for the Elder.

"You have seen the light and been burned.
You have done all you can for those who need you.
It is done.
May your soul find peace in the shade."

Eliza's fist touched my shoulder. She'd stopped singing. I turned and she pulled me closer.

I closed my eyes as she touched her forehead to

mine, then her nose to my nose, then her forehead to my forehead again, as she and the Elder had done on her return home. We put our arms around each other and held on for a long moment. I felt her breath on me. Then we let go.

Without a word, we returned to the village and put on our carrying bags. We walked into the fog together, leaving the ruins of the *Icarus* behind.

ICARUS RISING

CHAPTER TWENTY-THREE
WALKING TO DAEDALON

SIMON:

Rachel came to me in my dreams again.

I surged from the latest nightmare and found myself staring into Eliza's face. She kept her hands on my shoulders.

"You scream," she said. Then, « Are you all right? »

The nightmare faded, but not quickly enough. I shuddered. "Yeah."

She stayed close, frowning. "Who Rachel?"

I blinked up at her. Had I been talking in my sleep?

"Just a friend," I started, then stopped myself. That lie was far too obvious. "A good friend. She died when my city fell."

I rolled away.

I felt Eliza's eyes on me for a long moment. Then she sighed, turned away, and nestled down beside me to sleep.

•••

ELIZA:

We left the Elder, the last of my people. We left my home, for the last time. We walked.

Simon could see the pathways now. I hunted; he gathered fruits. We shared silences across our fires.

We came up through the cloud and into the narrow gap. On the other side, we paused. The hive that had been there the first time I came to this chasm was gone. Simon's city. *Eye-a-pix*.

Simon had paused the last time we were here, and now I knew why. Then we were leaving his world behind, and now we were leaving mine. I had been here before, but then the Elder had been back home. In a strange way, I had felt she was still with me. Now, no longer.

I heard the stones scrape. Simon came up beside me, looking at me.

"Eliza —" He was going to apologize. What for? It would not bring the Elder back.

I cut him off. "Where we go? Let us *go*."

"I've changed my mind about Octavia." He looked grim. "We're walking to Daedalon."

"Why?"

He got quiet. The dry wind whistled around us, tugging at our travel pouches, our hair. Finally, without looking at me, he said, "I've been thinking about the sickness that swept the Elder's people after the advance team arrived."

"*My* people," I said.

He paused at that, then went on. "Daniel Tal — Nathaniel's father — was the chief medical officer of the *Icarus*, and its chief xenobiologist."

"Zee-no-by- . . ."

"Sorry. He knew how plants and animals worked. He knew about how things get sick."

The silence stretched again. "The sickness. He did this?" I said.

His shoulders hunched up. "I'm not sure. But I think he did."

« We always believed this, » I said. « My people did not understand what happened, but we knew enough to connect it to the invaders. »

"We didn't know," Simon said quietly. "Most of us never knew. And I think that's what's happening here. Daniel Tal committed genocide, and his sons have killed to protect that secret."

The wind blew. My skin prickled in the dry heat. "Thank you," I said. "Not lie to me."

We had gotten around to "lie."

"I'm sorry," he whispered.

I tapped his shoulder blades with my fist. "This Na-than-i-el . . . He at Daedalon?"

He straightened up. "I overheard the guards talking about him when they were looking in our cave. I'm sure he's at Daedalon."

Suddenly, I saw Simon's goal. I was impressed. "Good!"

He frowned at me. "Good?"

« It is good that he is there. If he is there, we will find him. And when we find him, we shall have our revenge. »

"We'll have justice," he said sharply. He tapped the bag at his hip, where he had his black box.

I raised my shoulders and let them drop. "Same thing."

He looked at me a long breath, so silent that I had to look at him. There was a sadness in his eyes that I could not understand. "No," he said at last. "It's not."

"What mean?"

He bit his lips. « Truth. No more lies. A better story. » And he said again, "Justice."

"I not understand you."

« I not understand *you*, » he said.

Revenge, justice. We just didn't have the words. Maybe even it was more than words.

I felt the distance between us, and the silence. I turned away and walked down the slope into the fog. A few heartbeats later, I heard his footfalls as he followed me. It was a long while before Simon found something different to talk about. We did not talk about Nathaniel again.

• • •

SIMON:

Months of walking brought us to Daedalon, practically on the eve of Nocturne. Eliza pulled aside the ferns and nodded. « There. »

The fence stretched before us, buzzing with energy. Eliza clearly didn't like it, but we were home. I felt strangely ambivalent about that. I had been gone so long and had seen so much, home was nothing familiar. At the same time, I felt a tightness in my chest. Was it nerves? Anticipation? We had much to do.

"Plan?" asked Eliza.

« We go in, » I said. « We sneak past guards. Find clothes. »

« How do we get past the barrier? »

"We can't touch it," I replied. "We can't go over it or open it. So we have to make the guards open it for us."

She raised an eyebrow. « How? »

I brought out the full canister of firepills we'd taken from the *Icarus* crash site. « With fire. Get wood. I prepare. »

Eliza stepped away. Near the base of the fence, about five metres away from the gate, I started stacking up sticks for a fire, a fire with a difference. Rather than start a single firepill and pile kindling on top, I opened the canister and filled it further with more firepills from another canister we'd taken. I placed this carefully beneath the sticks, beneath a thick bough that I'd propped up with a precariously leaning smaller stick.

I didn't hear Eliza approach, so when she asked, « Simon! What are you doing? » I almost knocked the bough onto the loaded canister.

"Don't distract me," I muttered. "I need to con-centrate."

She folded her arms. "What you doing?"

I nudged the canister forward. "I don't want to wait while a little fire becomes a big fire to bring the guards out."

"But what plan?" she said. "You not good plans."

She might be right. How was I going to knock the small stick away so the heavy one could hit the fire-pills and ignite them? I should have used string. It was too late now. Instead, I grabbed another stick and poked it into the fire to knock the small stick down.

I heard Eliza backing up. "This smart?"

"It's fine," I muttered, and the stick knocked the prop, and the bough fell on the full canister with a crack.

Eliza dove for the ground.

It was a very big fireball. Above me, the fog went bright yellow, then angry red, and the distance be-tween it and me closed, very fast.

Eliza grabbed me as I was scrambling up. She yanked me away from the fireball, and we landed in a heap among the ferns.

She pushed herself up and glared down at me. « You idiot! You and your silly plans: *I know, I shall go and get between a mother slink and her hatchling! I shall set myself on fire!* »

Maybe it was shock, or adrenaline, but I grinned. Behind us, the fire was catching. "I think this plan will work."

She helped me up. We stepped behind a bulbtree

while the flames licked up, igniting the wet wood. The fog turned orange.

Beyond, a door banged. A man shouted. I translated his words for Eliza.

"Fire extinguisher!" the man said. "Now!"

There was a whine and a squeal. The gate was opening. « They are coming, » I said.

Two shadows appeared in the fog, materializing into security officers holding fire extinguishers, which they sprayed at the fire. I nudged Eliza and nodded at the open gate.

She hesitated. She frowned at the guards, and brought out her blowpipe.

No! I shook my head and beckoned her to follow. She didn't move.

The guards were still fighting the fire, but they wouldn't be occupied forever. I pointed emphatically at the gate.

Glowering, Eliza shoved her blowpipe away and followed me. I led the way through the gate and past the rows of crops.

There was no need to shoot these guards. If we could get in without their notice, it would be much better. And I thought we could get in without their notice.

Until the stem materialized out of the fog, and I saw they'd shut the door behind them.

I looked behind us. The fog no longer glowed orange. I heard no sounds of spray. The guards were talking.

"What do you think happened?" said one. "Did a branch fall on the fence?"

"No," the other replied. "Look at that stack of sticks. This wasn't an accident. This was a bonfire."

I jerked on the door handle, but it wouldn't move. There was no button release, just a deadbolt lock that I had no key to.

"Bonfire?" said the first guard. "What? Who? Tick-tock monsters?"

"Whatever it was . . . I think they set it to lead us out—"

Footsteps pounded through the undergrowth. I rushed for the gate. Perhaps I could shut it. But even as I took my first steps, I knew I wouldn't be in time.

Then Eliza stepped up beside me, putting her blowpipe to her lips, and I couldn't stop what happened next.

• • •

ELIZA:

I blew, reloaded, and blew a second time. The second guard lurched out after the first and keeled over on top of him.

I shoved the blowpipe back into my pouch. Then I looked up and saw Simon staring at me. « Why are you looking at me like that? »

"You killed them!" He knelt by the guards' limp bodies and pulled the heavier one off his partner.

I stared at Simon. Why would he think this? « I did not! »

"But — you hit them with your darts—"

Is that what he thought my darts did? « It wears off after a sleep. *Two* sleeps on people, » I said. « You *must* know this! Always I have to break the animal's neck after I hit it with my blowdart! »

He was suddenly unable to meet my gaze. "No . . . I did not know that. I thought . . ."

What in water did he think of me? « I do not kill unless I need to kill. »

Simon looked up at that. He looked at me, curious. « How do you know if real need? »

Somehow, that question stung. « I just do! »

"Come on," he said. "Let's get them inside."

Simon started to move the the guards. I noticed, however, that he checked to see that each man was still breathing. I tried not to be insulted.

We dragged them in beyond the fence. Simon pressed a button on one of the posts, and the fence gap closed. He searched the guards' clothes and found the key to the stem's doors. He opened them and we stepped inside.

The inside was brighter than I had expected, and smaller. Lights burned behind glass in the ceiling. There was a pair of sliding doors, leading to a smaller room.

Simon led me into this smaller room. And here our trail ended. There were no other doors. No steps leading up into the city. I looked up and around, searching for secret openings. To come all this way . . .

But Simon slid the door closed and pulled a lever.

Steam hissed and the walls rattled. The floor shook and I grabbed a handhold.

"Elevator," he said quietly, but smiling. « Remember? Lift machine. I tell you. »

« Oh, yes. » But I felt trapped. And I hated that Simon took all of this in stride. I straightened up, planted my feet and gazed at the closed door, just as he was doing.

« Will this take us to the top of the hive? » I asked.

"No," he replied. "Only a hundred metres or so."

After a breath of silence, he added, "It's for defence. You go up one short elevator because, if there's trouble, they can shut it down. They make you switch elevators so that someone taking over the elevator doesn't get an easy run to the city."

« Defence from what? »

He grimaced. « The Elder's people, I think. »

« My people. »

He did not look at me.

« When we come here, » he said, slowly, « we put our cities on fog floor. We could not see. Our machines — » he searched for the word, « red turned. » "Rusted." « Then . . . »

He took a deep breath. I knew the story my Elder had told me, but this was the first time Simon had talked of what he really knew. I waited.

« Stories say clicking monsters attack out of fog. Hundreds die. Many never found. »

Silence fell. The elevator suddenly seemed much smaller.

« The Elder had her reasons, » I said.

« I not blame her, » he said.

« I think you do, » I said. Then I added, « I do not blame you. »

The floor stopped rising. Simon opened the door. Even though he had told me about the lift machines, I was still startled to see that the room outside had changed.

We stepped into a corridor. The wall curved in front of us and, to our left, steps leading up curved behind the lift machine's shaft. There was a door a few steps up. It was open, and voices drifted out.

Simon tapped my arm, a warning. I nodded. I crept to the edge of the door and peered in. There were two men and one woman inside, seated around a table, holding small, square pieces of paper that, from time to time, they tossed onto the table. The two men had their backs to the door. The woman did not. No one was looking at us.

I signalled back to Simon. Three. No one watching.

Simon nodded. He motioned me back from the door and did not object when I pulled my blowpipe out and shoved a thorn inside. Then he coughed, loudly.

Feet shifted in the room. "Ben? Gaz? That you? Everything all right out there?"

Another voice chuckled: the woman's voice. "You two aren't sneaking up to the Nocturne celebrations, are you?"

"Gaz is out cold!" Simon shouted. "Come out here, quickly! Give me a hand!"

Scrapes and footsteps erupted from the room. Shadows darkened the doorway, and a guard emerged. I blew. He managed one shout before he fell forward. A second guard came out and tripped over the first. I shot again. He jerked as the thorn hit, then lay still.

I listened for one more set of footfalls, but none came. I looked at Simon. He shared my look, and crept to the door, peering in. Then he lunged into the room.

I rushed after him. I arrived just as he pulled the female guard away from a slot in the wall. The guard was holding a container that would have fit into the wall, and Simon seemed to think it very important that the container stay outside. The guard turned and smashed the container, end-first, on the side of Simon's head. He stumbled, almost fell, but grabbed the guard and tackled her. They struggled.

I could not use my blowpipe. I might hit Simon. But then Simon shoved the guard with all his might, and brought up his hand, fist balled, and struck. His knuckles connected hard with her jaw and she crashed to the floor.

Simon looked horrified, but I could see the fight wasn't over. I shoved a thorn into my blowpipe and blew. The guard flinched, then lay limp.

Simon gaped. "You didn't have to do that!"

I frowned at him. "I did. She would kick you. Hard. She stays down now."

"Yeah, but —"

"What?"

"She was *down*!" he yelled. Partly to himself, he added, "I almost knocked her out cold. I could have killed her!"

"Simon!" Then I switched, the better to say what I meant: « You are not going to bring the truth to your cities without hurting people. They will stop you, otherwise! »

He looked at me, breathing heavily. Then he looked at the body on the floor. I could see he had many objections floating in his head, but he could not give voice to them. Probably because he knew I was right.

• • •

SIMON:

I hated that she was right.

The last guard had been trying to send an emergency message. I'd stopped her before she'd gotten the canister away, and that bought us some time, though I didn't know how much. Probably until the shifts changed.

I looked around and found a storage locker, with uniforms stacked on shelves. "Good," I said. "Something to wear."

Eliza stared at the grey garments with distaste. "Have to?"

I nodded. "Forest camouflage won't work in the city. We need city camouflage."

She huffed. « Fine. Show me how to wear these. »

I thumbed through the locker and tossed her a uniform that I thought might fit. "Here."

She unfurled the bundle of fabric and stared at the grey tunic. "Why you wear these?" She slapped the tunic's chest. "You not *need* these. Why you wear them? You ashamed of your skin?"

"Yes," I said. "We are ashamed."

I meant a lot of things by that. The shame of what our ancestors had done on Old Mother Earth, the crimes that had driven us into the darkness. When people heard of what the *Icarus* had done to the Elder's people — the same crime, as if genocide were bred in our bones — I did not know what would happen. But I knew shame was the least of it.

I also knew Eliza didn't understand anything beyond the simplest part of my answer. Shaking her head, she pulled off her travel pouches. For the first time in months, I averted my eyes as she measured a tunic and trousers against herself.

We stowed our carrying bags, after taking what little we needed. I noticed that Eliza left her knives in her bag, but she took out her blowpipe and a dozen thorns wrapped in leather and put them in a pocket. I put on my uniform and transferred the black box to my pocket. When I looked back at Eliza, she was dressed, but struggling with her belt.

"Here, let me." I took both ends from her, slipped the latch on and tightened it. Then I pulled her hair back. She squawked at that, but didn't slap my hands away. I tied her hair back into a ponytail. "There." I stepped back to look at her.

I had to admit, wearing a uniform that fit her, with

slender, grey trousers, made her look very . . . different. It was . . . interesting . . . seeing her wearing it.

"You look nice," I said. She gave me a suspicious look and for some reason my mouth went dry. "You look . . . very nice. Really! You look . . ." There was a word I wanted to say, but I was afraid that if I said it, she'd hit me. So, instead I said, " . . . nice."

She tugged at the cuffs of the sleeves. « I feel strange! »

"It suits you," I said. « We must go. »

« Wait. » Eliza reached into the locker, and brought out two guns in their holsters. She handed one to me. « Here. »

I held it gingerly. "We don't need these."

"We do."

"They're dangerous," I began.

« I see that, » she cut in. « But the guards had them. So should we. »

I did not like where this was going, sneaking through Daedalon with guns. I was not that person. "Eliza, I can't—"

She cocked her head. « What was it you said about camouflage? »

I really hated the fact that she was right. "Fine." I clipped the holster to my belt. "But keep it in the holster. Blowpipe only."

She nodded and strode from the room with such purpose, I thought she should have scissors in her hand.

CHAPTER TWENTY-FOUR
NOCTURNE PREPARATIONS

SIMON:

When the elevator shuddered to a stop and the doors parted, I heard laughter.

A half dozen men and women walked past, the insignia of the flight bay on their sleeves, and bottles tucked under their arms. One woman looked at me, and I had a sudden fear I'd be recognized, but her eyes fell on my guard's uniform, and she flashed me a smile. Then they were gone.

Eliza stood tense. Her hand was in the pocket of her uniform, holding her blowpipe. I tapped her arm and gave her a look that I hoped told her to keep calm.

Guarding the elevator that led down to the stem compound was a large security desk and an empty chair. Somebody wasn't at his post, and neither were the flight bay attendants.

Then I remembered the date: Nocturne. Though the chasm had been darkening, it was hard to believe seven months had passed since Iapyx fell. It felt like yesterday. It felt like a century ago.

Nocturne, the end of white, the end of restraint. Nocturne: darkness and colour. We'd timed our arrival well. People weren't thinking about staying at their posts. The last flights were probably in, and there was nothing for the flight bay attendants to do but start their party.

I looked around, remembering the layout of the place when I was last here. The upper levels held the factories, which took advantage of all that heat. Then came the housing levels, then finally the lowest level of all, which housed the flight bay, the arboretum, some offices . . . and the prison.

I tapped Eliza's arm. "Let's go."

We walked away from the flight bay, following the crowds that were gathering at the arboretum — a satellite to the main event in Daedalon's Great Hall, with less music and more drink.

The arboretum was a long room that stretched the width of the lowest level of Daedalon. Though longer and wider than the Great Hall, it only occupied one level of the city. Light globes were mounted on the support piers, filling the room with an even, yellow glow.

There were plants everywhere. Specially bred crops from Old Mother Earth grew in tight rows alongside vegetables we'd adopted from this world. Couples giggled and darted among the cornrows.

A young woman ran out, red ribbons fluttering in her dark hair. She skidded to a halt in front of us and gave us a giddy grin. "You're not Ebenezer!" she said.

She shrieked as a young man sneaked up behind her and tickled her sides. "I'm here, love!" he said.

The woman grabbed Ebenezer's hand. "C'mon! I've got to show you something."

And she kissed him, as if we weren't there. Then, remembering that we were, the couple gave us grins that were both sheepish and wicked. They slipped into the cover of the corn.

Eliza stared after them, eyebrows up.

"It's Nocturne," I said, as if that explained everything.

We left the arboretum. Ahead of us, the corridor came to an abrupt end in a set of perspex doors.

The prison. Beyond was a large room with a big wall and two big doors. There was a desk there — a big one. It was not empty. As we approached, I counted the grey uniforms. One man sat at the desk. Another leaned on the desk, talking to him. Two more guards in front of the shining doors, one of them partly blocked by the man leaning on the desk.

My eyes flicked to the man behind the desk. *Was that . . . ?* Well, that changed things. But only a little.

I didn't slow my pace. « Four guards. »

Eliza matched my pace. « Yes. Four shots. »

« Three, » I said, quickly.

« What? »

« Three shots, » I snapped. « Two at door. One stand at . . . long flat thing? » I grimaced. "Desk."

She frowned at me. « Not the man *behind* the big wood block? »

« We need him. »

She scowled, but didn't object. That didn't necessarily mean that she was going to listen to me, but I decided to take it as a good sign. I shoved through the doors and made a beeline for the man leaning against the desk.

He turned as I approached. His expression went from jovial to bewildered as I swung my fist and caught him straight on the jaw. He staggered back and caught himself on the desk, but he didn't keel over. As I clasped my knuckles in pain, he turned on me, shouting. "What in sunlight did you do *that* for?"

A thorn zinged past my ear and caught him in the chest. He clutched at it, then went stiff, falling to his knees before keeling over.

The two guards by the door swung up their weapons, but they were looking for guns, not a woman with a reed in her mouth. She blew, reloaded and blew, all in the space of a second. The two guards lay face first on the floor.

The face of the guard behind the desk went as grey as his uniform.

"Hello, Sergeant Gaal," I said. "You remember me, don't you? From the fog forest?"

I caught Gaal's wrist just before he could grab an emergency message canister. We struggled. His other hand went for his gun, but I grabbed that wrist too. Then he grabbed my shoulders and twisted,

306

hauling me over the desk and onto the floor. Next moment we were grunting and kicking at each other, each desperately trying to keep the other's hand away from his gun.

"How — can you — be alive?" Gaal grunted.

"How can you still be a guard?" I gasped back. "You said yourself — they were arresting Grounders — after Iapyx fell." I smacked his wrist against the floor. "How — did you escape the purge? Did you sell out your friends?"

"Shut up!" Gaal hissed.

Eliza loomed into view, her blowpipe at her lips.

"No!" I yelled.

She glared at me, but put the blowpipe away and looked around for something to use as a club. Then she said to Gaal in her own language, « You there. You should stop, now. »

Alarmed, Gaal looked over his shoulder. It was a split-second reaction, but it was enough. I pulled my hand free and grabbed my gun. "She's right," I said. "You really should stop now."

Gaal stopped struggling. I snatched his gun from his holster with my other hand and held it ready. He sagged. Keeping his moves slow and careful, he let go of me and gently eased himself back. He looked at Eliza, and he looked at me. "I thought you were dead."

"I'm not."

"But how did you survive the fog forest?"

"I found friends." I nodded at Eliza. "I brought

one back with me. Eliza, this is Sergeant Gaal of the Daedalon security force. Gaal, meet Eliza. Introduce yourself, Eliza!"

Eliza looked at Gaal. She looked at me. She grinned. « What do you want me to say? »

"Monster!" Gaal crabbed backward.

I stood up, my gun ready. "Does she look like a monster to you?"

Gaal's face was a mixture of bewilderment and fear. "N–no."

"Good. But you saw what she did to your friends. If you don't want to find yourself laid out on the floor for the next two days, you'll do as I say. Understood?" I waved the gun at the big doors. "Now, open these."

As Eliza moved the unconscious guards into the corner and took their guns, Gaal fished a ring of keys from his belt loop. He unlocked the doors and opened them. We stepped inside.

The corridor was empty. There were no guards. Wooden doors lined both walls, stretching into the distance. I heard coughing, and the hush of people waiting.

"We're a skeleton crew," Gaal explained. "After the evening meal, everybody booked off for Nocturne. Except for me and the three guards you, um . . ." he glanced at Eliza's blowpipe, "shot. It was supposed to be a quiet night."

"Not this night." I looked at the rows of doors, unsure where to start, and worried at where it would finish.

Eliza nudged me. "Who here? Why we here?"

"Friends." I turned to Gaal. "Grounders, right? Did you sell out your friends?"

Gaal flinched. "No. I just . . . kept my head down. Nobody implicated me. They pled guilty at the trial. Their sentences were commuted to prison terms."

"Hmm." I felt grim. "Take me to their leader."

He hesitated. But I had the gun. "This way." He led the way down the corridor. The cells were quiet, with nothing more than the occasional cough coming from behind the closed doors.

Gaal stopped by a door that looked like all the rest. "This is the person you want to talk to." He sorted through the keys on his ring. A moment's rattle of the lock got the door open. The room was dim inside.

"Come on out," Sergeant Gaal called into the cell. "Someone's here to see you."

Someone coughed. A cot squeaked. "I've said all I'm going to say to Nathaniel that doesn't involve swear words," said a voice within. "If he wants to hear me swear, by all means, bring him in. I could teach him a thing or two."

I had to laugh. "You know the value of words, CommController."

There was a moment's silence. Then an incredulous, "Simon?" Feet hit the floor and an old man in white overalls came to the door. He gaped at me. "Simon!"

I clasped his hand. "Hello, Gabriel."

• • •

ELIZA:

We had released an old man. I did not know who he was, but he looked happy to see Simon. "You're alive!" he said. "How?"

"I might ask you the same question," said Simon. He was grinning

"We were lucky," said the man Simon had called Gabriel. But he did not look as though he thought himself lucky. "While they were taking us to the cells, the evacuation alarms sounded, and everyone ran for the ornithopters. It was chaos. Someone saw my rank, grabbed me and bundled me inside one of the last ones. I barely managed to get the battery girl on with me. But when we got to Daedalon, Nathaniel was there. He spotted me, and had us arrested." He looked up at Simon. "But where did you come from? Where did you hide all this time?"

"In the fog forest."

Gabriel looked at Simon in disbelief. Then his eyes flicked to me.

I stood there, silent. Yet another invader that I had to trust because Simon trusted him. It had taken half a sun turn to come to know Simon enough to trust him — more than trust him. How could I do that with this new invader in the space of heartbeats? My clothes itched. I pulled at the cloth that hugged my neck too tight.

"I've found the truth," Simon said to Gabriel.

"The truth? What—"

"Long story. We'll get to that. But right now, I need your help."

"Yes, anything."

"Let's get the Grounders out of prison. I assume they're all here?"

"Yes," said Gabriel. "The few who survived from Iapyx, and most of the membership from Daedalon — present company excepted." He gave Gaal a dark look. Gaal looked down and turned away, opening more doors.

"A plea bargain?" Simon shook his head. "You knew the truth. Why did you plead guilty?"

"The public wanted blood," said Gabriel. "The Tals held all the cards. Pleading guilty saved us from execution or banishment. It stopped the witch hunts. The battery girl who was with me . . ." He nodded up above him. "She's up there, a battery girl again, on condition she keeps her mouth shut."

Then he glanced at Gaal, who stayed very quiet. "It also kept some others on the outside, so there'd be a chance the truth could come out once the fury died down."

People were leaving their rooms — cells — which Simon had explained they weren't allowed to leave. Seeing these rooms, I could sense the horror of this place. To be confined in so small a cave . . . .

But as more invaders left their cells and joined us, looking bewildered, looking at me, I felt the cave closing in. I slowed my breath as if a slink was near.

"But what about the evidence I gave you?" Simon asked. "The arrivals log? The requisition form?"

"Just pieces of paper against the tumult," Gabriel replied. "Not enough to prove our innocence, and that was what we had to do, given the public mood." He gave Simon a sly smile. "We still have them, though. The battery girl was able to hide them during our brief run of freedom on Daedalon. She keeps them safe. Nathaniel doesn't know."

Simon seemed happy with that, but unsure. "Couldn't you have appealed to the Captain—"

"The Captain's dead, Simon."

Simon stared in horror. "No! Did — Nathaniel didn't—"

Gabriel shook his head. "The Captain died in his sleep. Cancer. It wasn't unexpected."

"But —"

"We're in the midst of an election," Gabriel said. "In some ways, that helped. It's one reason the authorities wanted us dealt with quickly — hence the plea bargains."

Simon looked grim. "Who's running?"

"Mayor Tuan, from Daedalon, as expected." Gabriel matched Simon's expression. "And Matthew Tal."

"Will Tal win?"

"He's the mayor of a murdered city, Simon. Of course he'll win."

This place was getting crowded, and loud. People were chattering like animals in the forest. I could not follow their speech, but I could sense their nervousness and fear. I did not like being here. But Simon, though he looked concerned, was relaxed. Like this was his place. His home.

As the crowd gathered closer, I stepped back, then back again, seeking shadow, and whatever open space I could find.

"The mayor of Octavia's backing Tal. So are most in the outer cities," said Gabriel. "Tal would be acclaimed, except Mayor Tuan is staying in the contest. Out of pride, I think."

"When's the vote?" asked Simon.

"Right after Nocturne."

Simon nodded, but I could tell he was upset. He motioned for Gaal to continue opening cells, and while Gabriel moved to talk to others, Simon saw me and came over. "A lot of people, isn't it?"

I scratched at my skin through the stupid grey coverings. I nodded at the frightened and nervous crowd. "We trust them?"

He looked shocked. "Of course!"

He was going to say something more, but somebody approached; a young man. "Look, thank you for getting us out of the cells, but what do we do now? It doesn't take many guards to outnumber us."

Others nearby nodded. "We don't need any more trouble," said a young woman. "We're safe here."

"Look, I've got a plan, but I need your help," Simon began.

But the fearful voices in the crowd overwhelmed him. Simon may have thought he was doing these people a kindness, but they did not seem grateful. I stepped farther into shadow.

I found myself by the door leading to the room with the desk and the three guards I had shot. I glanced outside, longing for the extra space.

Someone was moving in the outer area of the prison.

I pressed my back to the wall as a young man, dressed in white, knelt by the fallen guards. The boy called Ebenezer. This was not good. He could alert others.

I pulled out my blowpipe and shoved in a thorn.

Before I shot, a man and a woman, clad in grey, came into view. I pressed back into hiding. They stared at the guards, and each put their hand on their gun.

"Simon!" I hissed. "Simon!" But my voice was lost in the clamour of the prisoners.

The guards looked at our door. I ducked farther back into shadow as they pushed open the doors, hard. "Nobody move!" they shouted.

People jumped, some shouted. The guards entered, Ebenezer behind them, passing me.

The guards did not draw their guns. They did not need to. Except for Simon and Gabriel, the crowd from the cells drew back, cowed. Some even backed into their cells and closed the doors. *These* were the people Simon needed help from?

"What is going on here?" one guard demanded. "Back into your cells!"

Simon drew himself up and got ready to speak.

But he had no plan. How could he, when it had gone this wrong? But he did have me.

I stepped from the shadows, blowpipe in hand, and blew. Reloaded, and blew again. Both guards stiffened, then fell to the floor. Everyone stared in shocked silence. Especially Ebenezer. Then he turned and saw me.

"No! Wait!" Simon shouted.

I recognized Ebenezer's look: he was cornered, and like a slink, that made him dangerous. He grabbed up a fallen guard's gun.

I did not have time to reload, so I rushed him, grabbed his wrist, swung it toward the ceiling. The gun went off, an ear-battering noise. Screams followed.

"Please! Stop!" Simon yelled.

But the fear in Ebenezer's eyes blotted out reason. He fought like a slink, clinging to the gun, and he was strong. I could not let go to reload my blowpipe. He brought the gun down between us, where I knew it would be deadly. His hand still clutched it. I strained to keep it pointed safely away.

The gun fired a second time.

We stopped. I stared into Ebenezer's eyes, seeing the shock, disbelief and horror, and then a strange peace. He collapsed to the floor, blood staining his tunic in a widening circle. The gun slipped from his grip.

"No!" Simon shouted, rushing forward. "No! Somebody! Help him! He needs a doctor!"

People rushed forward. Someone pulled off his tunic and wadded it up, pushing it against the wound.

I felt warmth on my hands, looked down, and saw blood there.

Ebenezer gaped, then let out a groan. He looked through people, the same way my mother had stared. I shuddered.

People pulled back, but Simon worked frantically, pressing the tunic on the wound, shouting for help. Gabriel touched the boy's wrist, then let it drop.

"Simon, I'm sorry," said Gabriel. "He's dead."

CHAPTER TWENTY-FIVE
TO LIVE AND TO FIGHT

SIMON:

His name was Ebenezer Todd. He was eighteen. He grew up on Daedalon and apprenticed at the flight academy. We'd never met. He'd preferred mechanical work to flying and was soon routed to the maintenance crews. By the time he died, thanks to me, he'd been working a whole year at Daedalon's flight bay. We may have passed each other dozens of times, during which he was only a face and not a name.

His fiancée never forgave me.

"No," I whispered. I rose to my feet. "No!" I was yelling at a dead man. "Why did you have to follow us? Why did you have to be a hero?"

"Simon!" Eliza shouted.

I stood there, breathing heavily. The echoes of my shouts faded. I was aware of people staring at me, but I could only stare at Ebenezer.

I hadn't meant him to die. But he died anyway, because of what I was trying to do. Just like at the anchor, when Iapyx fell because we'd tried to stop Nathaniel's sabotage.

If I kept this up, more people were going to die. Maybe what some had said here was true: maybe we shouldn't speak out. Maybe I should step into a cell myself and close the door. Let Nathaniel have his secret. Let the world move forward on its own.

Then Gaal walked to his desk and pulled a lever. A rope stretching up from his desk snapped, and the outer room started to rumble. A black shutter fell into place in front of the prison's front doors. I looked at Gaal, bewildered.

"Lockdown." He pointed at another lever in the wall. "The alarm is still inactive, though. If nobody else comes, you have about a half-hour before someone notices. That barrier will keep people from just stumbling in."

Gabriel frowned. "Then how do we get out?"

"There's a secure door set into that barrier," said Gaal. "Wide enough for one person to get out at a time. Easily defended, and right now not under guard, so long as you move fast."

Eliza straightened up. "Why you do this?"

Gaal looked from her to me. He didn't quite meet my eyes. "Because I know you didn't destroy Iapyx. And, now you're here, you're going to do something about it. Last time I saw you . . . I sent you away to die." He looked down at Ebenezer. "I stand around, and people die." He looked up at me. "Well? What are you going to do? Whatever it is, now's the time to do it."

I stared at Ebenezer's limp form again, and thought of the Elder, lying in death, her civilization taken away by a lie. I had the truth. Stopping now meant Nathaniel would get away with it all. It meant a lot of deaths had been for nothing. Ebenezer's among them.

I looked at the Grounders. "You know as well as I do what Nathaniel did, his campaign of sabotage to turn the people against you. I can bring him to justice, but I need your help. More guards are coming. When they do, I need you to keep them occupied."

The crowd shifted nervously. The man who'd approached spoke up. "You're talking about a prison riot. There's already blood on the floor. We only have a handful of guns, and not many of us know how to fire them."

I raised my voice in the hubbub. "If all goes well, you'll be acquitted."

"So you say," said the man. "You weren't here for the mass arrests. You didn't hear people calling for our blood. We came away with prison sentences instead. Some people were starting to forget about us. Who are you to come and stir things up?"

"My name is Simon Daud." My voice echoed in the sudden silence. "You thought I was dead. You may have heard rumours that I was cast out into the fog forest. Well, those rumours are true."

People shook their heads. "Nothing survives the fog forest," a woman said.

"I did. And I can prove it." I brought out the black box.

I walked into the crowd, holding it out so they could see it. The light gleamed off the glossy seal of the Captain of the *Icarus*. Jaws dropped. People gasped. Everybody knew original technology when they saw it. They recognized the seal, and knew that the Captain didn't just give that stuff away. I finished my walk through the crowd in front of the man who'd spoken out. He gaped at the black box.

"What's your name?" I asked.

"David," he said. "David Hall."

"David," I repeated. "I'm sorry you were arrested. I'm sorry people called for your blood. But none of that was my fault. The person whose fault that *is* is walking around out there, and we've got to stop him. I can understand why you want to keep your head down. But now it's time to look up and around. Will you help me?"

David looked at me. He nodded.

"But what's your plan?" a woman shouted. Others murmured and nodded.

I hesitated. The truth was, I used to have a plan. Now I had to change it. With the Captain gone, I had no idea who to tell the truth to. I needed to get it out as widely as possible, so that Nathaniel had no chance to silence it. And I had to do it fast, before Matthew's position became unassailable.

But in the silence, I heard . . . music. I looked up, and found myself staring at one of the ventilation ducts. The music was soft, echoing down the tubes. Pipes and drums. Nocturne. The end of white. The end of restraint. Celebrating the setting of the sun.

I rounded on Gaal. "What time is it? How long until Nocturne? How long until the sunset?"

He thought. "A couple of hours."

I turned to Gabriel. "Give me an hour or so, then send people up to the Nocturne celebrations. Dress them up as guards so they blend in. The rest of you, when the guards come, make as much noise as you can, so you keep them off our backs. Okay?"

People looked at each other, but where they'd been cowed before, I saw something else: a quiet determination. Had the black box given them hope? Or was it me?

Gabriel clapped me on the shoulder. "We will. Good luck, Simon!"

I took a deep breath. This was it. Now or never.

I went over and tapped Eliza's wrist with my fist. "Come on. We've got work to do."

• • •

ELIZA:

We left the prison and walked through the arboretum again, hearing laughter among the plants. As we passed, a girl's voice called, "Ebenezer? Ebenezer? Have you seen Ebenezer?"

Simon hunched his shoulders and hurried past.

We came to another elevator, rose up a few floors, stopped, and then shifted sideways. Through gaps in the cage door, I caught glimpses of the city: people walking, people working, people laughing and running.

I wet my lips and frowned at him. "What we doing now? You plan tell people truth what happened?"

"Yes."

"And that all?"

"Yes . . ." he said, slowly.

I pulled the lever Simon had used to start the elevator up. It ground to a halt.

"Eliza, what are you doing?"

I rounded on him. "You have no plan! You tell people truth, *and that all*. What next? How you fix—" Curse this howler-climber language! I switched to my own. « What happens after you tell people the truth? What will they do then? »

He looked hurt by my anger. « I not know. »

I thumped the side of the elevator. « *That is not enough!* » I snapped. « They broke my people! They need to fix what they broke! »

« Is broke. Is forever. » He looked away. "Eliza. Genocide can't be . . . fixed."

I folded my arms. « What do you hope they will do when they learn the truth? What do you hope they will say? »

His brow furrowed. "I hope . . . I hope Nathaniel and Matthew are put in prison for what they did. I

322

hope people understand the terrible things they covered up. I hope they will . . . remember."

I shook my head in disbelief. « Remember? »

"I hope they'll be sorry."

I turned away in disgust. « Sorry! »

"Look." He put his hand on me. "What do *you* want? What was *your* big plan when you got to Iapyx? I mean, look at you: one girl against thirteen cities! You didn't even speak the language. What could you possibly have done to make people pay attention . . ."

The light dawned. He stared at me, and suddenly I found I could not meet his eyes.

"Oh, no," he said.

I looked at the wall.

"That was your plan, wasn't it?" he said. "Your plan was to get yourself killed in some blaze of glory, some great violent act, that we'd never forget. That's why you brought six knives." Silence stretched for heartbeats. Then he added, "Why?"

I took a deep breath. "Mother dead—" Never had the gulf between us been so wide: this stupid language. I switched again. « My mother had just died. My father and my brothers were already dead; everyone was dead. It was only the Elder and me. There was nothing left for me but anger. »

"And now?"

My brow furrowed. "Now . . . ?"

It was different now. I still wanted to make the invaders pay. But half a sun-turn ago, I had not cared if I lived to see them pay. Now was different. Now, I suddenly realized, looking up at Simon, I had something to live for.

I pushed the lever back up. The elevator shuddered and rolled on its way.

Simon stared at me a long breath longer, before turning away.

• • •

SIMON:

The elevator opened onto more laughter. We saw people walking the corridor in twos and threes, holding hands, or holding each other around the waist, wearing bright sashes over their clothes and ribbons in their hair. No one paid us any notice.

We were across from Daedalon's Communications Hub. The counter window was closed. Someone had taped up a sign reading SORRY, COME AGAIN! Nobody was taking messages, and the office was probably on skeleton staff. At least, I hoped it was.

The door opened easily and we stepped inside.

Daedalon was the largest city on Icarus Down, and its Communications Hub was accordingly larger than Iapyx's. The long, wide, low-ceilinged room hissed and breathed. The translucent pneumatic tubes snaking above our heads blinked as canisters zipped past, inbound and out, though at a slower pace as Nocturne approached.

I saw isolated workers in the distance, pushing bins. In a distant staff room, boisterous voices were raised: people eager to be out for Nocturne. Nobody was near enough to see us or challenge us as we crossed the floor. The clerks' desks were all empty.

Along one wall were the doors of several rooms. The office of Gabriel's counterpart here in Daedalon was closed. No light shone out from beneath the door.

Farther down the wall I spotted a door marked FILM TRANSFER and peered inside. This room had similar video equipment to that in Iapyx's Communications Hub. Good. My plan might just work. But how did I work the equipment? I had no idea, and there was nobody here who could help me.

« What are you looking for? » asked Eliza.

"Help," I replied. Then I heard voices in the room next door. Eliza reached for her blowpipe, but I held up a hand. I crept to the door marked OUTGOING and looked inside.

The room was full of the *hiss, click, hiss* of pneumatic canisters arriving and departing. The tubes snaked down the wall in two long vertical displays, one for arrivals, the other for departures. Between these, a long sorting table stretched into the middle of the room.

Two men were at work at the arrival and departure tubes. A young man waited by the arrivals, snatching up the tubes as they slid into place, and stacking them on the sorting table. An old man stood on the other side of the table, working the departure tubes.

The old man, I saw from his insignia, was

Daedalon's CommController. His back was bent and his hair was grey. He looked rather like Gabriel, but older and with glasses.

We slipped into the room.

The CommController glanced at us, took in our uniforms and said, gruffly, "I'll be with you in a minute! Just you wait." He peered at the canisters as he grabbed each one up, taking less than a second to read the label before popping it into the correct departure tube.

Nudging Eliza, I pointed to the apprentice. We stepped forward. I kept my eyes on the CommController. The apprentice looked up as we approached. His mouth opened wide when he saw the look in Eliza's eye, but his protest never aired. Eliza clapped a hand over his mouth, twisted him around, and wrapped an arm around his throat.

The CommController continued to grab from the pile of canisters the apprentice had stacked on the table. The pneumatics hissed as they shot away.

"What is with the stem guards, today?" he muttered. "It's been half an hour since their last canister. Nocturne's no excuse to shirk their duties." His hand shot out and swept the now empty spot on the table. Without looking back, he added, "Zachariah? You sleeping on the job?"

I picked up a canister, glanced at the label and handed it to him. "This one's for the mayor's office."

"Thanks." He gave the label a quick glance before shoving it into the right tube. Then his head jerked and he peered at me through his thick glasses. "Who the devil are you?"

I gave him a wave. "Hi. I'm Simon."

"Where's Zachariah?"

A grunt, followed by a thud and a groan, made the CommController squint past me. He stared to see Zachariah lying dazed on the floor, with Eliza standing over him.

"Taking a break," I said.

He shied away from me. "What is this about?"

I took his arm and guided him away from the tubes. "Will you come with me, please? I need somebody to work the video equipment."

"What are you *doing*?" He tried to twist away. "You can't disrupt the delivery of the mail."

I gave him an apologetic grin and held on. "My superior on Iapyx shares your passion. When the breakdowns happened, he took it personally."

The CommController blinked at me. "Wait . . . Simon . . . ?"

I sighed. "Yes."

The old man tried again to twist away. Gently but firmly, I pulled him to the back of the room where Eliza stood over Zachariah. The boy was getting his breath back. Eliza watched him warily, fists ready.

"It's okay, Eliza." I held up my gun. "Both of you, I'm armed, so please stay calm."

The CommController glowered. "What do you want?"

I stepped to the door and opened it. "I want to

show you something. Actually, I'd like everybody to see it, but you get to see it first. Come with me to the film transfer room, please. Don't make a fuss."

Though Zachariah had been knocked down, he pushed himself up and took the CommController's arm as they stepped into the room with me. I left Eliza to guard the two, while I turned to the salvaged video screens. I fiddled around their edges until I found a wire that fit into a receptacle in the black box. "There," I said. "I knew the connection was compatible."

The CommController peered over my shoulder. "Where did you get that? That's original technology!"

I angled the black box so the light gleamed off the seal of the Captain of the *Icarus*. "Where do you think?"

His face was blank a moment, and then — I imagined this was what it looked like when stars came out.

I nodded. "That's right." I set the black box on the table and flipped a switch. The screen flickered to life, showing heavy static. "Gather around, everybody." And for the second time in nearly sixty-three years, the ship's log of the *Icarus* began to play.

The CommController and Zachariah stood transfixed as the old Captain began to speak. They stared in horror as they witnessed the fall of the mother ship. They went still and silent as they heard Navigator Salk's confession, and saw the attack of the ticktock monsters.

When the Elder's people attacked, I glanced at

Eliza. I saw her grimace. Then she sensed my eyes on her and looked at me. Her face became like stone and she turned away.

When the video was done, the CommController and Zachariah kept staring at the screen. Zachariah had his hand over his mouth.

I cleared my throat. "That's what I want to show the people of Daedalon," I said. "I want to do it during the Nocturne ceremony. Will you help me?"

Zachariah's brow furrowed. "How are you going to get that out to the people? You'd need a screen the size of . . ." The light dawned. "Oh!"

"I ask again: Will you help me?"

"We've got the sunset film here," said Zachariah. "The pick-up request hasn't been sent yet, but it's due soon. You'd have an hour to make the transfer to film."

I rubbed my chin. "An hour." The video was fifteen minutes long. We had the technology to develop film quickly, but we were cutting things fine.

"I don't understand," said Zachariah. "Why do you need us?"

"I know how to work the video equipment," I said, "but working it and the projector? Getting the film developed? I could use a hand."

I looked at them. The CommController's eyes had lost the hostility they'd held only minutes ago. Now he and Zachariah just looked bewildered.

"It's up to you what you do now," I said. "I'm not a violent man. I wasn't the one who killed Iapyx. I'm not going to hurt you or tie you up. Now that I've shown you the truth, it's up to you. You can help us, or you can go back to your office and sit down. What do you choose?" I held out my hand.

The CommController turned to me, and in his eyes, I saw his bewilderment was tinged with horror.

"The truth?" he echoed. His voice was barely a whisper, but he struggled to get the words out. "After all this time. Sixty-three years, we lived the way we lived because of the horror of what we left behind, and you're telling me that we did it again? Genocide? Destruction? That's what you want me to tell every-one?"

Eliza, Zachariah and I stood in the video trans-fer room, silent. The CommController looked down, trembling. He swallowed hard. Then he looked up at me, his eyes haunted. "Leave me out of this. Please, just . . . leave me alone."

He turned away, walking toward the door, past Eliza. She tensed as he approached, but I raised a hand. I followed as he shuffled toward his office. He gave me one final look before he stepped inside and shut the door.

I clenched my teeth. This was what I was afraid of. My own words to Rachel and Gabriel echoed back at me, when they first told me th eir suspicions about the Tals. We were here because we'd fled here. We'd suffered and scrabbled these past six decades, not just because we had no choice, but because as bad as it got, it hadn't been as bad as what had driven us from Old Mother Earth. We took pride in our suffering, because we thought we were better than what we'd left behind.

I was going to shatter that illusion. Confronted with that truth, the CommController had curled up into a ball.

If this was how people were going to react, maybe I'd have to get violent after all.

Zachariah tapped me on the shoulder. I turned, and saw a different look in his eyes. Determination.

"I know how to operate the projector," he said. "I'll help you."

CHAPTER TWENTY-SIX
NOCTURNE DAEDALON

ELIZA:

We left the place of tubes after a long, frustrating time while Simon and the other boy fussed with the moving picture machine. Finally, the boy took the film, and Simon and I walked the closed-in paths of Daedalon, joining a river of people.

We dodged people who laughed and chattered as they flowed forward. The music and drumbeats boomed through the pipes above us. I tried not to flinch when people brushed against me. I could see Simon smiling. Though he was nervous, he was still happy to be here, among all his people. Even if this wasn't Simon's city, this was still home for him.

Simon looked back, saw me squeezing against a wall to push past a group of people who had stopped to talk to each other. He reached out his hand — as

I had made myself do when I guided Simon through the forest.

"We're almost there!" he said.

"Where?" My chest felt tight.

He led me up some steps. The crowds parted as they levelled off. Suddenly, I stood at the edge of a cavernous space.

For several breaths, I could hardly move: to see a room as big as a real place, but still a room. There were trees and hills, but there was no fog. The walls were far away. They had curved struts, like the rib-cage of an animal, holding up a solid sky. It was all too open and too closed at the same time.

We climbed to the crest of a hill that was fringed with trees, stepping between the trunks, and looked down at a sea of people.

How could so many people fit into one place? How could they enjoy it so?

But they were enjoying it. In a large flat area, people paired up, grabbing hands and twirling. There were tables set up, with more food than I'd seen in my lifetime. The music hammered in my ears.

"What is this place?" I gasped.

He looked around him, strangely wistful. "The Great Hall of Daedalon."

"How you put so much space inside?"

He thought about this. "We needed to take it with us," he said. "From Old Mother Earth. I think it kept us sane."

I leaned on the tree. I did not like how it pulsed

beneath my hand with the invaders' drumbeats. This was *not* sane. I nodded at the shifting mass of people below. "What they *doing*?"

Simon looked. "They're dancing."

"What is dancing?"

He opened his mouth to answer, then stopped. His forehead wrinkled. "It's, uh . . . It's something people do . . . when they want to show that they're happy or . . . that they like each other. To celebrate. Couples join hands on the dance floor, and move in time to the music. It's . . . fun."

"What is couple?" I asked.

"Um . . ." His cheeks were turning red. He cleared his throat. "Two people. Mostly friends. *Good* friends. *Really* good friends."

I began to understand. « Is this a mating ritual? »

He coughed again. "Sort of. Yeah." He peered out at the crowd and pointed. "There's the stage. Look, at the end of the amphitheatre."

I looked. In a dip in the ground there was a raised area where a dozen people sat apart, arms folded or hands on their laps. Behind them, on a giant white screen, flashed symbols I'd seen before. The arrowhead that signified Simon's dead city. The notched wheel and big stick of this city, and an unfamiliar symbol: an eight-sided web.

"What is that?" I asked.

"The symbols of Iapyx and Daedalon. The spider-web belongs to Octavia," Simon replied. "Their dignitaries are on the stage. There's Mayor Tuan

334

of Daedalon." His jaw tightened. "There's Mayor Matthew Tal." He shuddered. "And there beside him is Nathaniel—"

Suddenly, his eyes went wide, and he pushed me hard against the tree as he tried to duck behind it.

« What? » I grunted.

« Sorry, » he whispered, pushing away. "I thought Nathaniel saw us."

I glared. He thought he had been spotted, and made a mistake that got young hunters killed. Do not dive away and attract attention.

I nodded at a tree ten steps away. The view of the stage was blocked by a row of bushes from here to there. Simon nodded, and we snuck to the new vantage point. We looked out carefully.

I focused on the grey figure Simon had pointed to as Nathaniel. He was no longer looking at where we were, but he was talking to someone leaning over his shoulder, another man in grey. The man in grey nodded and slipped away. Nathaniel turned back and stared hard at the place where we'd been.

"What's he doing?" Simon muttered.

Simon was getting distracted. I nudged him. « Where do we have to be? »

He pointed at the stage. "There. I have to tell everyone what I know as soon as the *Icarus*'s black box plays. We don't have much time . . ."

I tensed. Someone was approaching. Simon felt my tension, and we turned to look. The guard known as Gaal hurried to our cover of shadow and trees.

"Hey," he said. "We have a problem." He nodded at the entrance we'd come through. On either side were people wearing the same grey clothes we were wearing. They were on guard, and had not been there when we had entered.

"Those aren't Daedalon guards," said Gaal. "They're Iapyx."

Simon's eyes widened. "Nathaniel?"

"Something must have spooked him," said Gaal. "More guards are taking up positions at other exits. They're not looking for Grounders; we passed without problem."

"They look for you," I said to Simon. Nathaniel must have seen us. He really did have the eyes of a predator.

Simon grimaced. He took a deep breath. "Is everybody ready?"

Gaal nodded. "A few guards came to investigate why the prison was in lockdown. We overpowered them and they're in cells. Nobody knows what's happening, yet. The Iapyx CommController sent me and a few others up to help you. He's over there."

He tipped his head. Across the field, the invader known as Gabriel looked over at us. He wore a grey uniform that was too long for him and too tight around his waist, but nobody around him seemed to notice. Simon would probably say it was because it was Nocturne.

"So, when do we go?" I asked.

"There'll be speeches in a few minutes," Gaal replied. "Then the oath, then the sunset film."

Simon sucked his teeth. "I'm not in position, and I can't go out through the exits or Nathaniel's guards will stop me."

I tapped Simon's wrist. "Walk down to dancers. Gaal, stand between Simon and stage."

Gaal led the way. We came down the hill toward the amphitheatre and the great field of dancers. Simon kept calm, but he walked tense, until the stage slipped behind the rows and rows of dancers. Then he breathed a sigh of relief.

"Gaal," he said. "Take some people and go to the projection room. I've got something special queued up in place of the sunset film. Your job is to make sure they keep playing it when they realize something is wrong. Can you do that?"

Gaal nodded and slipped away, and again we were alone among the revelling crowds.

« What now? » I asked.

"We have to get to the stage," he replied. He looked around at the exits, but there were grey uniforms at every one we could see.

The only way to the stage was through this shifting, jostling crowd of dancers. And we had to do it quickly, and stealthily. If we shoved our way through, we would attract attention. So, how did we get through?

I looked at Simon, and saw him come to the same idea as me. His cheeks grew red again. "Eliza—"

He had just said that dancing was a mating ritual. But . . . « You need to get to the stage, » I said softly. "Best way is through dancers." « Camou-flage. » But I felt my own cheeks betray me, and heat up.

He looked at the ground, and then looked back at me, a small smile on his lips. « *Ek-Taak-Tock-Taak?* » Then, "Would you dance with me?"

I fought down the strange, swirly feeling in my stomach and took his hand. We stepped in.

I had never danced before. I had no idea how to follow the steps, and I doubted Simon could, with his old injuries. But we didn't need to know the steps. I just needed to shift my body in time with the drumbeats. And anticipate where Simon's feet would land, and keep my feet out of those spots.

But as I avoided a young woman being turned by her partner, I realized that I had moved like this before. When you fight a slink up close, you have to react as you stalk.

Simon and I pulled back and pulled forward, step-ping into gaps as they came open, moving closer to the stage. Sometimes we were an arm's length apart. Sometimes his breath brushed my cheek.

I was stalking Simon! To what end? The possibil-ities were exciting, and I found I was enjoying this. I smiled to see Simon smiling back. It was good to dance with him. It was good to dance, *with him*. I laughed as he swung me around, and as I saw the faces of the couples swing past me. In that instant, I felt as though I was home.

Home . . .

I staggered to a stop. Simon bumped into me, and stared. I looked around, at the metal sky, the crowds of people. Horror rose in my chest.

• • •

SIMON:

We stumbled at first as we entered the dance, Eliza unfamiliar with the moves, me unfamiliar with Eliza, but after a moment's effort, we figured it out. We managed not to look too conspicuous as I moved us through the crowd, toward the stage.

Though I focused on reaching the stage, I could not help but think about the dance. *Did I mention that you were a good dancer,* Rachel had said. I hadn't known. But I liked dancing with Rachel. And I liked dancing with Eliza. Her breath, smelling of the fruit of the forest, reminded me of the smell of candy on Rachel's.

As we danced, Eliza's look of bewilderment faded. She gasped as I pulled her through a turn, then laughed as I pulled her back to me. It was good to see her happy.

Slowly we were getting closer to the stage and its screen.

Then Eliza's smile vanished. She pulled away. She looked at me, at the crowd around me, with wide, horrified eyes.

"Eliza?"

It happened so fast. I'd barely registered the change in Eliza's expression before she shoved me away and looked at all the people — and at me — in horror.

"Eliza?" I reached for her. She recoiled, then turned and ran.

• • •

ELIZA:

Home, I thought, and my mind flashed to the Elder, her life draining out of her. My mother, staring right through me. *The invaders are not my people!*

I remembered my brothers. Living in a village that was too hot but was still where my family lived. Only, not anymore. I saw the ragged lines of the metal huts and I saw the stark lines of this gigantic room, and revulsion swept through me. Dancing with Simon, I had thought I was home. For an instant, I had forgotten what these invaders did to my people. The realization made me hate my own skin.

"Eliza?" Simon reached for me. I pulled away. I could not be here anymore. I could not stand being surrounded by so many monsters.

I shoved my way through the crowds, running for the nearest doorway out of this false forest, looking for somewhere to breathe.

• • •

SIMON:

"Eliza!" I pushed forward. People protested. Others started to look. Eliza disappeared among the crowd, but I followed, wanting to know what had happened, and desperate not to be alone. On the stage, Mayor Tuan and Mayor Tal stood up and approached the podium.

Behind me, Gaal shouted a warning. I didn't listen. I was almost at the edge of the crowd, and I'd seen Eliza disappear through one of the Great Hall's entranceways. I didn't realize what Gaal had shouted until it was too late.

I burst into the open and found myself face to face with two of Nathaniel's guards.

CHAPTER TWENTY-SEVEN
ACCUSATION AND REDEMPTION

ELIZA:

I ran through the closed-in paths of the hive, not wanting to touch the walls. To be in the belly of the monster and all alone was horrible.

But there was only so far I could run. Before long, I had to slow down and think of what to do next. Maybe there was some way I could hurt this place. Simon had said his city died when Nathaniel attacked something called the anchor. Perhaps I could go there, find some way to cut the wires without sunlight.

That's when I heard the voice.

"Ticktock!"

I looked around. What was that word? It felt like it should be a word in my language, but it was only gibberish.

"Ticktock! Ticktick!"

I saw children ahead. I ducked behind a corner and peered out.

Giggling children, hiding behind corners of their own, watched as a young girl walked around, eyes closed and arms outstretched. When she got too close to one of the other children, he or she would lunge out and shout that strange word. "Ticktock!" or "Ticktick!" The last word I knew as *hello*, but I do not think the children knew it as *hello*.

I realized what the children were playing. Anger burned hotter in my chest. Is this what my people were now? Some play-fright that children laughed over? I bared my teeth. If the children wanted monsters, I would give them one.

Keeping behind the corner, I leaned out and clicked at them. « *Tik-tik-tik-tik.* »

Most of the children did not hear me. One or two stopped and looked around. I clicked again. « *Tik-tik-tik-tik!* »

More children looked nervous and fearful. They asked each other what they had heard, what it meant. And the more they talked, the more fearful they became. A brave few came closer, looking for the source of the noise. I waited, until they were within striking distance . . .

I leapt out at them, chittering as a true monster would.

The children scattered, screaming. All save one little girl in the centre of the group, now alone, so startled she had fallen to the ground. She stared up at me with wide, terrified eyes. Then she curled up into a ball and wailed.

I stared down at her, my arms limp at my sides. She was so small. Her long hair hid her face. Her long, dark hair. Like mine.

She looked so small to be frightened, and I was ashamed to have frightened her.

I knelt before her and brushed back her hair. She flinched at my touch, but I hushed her gently. "Listen, listen," I said, choosing my words carefully in Simon's language. "No fear me. I . . . sorry."

The girl sobbed, but one eye peeked at me over her knees. I brushed her hair again, and this time she did not flinch.

The other children peered out from hiding. Some crept closer.

"Soft, soft," I said, quietly. "No fear. Nothing fear."

The girl stopped crying. She looked up at me, her eyes wide. They were like my mother's eyes, before they went blind.

"Nothing fear," I said to the girl. "Nothing here." My voice caught as I looked around me. "No monsters here."

The other children gathered around their fallen friend and helped her up. They looked at me, unafraid, but perplexed by this strange woman before them.

"I sorry," I said to the girl again. "Please . . . forgive."

The girl looked at me a breath longer. She patted my hand. Then she turned and ran, but she was smiling. Her friends followed her, casting nervous glances at me as they went.

I rose to my feet and watched them go with new eyes.

Maybe I could not forgive all of Simon's people, but I could forgive the children, just as the Elder had done. Though someone would have to teach them a different game to play. Maybe that someone would be me.

But first, I had work to do. Maybe there were no monsters here, but I knew where I could find some. And I had left Simon to fight them alone.

● ● ●

SIMON:

For a moment I stared, dumbfounded and caught. It took me a second to realize that the security officers — Iapyx security officers; I could see the arrowhead icon on their sleeves — looked just as stunned as I did.

"Well, I'll be," muttered the shorter of the two officers. "Simon Daud. Tal was right."

"How'd he survive the fall? Or the fog forest?" said the other officer.

"Doesn't matter," the first officer muttered. He stepped forward, reaching for my arm. "Come with us, Mr. Daud."

I didn't recognize either of these officers. Iapyx had been big enough that they could be faces in a crowd, so I didn't know their names. I didn't know what they knew. But I knew that if I went with them, I would be dead. I backed up.

The two put their hands on their holsters. "Don't make a scene," said the second officer.

Making a scene was a very good idea. But right then, I didn't know what scene to make.

Just then, Gaal ran up. "What's going on here?" His voice pulled an edge of command that I hadn't heard from him before. "Is there a problem?"

That's when I remembered that Gaal was wearing grey, just like these Iapyx security guards. More importantly, he had Daedalon's cog and hammer on his sleeve.

The two Iapyx officers worked for Nathaniel, but they were not on their home turf. Still, they weren't about to give up.

"This is Simon Daud," said the guard. "He's under arrest."

We didn't have to shout anymore. The crowd had grown quiet. They were watching the stage as Mayor Tuan gave an address.

"Nocturne is a time of celebration and thanksgiving," his voice rang out. "A time when all the citizens of Icarus Down remember the past, and reaffirm their allegiance to the future — our future — together. As we deal with the loss of our sister city Iapyx and decide on who will next ascend to the Captaincy, I am proud that we know how to open our arms to each other and work toward the common good of our colony, leaving the mistakes of our ancestors behind."

"Simon Daud," Gaal deadpanned. "The man who was at the fall of Iapyx seven months ago and hasn't been seen since? Somehow turns up, wearing a Daedalon security uniform like me?" He pointed at his insignia. "You'd think I wouldn't know if I was serving with a terrorist?"

The Iapyx security officers looked uncertain. I kept my mouth shut. One mustered, "But Security Chief Nathaniel said—"

"Does Nathaniel give the orders here?" Gaal snapped.

On the stage, Mayor Tuan introduced Mayor Matthew Tal, who started to give what I could hear was a campaign speech. The reception of the audience was polite, but cool — different from what I would have expected from Iapyx, or perhaps even any other city. On Iapyx, there had been resentment over the apparent presumption that the mayor of Daedalon would be the next Captain. I wondered if, on Daedalon, there was resentment over the apparent presumption everywhere else that the mayor of Daedalon wouldn't.

The two officers shifted on their feet, neither bold enough to challenge Gaal's rank and authority — at least, not in public like this.

"Remarkable resemblance," the first officer rallied.

"More likely than a remarkable survival," Gaal shot back. "Now, if you have things to do, go do them.

Or enjoy Nocturne, at least." He and I turned away. "That's a relief," he whispered.

Then we faced the stage. We were fifty metres away, and the crowd was impenetrable.

The mayor of Daedalon called for the colonial oath, and the chant rose up from the people around me. This had been so ingrained in us that I found myself chanting along with the audience: "We pledge ourselves to the future of Icarus Down. Together we shall build the future, for ourselves, and for the generations that follow. We shall leave the mistakes of Old Mother Earth behind."

As I said the oath, a knot formed in my throat. *Whose generations?* I thought. Hadn't the Elder's people deserved that same chance? What about Rachel and Isaac? Why had we brought the mistakes of Mother Earth with us?

We should be ashamed, as I had told Eliza. Ashamed of our very skin.

I turned back to the Iapyx security officers, who were walking toward the exit. "Actually, I am Simon Daud," I called.

Gaal flinched. "Simon—" he hissed, before he could stop himself.

The Iapyx officers turned on me. They put their hands on their guns.

"And you are going to help me get to the stage," I said.

The first officer scoffed. The second shook his head in bewilderment.

"Because I think that you would never have helped Nathaniel if you knew the truth about him," I said. "I did not destroy Iapyx. But I know who did. And I survived seven months in the fog forest to find the truth."

At the podium, the mayor of Daedalon raised his arms to the screen. The projection flickered to life and displayed last year's image from atop Daedalon's semaphore. The diamond lands sparkled as, taking up just an eighth of the horizon, our sun finally descended from the sky.

Then, in the blink of a frame, the setting sun disappeared. The mayor dropped his arms, startled to find himself staring into the larger-than-life face of the second Captain of the *Icarus*. The crowd gasped.

I gave the officers a grim smile. "And I'm going to show the truth to everyone."

Through the projection room's megaphones, the Captain's voice boomed out.

"Ship's Log. Day 26,298 of our journey from Old Mother Earth. The advance force leaders are due back tomorrow . . ."

On the stage, Nathaniel shot up from his seat and rounded on the screen. The projection shook, as though someone in the projection room had grabbed the projector, only to be knocked down by someone else. The film played on.

The Great Hall had gone quiet, but Nathaniel didn't seem to notice. "Who tampered with the projection?" he shouted.

Through the crowd, murmurs of awe rose up. "It's the Captain! It's the *Icarus*!"

It was time for me to make my move. I nudged Gaal. "Move back!" I shoved him away to clear a space in the grass. Then I pulled out my gun, flicked off the safety and fired into the ground.

The bang echoed through the Great Hall, making people jump and scream. People nearest me scrambled back, opening a hole in the crowd. Suddenly, all eyes were on me.

"It's the truth, Nathaniel!" I shouted. "It's what you killed a city for; the truth you tried to hide!" I turned back to the two Iapyx security officers. "Are you going to take me to the stage, or what?"

On the screen, the Captain held up a binder. " . . . this report. My clerks have examined every paragraph, and my security people have debriefed the advance force personnel . . ."

Eyes were not the only things on me. On stage, Mayor Tuan's security squadron had drawn their guns, but they weren't about to start firing randomly into the crowd.

Before they had a chance to aim, I raised my hands above my head, keeping my gun in sight, and my finger well off the trigger.

I stepped forward, and Gaal led the way. I felt as though my feet were walking on automatic; my brain could hardly believe I was doing this.

What if this didn't work? What if everyone reacted as the CommController had done, with horror and disbelief and inaction? What if I told everyone the truth, and they did nothing?

Without Eliza beside me, I felt so alone.

But one of the two Iapyxian officers followed, gently moving people aside as we approached the stage. I chanced a look back at the other guard and saw him rooted to the spot, staring up at the image of the Captain.

I focused on the Tals. I had to do this. For my people. For Rachel. For Isaac. For Mom. For Eliza's adopted people. For Eliza.

Gaal and the Iapyx officer stopped at the stage and I mounted the steps, keeping the gun in clear sight. When I reached the platform, I bent down and placed it on the floor. Then I straightened up. Exposed and unarmed. They could shoot me, but they'd be shooting an unarmed man. I hoped that the confusion wrought by the ship's log would buy me enough time to speak.

Nathaniel seethed, but he was surrounded by the Mayor Tuan's guards, and being held by his brother Matthew. Everyone was shocked into stillness by the image of the old Captain.

"My name is Simon Daud," I said, and my voice sounded so small. Even projecting as much as I could, even with the acoustics of the amphitheatre, I feared that I could only be heard by the first few rows.

But then I heard whispering. "His name is Simon Daud. His name is Simon Daud. Simon Daud. Daud.

Daud . . ." Those rows whispered my words to the row behind, and they whispered to the row behind them, and so on. My words carried on their own wave, out of the amphitheatre, through the Great Hall, even to the rafters, where I saw schoolchildren watching.

But in the waves of whispers, a word came back at me. "Terrorist? Terrorist?"

I took a deep breath. "My name is Simon Daud," I said again.

The echoes rolled back, louder. "Name is Simon Daud."

"And I am not a terrorist. I did not cause Iapyx to fall."

"Not a terrorist . . ." said the echoes. "Not cause Iapyx to fall . . ."

I pointed at Nathaniel. "*He* did, to cover up the secret that you're about to see revealed on this screen!"

Nathaniel leaned over and whispered to a young man in grey. He was making sure that no one else on the stage could hear. The young man nodded and slipped quietly away, taking the other stairs. Now where would he be going? *Oh, yes. Thank you, Nathaniel, for proving my point. I'll give you a few minutes so you can properly hang yourself.*

In the audience, the whispering continued. And I noticed something else: men and women in grey uniforms fanning out among the crowd. I saw Gabriel among them, and Grounders from the prison cells. The whispers got louder.

"This man's father," I said, speaking clearly, loudly, "Daniel Tal, committed genocide against the indigenous people of the blue planet we were supposed to colonize. Daniel Tal's son suppressed all knowledge of this event, and persecuted the people who sought the truth. In trying to discredit them, he sabotaged Iapyx's anchor, and caused my city to fall."

On screen, the second Captain of the *Icarus* continued his ship's log. "If nothing else, I can't leave behind the people we still have on the planet. Maybe when we get there, I'll see what really happened during Tal's year-long trip."

Behind me, the people's echoes fanned out. "Tal . . . Tal . . . Tal . . ."

Then I heard it: shouts and a crash from near the projection room. I rounded and pointed. "See! He's doing it now, trying to silence our own Captain!"

The audience turned, and saw a melee of grey uniforms by the door of the projection room. People in the audience shouted. "Stop them!" "Let the film play!" "Let the Captain speak!"

Nathaniel further proved my point by losing his cool and lunging for me. This knocked his brother, who knocked into one of the guards. Sensing an immediate threat to their mayor, the Daedalon security guards grabbed Nathaniel and held him.

"This is preposterous!" He shook himself free and pointed at me. "This man is a convicted terrorist! You can't trust what he says!"

"You never convicted me," I shouted. "I was never tried. I never pled guilty. I spent the last seven months in the fog forest, as good as banished. But I survived, and do you know why? I'll show you!"

I pulled the black box out of my pocket and held it high for all to see. The light gleamed off the Seal of the Captain of the *Icarus*. "I found the *Icarus*!"

Nathaniel paled. There were gasps from the first row, and more whispers buzzed through the audience. A Daedalon security officer, who had been lumbering toward me with a mean look in his eyes, saw the seal and his mouth dropped open. He actually fell to his knees.

Through the crowd, the fervent whispers spread. Now the town criers in the back were taking up my words, sending them farther. "The *Icarus* . . . *Icarus* . . ."

"I found the *Icarus*. And I found the truth." I pointed at the screen. "Those of you out there who helped Nathaniel Tal implicate the Grounders, *this* is what you were trying to hide."

On the screen, the Captain's log continued. "Clearly, he wants to tell me something, and he doesn't feel safe telling me in the open. I think I may be closer to figuring out what CMO Tal is hiding from me."

Mayor Tuan stepped to the podium. "Look, maybe we can talk about this." I wasn't sure if he was talking to me, or Nathaniel, or just throwing the idea out there. "The boy's unarmed, and he's brought alarming new evidence. We should hear what he has to say. In private."

But the crowd was hearing far more than Nathaniel wanted. I couldn't help but smile. People were making up their own minds. Before Iapyx had fallen, the Grounders had started to wonder what Nathaniel was really up to. They couldn't have been the only ones to ask questions. And not all Grounder sympathizers had been arrested. Some would still be in the crowd, listening, giving voice to the questions in their minds.

Voices rose. "Let him speak!" "What did you do, Tal?"

Nathaniel's face darkened.

I jumped when a hand clamped on my shoulder. I jumped again when I saw who it was. "Leah!"

My friend from the flight academy. I hadn't seen her since she'd come with my classmates to the infirmary. So she'd survived the fall of Iapyx. I glanced at the pilot's insignia on her tunic, and saw my city's arrowhead, haloed in black beside the hammer and cog of Daedalon. She'd transferred, but she still remembered our old city.

There was a complicated look in her eye. "Was that you?" she said. "On the anchor? I was flying in. I didn't have time to land." She shuddered. "Just before the city fell. I saw—"

I remembered the daring ornithopter that had flown close just as Nathaniel had jumped. Somehow, I wasn't surprised that it had been Leah.

I looked at her. I waited.

"I saw a man and a woman in white," she said. "I thought the man was you. And I saw a security officer in grey, grabbing a parachute and jumping off. The man in white — was that you?"

I nodded.

I could see Leah putting it together. If she'd seen the anchor, she'd have seen what was done to it. And if a security officer had been there to try to stop it, would he have taken a parachute and jumped? Add to that the fact that she knew me, knew I wouldn't kill my own city.

But if we hadn't done it, who had?

Leah went red. She stormed at Nathaniel, and had to be held back by a guard. "You killed my city! It was *you!*"

The crowd shouted with her. I looked at Nathaniel. He looked back, stone-faced. He touched his holster, but he was unarmed. He was a guest, after all; a security chief without a city.

I wish you were armed, I thought. *Go ahead and shoot an unarmed accuser. Prove to the world that you have something to hide.*

But then, flanked by his guards, Mayor Tuan came up to me. "Mr. Daud," he said. "This is getting out of hand."

"Getting?" I stared at him in disbelief. "This is only now getting out of hand?"

"I promise you a full investigation," the mayor continued. "I'll reopen the cases of all the

Grounders. I'll order new trials. You've been to the *Icarus*, Mr. Daud, so I promise to hear you out. But right now I need you to tell the people in the Great Hall that you're coming with us willingly, to tell us the full story. I promise you full safety and protection."

"But Nathaniel—"

"Nathaniel Tal is still a well-respected officer of the colony," said the mayor. "Entitled to the same rights you think the Grounders may have been denied. There are proper ways to deal with these allegations—"

"No!" I pointed past him. "Where is Nathaniel?"

Mayor Tuan turned, and swore. Neither Nathaniel nor Matthew were on stage. I pushed past the mayor and ran to the steps, scanning the crowd. "There!" I shouted. Nathaniel and Matthew were running for the nearest exit.

Mayor Tuan ran back to the podium. "Everyone," he shouted. "Stay calm!"

You know, somehow shouting "Stay calm!" never works.

Other people converged on the Tals. I saw Gabriel get there first, but Nathaniel dropped him with a punch. Without another thought, I grabbed my gun from where I'd left it and jumped off the stage.

When I got to Gabriel, he was surrounded by Daedalon security officers. They all wanted to help him up. He batted the hands back angrily. "I'm all

357

right! I'm all right! Will somebody get after those two men?"

I looked around at the Great Hall. People were shouting. Others gazed up at the screen, where the projector now showed the fall of the *Icarus*. People screamed when the screen flashed white. Security officers ran this way and that, trying to keep order. The mayor of Daedalon stood at the podium, shouting, but no one heard him.

I left Gabriel and ran through the door after the Tals.

CHAPTER TWENTY-EIGHT
THE FALL OF NATHANIEL TAL

SIMON:

I pelted down the stairs to the lower levels. I ran through the arboretum, past giggling couples. I couldn't see Nathaniel or Matthew anywhere, but I knew where they'd go.

I crashed through the flight-bay doors and spotted two attendants lying on the floor, unconscious. I put my hand on my holster and looked around.

Except for the two attendants, the flight bay looked empty, shut down for Nocturne. Outside the doors, ornithopters dangled by their tailhooks. Which one would Nathaniel pick?

Then I heard Nathaniel's calm voice, along with Matthew's frantic one. They were coming closer. My hand still on the gun, I ducked behind a support pillar, waiting for my moment to strike.

Nathaniel emerged, wearing a parachute pack. He

pulled his brother along and shoved another pack into his arms. "Put this on, now!"

"Is it true, what he said?" Matthew gabbled. "Well, is it?"

"What does it matter? The important thing is too many people believed it. We have to get to Octavia to get ahead of this."

"What does it *matter*?" Matthew echoed. "Of course it matters! Our father? Committing *genocide*? To be tied to the shames of Old Mother Earth, such evil . . ."

Nathaniel grabbed his brother and shook him till his head flapped. "Seventy-two years the *Icarus* was in deep space! Seventy-two years! Our father knew that if the Captain followed Earth protocol and turned the ship around, there'd be mutiny. He also knew that there'd be mutiny if the Captain *didn't* turn the ship around! And all for a bunch of lizards who'd just figured out how to put tools together? We're here and we're alive because of our father's impossibly hard choice, and I'm going to see to it that you ascend to the Captaincy and that this colony finally gives us the honour our family is due!"

"Wow." I stepped out from behind the pillar, my gun pointed. Nathaniel rounded on me. The mayor looked pale. "Wow," I said again. "You *did* know. All this time you knew. And you were okay with it."

Nathaniel smiled that infuriating, calm smile. "Mr. Daud. I see you've come alone."

"Others will be here soon. You're under arrest, Tal."

"Under what charge?" he said.

"You know what charges. Murder. Terrorism. Conspiracy to cover up genocide."

"I have nothing to be ashamed of," said Nathaniel coolly.

"Your *father* had the decency to be ashamed!" I struggled to keep my voice level. "It's obvious he did: the last known survivor of the *Icarus*? He could have ascended to the Captaincy if he wanted to, but he didn't. He took a quiet posting on Iapyx and he tried to hide himself away. And though he told *you* what happened, Nathaniel . . ." I nodded at Matthew. " . . . he never told your baby brother."

Nathaniel's face went dark red. Matthew, seeing this, took a frightened step back. But Nathaniel did nothing. After a long moment, he tamped down his anger. When he spoke, it was almost a whisper. "What happens now, Mr. Daud?"

"You come with me and face the charges against you. Mayor Tuan has promised a fair trial, which is more than you deserve."

Nathaniel tilted his head. "And if I refuse?"

"Why would you? You've got no place to run."

Nathaniel's smile widened, and I wanted so much to smack it off. "I wouldn't be so sure," he said. "It's Nocturne, Simon. The sun won't be up for another few hours. Nobody can see Daedalon's semaphore, especially now that Iapyx is gone. So we can outrun the news. My brother and I can make it to Octavia and tell them why they shouldn't believe the fantastic tales Daedalon will spread to ensure their mayor ascends to the Captaincy for the second time in a row, and how the Mayor of Daedalon is working with the Grounder terrorists that brought down Iapyx. By morning, we'll have ornithopters at our command."

I gaped at him. He was going to use the reactions of people like the CommController to protect himself. "You'd set the cities against one another to protect a lie?"

He shrugged. "I'm not protecting a lie, Simon, I'm protecting people from the truth. My father saved this colony from a cruel decision, and I'm saving the people from the horrible knowledge that we'd made that decision. We're not so different, Simon. We both believe the truth is worth fighting for."

I brought up the gun and pointed it right between his eyes. "Thousands of people are dead because of you, you son of a bitch!" My voice shook. "I am not like you! You killed Aaron! You killed my city! You killed — You killed —" I swallowed the lump in my throat. "You killed Rachel."

Nathaniel just stood there, his hands by his sides. "Yes, I did, Simon," he said quietly. "In most of those cases, I didn't mean to, but I still did what I had to. I'm walking away now, and if you want to stop me, you're going to have to shoot me. If you think justice demands vengeance, go ahead. Pull the trigger." He showed his teeth. "Be a man."

My finger tightened on the trigger. Nathaniel didn't flinch. My hand trembled.

All I had to do was move my finger another

millimetre, and it would be over. Nathaniel wouldn't be able to hide behind the lies and manipulate the other cities with them. The truth would come out, all of it. I could do it. All I had to do was, for just one moment, be like him.

A moment passed.

Another.

I flipped the safety back on the gun, lowered my hand, and stepped back.

Nathaniel's mouth curled. "You see? It's not so easy, making the hard decisions."

"Go on." I stepped aside, leaving the way clear to the ornithopters. "Get out." I turned and walked away.

Behind me, I heard Nathaniel grab the mayor and hurry to the ornithopter bay.

• • •

ELIZA:

I watched Simon walk away. A part of me felt that I should be disappointed, but the rest of me was proud of him, though I wasn't sure why. I knew now, however, why the luck of the Elders had brought us together.

I had dropped my gun during my angry run through the corridors, but I had no need of it now.

Nathaniel hurried his brother toward the see-through doors. A mechanical insect dangled from its tail outside.

363

"I thought he was going to kill you," Matthew gabbled.

"I knew he wouldn't," said Nathaniel. "I know his type."

"What type is that?" Matthew asked.

"Good," I said.

Both men froze. I stepped out from behind the pillar.

Nathaniel frowned. "Who are you?"

I ignored the question. "Simon is good. That why he not kill you. *You* kill; he can not." Even if it meant letting go the one who killed his friends and his love and his city, he could not kill. Not without killing part of himself. And, though the thought surprised me, I found I was glad he could not. And I said so. « I would hate to see that part of him die. »

The clicks made horror rise in their faces. Nathaniel let go of his brother and stepped forward. I planted my feet. "Do not." It was a clear warning. It stopped him.

"Who are you?"

"The *Icarus*," I said. "I am last survivor."

Matthew looked bewildered. Nathaniel stared at me. Then he took a step back, and another. He nodded at my empty hands and the empty holster. "You're not armed. You can't stop us. If you want to live, don't try."

He grabbed Matthew's arm and pushed open the see-through doors. Matthew stumbled after him, looking back. I followed quietly. When Nathaniel put his hand on the mechanical insect, I pushed open the door and called out, "Nathaniel Tal!"

He stopped. He looked back at me.

I pulled my blowpipe from my pocket. "Unlike Simon, I *am* like you."

For the Elder, I thought. *For my people. For Simon. For Simon's people.*

"For Rachel."

I put the blowpipe to my lips.

CHAPTER TWENTY-NINE
ICARUS RISING

SIMON:

At the top of the stairs from the flight bay, I was met by what looked like Mayor Tuan's entire security retinue.

"You're too late," I said. "They're flying to Octavia."

The mayor's chief of security waved the men and women down the stairs. "Scramble the pilots! Get after them!"

As they rushed to organize pilots and get the ornithopters ready, I made to push past the group and head back to the Great Hall, but Daedalon's chief of security stepped in front of me. "Wait over there, please." He nodded to a spot by the wall.

"Am I under arrest?"

He gave me a narrow-eyed look. "Do you want to be?"

The meaning was clear. I didn't like it, but I was

tired and alone. Eliza — where had she gone? I went to the wall and leaned against it.

In the corridor leading to the Great Hall, some bureaucrat was gabbling at Mayor Tuan. "I assure you, the mayor of Octavia had no inkling of the accusations that could be raised against Mayor Tal. When the mayor gets a full report, I'm sure she'll tell you—"

"I'll hear that from Octavia herself, thank you very much," said Mayor Tuan. "I expect you to send a message to your mayor at first light, telling her the things Nathaniel might not have said upon his arrival at your city."

As he spoke, he slapped something against his other hand. I recognized it: my arrivals log, that I'd rescued from the to-be-pulped bin in Iapyx's record rooms. Beyond the mayor, I saw Gabriel standing beside the battery girl. The mayor of Daedalon looked at the report in his hand. His frown deepened.

People rushed back and forth in front of me. I heard ornithopter engines start up beyond the stairwell below. *If I closed my eyes now*, I thought, *I could sleep.* Maybe I should. I'd been walking for months, carrying the truth with me, and I was so tired.

But then I felt a presence beside me. I looked up to see Eliza leaning against the wall beside me. She gave me a smile, tapped her fist to mine, and I smiled back.

There were sounds of buzzing ornithopters, passing close. I heard more shouting, someone calling for people to contact the stem guards, and then, moments later, someone calling for a search party to locate the stem guards.

"We're in trouble, now," I said.

Finally, a pilot and guard came running up the steps. They stopped before Mayor Tuan and Daedalon's chief of security, breathing heavily.

The mayor frowned. "Where are the Tals?"

"They didn't take an ornithopter," said the pilot. "We counted. Nothing's missing."

"They jumped," the guard cut in. "I just heard back from a group that went out to the stem compound. They found, um, parts of them, sir."

Jumped.

I blinked.

Other people were whispering, and I heard the news travelling up the stairs. The Tals committed suicide . . . They've admitted their guilt . . . The Octavian official looked shocked, then grim.

It was — as such things go — good news. Nathaniel's suicide could well have saved the colony from a nasty conflict. He'd done us a great service. But I didn't buy it. I couldn't. Nathaniel had promised to outrun the news. He'd promised to fight on, destroying the peace of the planet to protect his lie. It made no sense that he should suddenly give up.

And I couldn't help but think that Mom had fallen. They'd found . . . parts of her, too. Nathaniel certainly hadn't flown, but I didn't think he jumped, either.

But if he didn't jump . . .

Nathaniel was a big man. No one could have pushed him, surely? He'd fight back . . . unless he couldn't. Unless he was shot down, and not by bullets, since the guards would have seen that.

A poison thorn, on the other hand, shot by a blowpipe . . .

I looked hard at Eliza. She looked back at me. Her expression didn't change. Finally, I looked away. "Yes," I said out loud. "Suicide. That's probably what happened."

Mayor Tuan, hearing my voice, turned toward me. "Simon Daud."

I pushed away from the wall. "That's me."

"Do you have any idea what you've just done?" He was seething.

I stood my ground. "I told the truth. What happens next is not my fault."

"Not your *fault*?" he echoed. "You've broken this colony apart!"

"Maybe this colony needed to be broken," I said. "The better to put it back together again."

"Everybody is in shock," said the mayor. "They can't believe what the advance team did. People are demanding we make restitution even though there's no one to make restitution to—"

Behind me, Eliza cleared her throat, with quite an alarming click.

"Well, that's for the people to decide, isn't it?" I said. "We're already having an election. Aren't elections a good time to decide things?"

"Don't get smart with me, Simon," the mayor snapped.

"I survived seven months in the fog forest," I said. "I've been to the *Icarus*. I've learned the truth behind this colony, the truth that Nathaniel killed for, and I've shared it. What happens next is up to you."

"But what do we do?" He looked at me, and this time I could see the fear in his eyes. Fear about the future. "If you're so smart, tell me: What do we do?"

I had no idea. I didn't know what to tell him, until, behind me, Eliza came closer and whispered, "The eggs."

Yes, I thought. *The eggs that could only hatch on the planet we were supposed to land on.* And while I was thinking about the truth, I couldn't ignore this fact: the truth was that the next step *was* up to me. I was a part of this colony. I had a responsibility to help decide what we did next.

A certainty rose inside me. The eggs were our responsibility now.

I looked at Mayor Tuan. "Okay. The *Icarus* — the engines, the metal — that gives us options. But we've got responsibilities, too. I have . . . something to tell you." *Something impossible: we need to leave this planet.*

The mayor frowned at my expression, but something in it must have convinced him. "All right," he said at last. "Come with me. Let's hear it."

With renewed energy, I pushed myself away from the wall and gave Eliza an encouraging smile and raised a hand to show the way. We had work to do.

●●●

I've read the textbooks. I know you know what happened next. You'll have heard about the election, and how the imprisoned Grounders returned to their cities and spread the truth. You'll have been taught about how our people threw their effort behind moving our cities to the planet we were originally supposed to colonize, a planet we were already calling Icarus Rising.

Yes, most people wanted to be someplace better, with night, and oceans and blue skies. But many also spoke about justice and making amends, about the need for the eggs of the Elder's people to be returned to their proper breeding grounds. Eight years we worked, lowering our cities into the fog forest and upending them, making them ready to go into space again. We salvaged the technology of the *Icarus*, reverse engineered the equipment, and made the jump engines fire one last time.

I was there on the first Landing Day — the event we now celebrate like we used to celebrate Nocturne. I saw an ocean for the first time. Can you imagine? I held Eliza's hand and we stood together for hours, staring and listening.

But all of that was in my future. As I prepared to follow the mayor of Daedalon to the Great Hall, these ideas weren't ones I'd dared to think yet. They weren't what impressed me most about that moment.

What impressed me was Eliza. As I held my hand

out to show the way, she looked at me, and gave me a smile that seemed . . . shy.

Then she reached up and kissed me.

It wasn't a perfect kiss, but considering she must have learned it only by watching others do it during the Nocturne celebrations, it was more than a passable attempt. She held her face to mine by pressing her wrist to the back of my neck. We knocked noses, bumped foreheads, and then for a second we were eye to eye. I could see her concentrating on getting it right.

Then her lips met mine. And that was perfect. For that moment, I had wings.

"You coming?" Mayor Tuan called, snapping me back to the present.

Eliza and I pulled back, reluctant, but there was work to do. "Yes," I said. I smiled at Eliza.

She reached out — her hand open, with no weapon, no threat — and took my hand. I gave it a gentle squeeze, and we followed the mayor up the stairs, to what I hoped would be redemption.

EPILOGUE

ELIZA:

This is a history.

An appendix to a history, which I have both lived and read.

To you, maybe, it looks like a good story. The brave struggle to leave the planet that was nearly the tomb of two races. The happy ending of twelve limping, makeshift ships touching down on a kind planet, a blue planet of salt flats and tides. Icarus Rising. The wrongs of the past undone.

You will read the great speeches that were made when the eggs of my Elder Mothers were returned to the hatch flats. They were speeches about responsibility, about facing up to the past. They were good speeches, as nearly as I can judge. Simon and his people, who are my people now, are a good people. They are kind.

But also I know this: after the first hatching, it was humans who built the mud domes. For no one else was there to build, only bones, and the old domes were cracked and falling. And after the first moult, it was I who taught the hatchlings our speech. Only, I cannot make all the sounds I remember. And the hatchlings do not remember them. My children have human accents.

The people of my Elder Mother are slow to grow, and I have grown old before they are even full grown. I wonder what will happen next tide-turn, when the second moult leaves the hatchlings a metre taller. Will there be quite so much tenderness for them then? Quite so much kindness?

I never told Simon what I did to Nathaniel Tal.

But I will tell history. This world, this Icarus Rising, is founded on a murder. A killing committed by a strong person, because others were too good to do what had to be done. It is the same founding, in a smaller way, that Daniel Tal gave to Icarus Down.

If the shadows are less dark here, it is only because we are not so close to the sun.

ABOUT THE AUTHOR

James Bow was born in Toronto in 1972 to librarian parents who fostered his love of reading. His mother, writer Patricia Bow, got him interested in science fiction and fantasy, reading him Issac Asimov and Ursula K. LeGuin at an early age. She also encouraged him to write.

James has been an unapologetic *Doctor Who* fan since 1984, and spent most of his spare time during high school and university hanging out with fellow fans, writing stories and editing fanzines, all while studying for what he thought would be his real job as an urban planner.

The economy had other ideas for him. After graduating, he found few jobs in his chosen profession and drifted through other work that paid the bills but starved the soul. Taking a leap and concentrating on what he loved best — writing — he published three books of YA fantasy and more than thirty non-fiction science and history books for children. *Icarus Down* is his first science fiction novel.

He remains a big fan of *Doctor Who*, though he also loves *Star Trek* and Harry Potter as well as the books of Kenneth Oppel, Arthur Slade, Philip Reeve and Madeleine L'Engle, to name just a few. He has met most of the important people in his life through fandom, including his wife (fellow writer Erin Bow), the best man at his wedding, and the godfather to his eldest daughter. He currently lives in Kitchener, Ontario, with Erin and their two daughters, Vivian and Nora.